Arms of Courage

WYOMING ARMS
BOOK TWO

TESSA CARR

A note of dedication...

to all my dear friends who are the polio survivors
of the world.
They fight valiantly from day to day
To overcome challenges; determined to live life to the
fullest.
They do what they can;
They find ways to accomplish what they can't;
and they express the joy of living in each
task they perform.

As my dearest friend GG said,
"These are my people."

One

The nightmare...

Katlynne's blood-curdling scream from across the room caused Shelley to awaken with a start. Throwing back the coverlet, she ran to the next bed, turning on the lamp as she reached her.

"Kat, *Kat,* wake up. It's just the dream."

Alarmed, Kat opened her eyes, seeing Shelley's concerned face. "Oh, Shelley. I'm sorry. I did it again, didn't I?" she whispered, covering her face with her hands.

"Don't be. It's probably just all that's been going on. The past few days have been atrocious." Shelley sat down on the edge of the bed. "But now that exams are over and graduation is here, things will calm down. You'll see."

"I'd never have made it these past few years without you, Shelley. And not just because no one else would have put up with my nightmares." Kat shook her head. "I think I'll be okay now. Go back to bed."

"I wasn't sleeping well anyway. I was thinking about summer. I wish you'd consider coming home with us for a while. Gabe and my stepmother both want you to. And they're not just being nice. They really do."

"They're sweet, and so are you. But Ted and Lorina would be so hurt if I didn't go home—at least for a while. I know they've missed me, and I owe it to them to at least try to stay there as long as I can."

Shelley sighed. "All right. But if you find you just can't do it? Call-any time. And Gabe will send our pilot out to get you. Or he'll come himself. He already said he would."

Kat stared, fully awake now. "Gabe doesn't even know me."

"Of course, he does. Every time I go home, I take videos of your performances. He's seen them all, and he was livid when he found out what happened to you."

Kat sank back into the pillow. "You told him?"

"Yes, I told him after it happened."

"And he still wants me to come?"

"If he didn't, he wouldn't have asked. Trust me."

When Kat didn't answer, Shelley added, "Night, Kat. Go back to sleep."

"Night, Shelley." Kat watched as her roommate climbed into bed and let her eyes drift closed.

At seven-thirty, Kat opened her eyes once again. The eastern sun was shining through the window. Had that been yet another nightmare during the night? Realization returned, along with the memory of talking with Shelley.

Call any time, Shelley had said. Kat sat up and glanced at her reflection in the mirror across the room. Her face was unusually pale this morning, and if she allowed herself to be honest, she felt awful.

As she glanced down at the book on her bedside table, she caught sight of the envelope peeking out from under it. There was no need to look at it to know what it said.

Department of Corrections.

She'd been notified that four men were being reviewed for possible parole. It had arrived in the middle of term exams. A second letter had followed the first. Could she make herself go? The idea alone scared the socks off her.

She scooted across the shower seat into the hot water, hoping to wash her hair and shower as fast as possible and get out. The college wasn't known for its abundance of hot water.

The truth was, she dreaded the thought of going home. The house she'd grown up in and loved so dearly was now forbidding and dark. Her bedroom now seemed threatening. Nothing had outwardly changed; the curtains were the same; the matching bedspread and desk, adapted to her needs. What had changed took place a few years ago when four intruders made their way into her bedroom and clapped a strange-smelling handkerchief over her face. And the comfortable world she had grown up in faded away forever.

Judge Abramson had always known there might be the danger of retribution for decisions made from the bench. He was careful to try to protect the household in any way possible. An alarm system had been installed before Kat was born.

That night, however, it had failed to announce the visit of the four men who managed to make their way into the house and then to Kat's upstairs bedroom. Somehow, they'd known exactly where she was.

She leaned into the spray of the shower, memories flooding her mind.

Memories of awakening, tied to the posters of her bed; the knife they had flashed in front of her face before cutting off her nightgown; the hissing sound echoing through the room repeatedly; her father's screams to let her go.

It had viciously continued. The voices of the four men were no less vivid now than they had been that night.

Just watch, old man...

You sit up on your bench and send my brother to the slammer? This is payback.

One of the men gave a high-pitched laugh each time a blow struck, as if watching was tremendously amusing to him.

Kat knew she didn't remember it all. There seemed to be patches of time missing. The thing she did remember the most vividly, however, was the moment her father's voice had suddenly gone silent.

She froze each time she thought of that moment. She'd known, then, that her father was dead.

The footsteps announced their departure even before she heard the sirens.

"Don't forget me, sweetheart. I'll be back to finish this," a voice had said in her ear.

And all Kat had been able to do was whisper sorrowfully into the quiet room, "*Dad... Dad*," as the tears streamed down her face.

The rest had been a blur; the police had stormed the house but failed to locate the intruders. Next, two officers had come into her bedroom. One pulled the sheet from the bed and wrapped it around her as another had untied her, carrying her from the room so she didn't see her father's lifeless body.

It had been easy enough for the investigators to find those men. Looking back through files of previous cases the Judge had presided over in the courtroom, the four men were brought in for questioning. One of them had confessed. They swore they'd never meant for the judge to die. Kat had been forced to testify against them, but in the courtroom, she'd only seen their faces for the first time when she testified.

Those faces... the one of Don Heraldson stood out the most. Kat was sure if she looked the word evil up in the dictionary, it would show his face in the description. He'd stared at her as she testified, with such an ugly smirk on his face. She wondered idly if his brother was still in prison. She hoped so. Tommy Miller and Billy Raine had received the same sentence. That left

Larry Connor, the man whose confession had brought their arrest.

And now, only four years later, they were being brought before the parole board for possible release.

Kat leaned back into the stream of hot water and sobbed quietly. The nightmares would be back to stay if she moved back into her house. The threats that they would be back to 'finish this' clouded every step she took.

She also knew Lorina and Ted would be extremely saddened if she didn't come home for the summer. They had moved from the cozy pool house into the house with her the day after her father's death, and stayed there ever since. They had also had a newer security system installed, and had urged her to change bedrooms, but she'd refused. If they'd found her once, they could do it again.

Kat knew she'd lingered in the shower too long when the water turned cool. Wrapping a towel around herself, she went back out to see if Shelley was awake.

"Morning, Kat," Shelley said cheerfully, yawning as she entered the bedroom. "Any hot water left?"

"Nope," she said, her face penitent. "Sorry, Shelley. Give it fifteen minutes."

"Good. I wasn't ready to get up anyway." Shelley

grinned, lying back down and bringing the covers up to her chin. "How are you this morning?"

"Ready for graduation. You? I'm so sorry I woke you last night."

"No worries. I went right back to sleep. Are you sure you won't come home with us?"

"Oh, Shelley. The truth? I'd dearly love to come. It's very sweet of you all to invite me. If it weren't for Lorina and Ted..." she bit her lip and turned back to the mirror, picking up the hairbrush to remove the tangles from her hair.

"I know. But we're not leaving until Tuesday, so if you change your mind, you still have time. I'd like you to spend as much time with us as you can until then. I'd love for Gabe to get to know you. Cynthia says she already feels like she does." Shelley stretched and wiggled her toes. "I don't know where the past four years have gone, do you? It just seems as if yesterday we were all freshmen. Except Maddie. I've missed her this year." She shook her head and threw back the covers, padding over to the window. "At least we have a beautiful day for the ceremony. Are you ready to sing?"

"I suppose. It's the last time I'll get to sing here, I guess. And certainly, the last time I'll be singing with David."

"Everyone thought you two would be an item," Shelley said thoughtfully. "Will you miss him?"

Kat laughed. "We were never an item. I was always a bit off-limits to him. David's very conscious of his," she held up her hands, cupping her fingers, "image. No, don't you dare feel sorry for me, girlfriend. I've always known my disability put him out of my reach, but you know what? That's quite all right."

"It's his loss," Shelley said distastefully.

Kat smiled at her friend's loyalty, tilting her head. "And you, Miss Valedictorian—are you ready for your speech? I wish Maddie could be here to hear it."

"I'll bet Gabe will record it," Shelley said. "Am I ready? Well, the honest answer is *no*. I know what I want to say, but how to say it? Not a clue. And as far as this summer is concerned, I'm looking forward to being home and seeing Maddie again. I wish she could be here. It's been way too long. Anyway, I've told you what I think about David."

Kat grinned, swiveling to face her. "Once or twice. But I'm dying to hear it again."

"It's what I've always thought. He's a complete jerk. He's like a peacock, showing off his colorful feathers whenever he's on stage. One of these days, he's going to bow so many times he'll forget where he's standing and fall off the stage." She raised a brow. "We can only hope."

Kat shook her head, laughing. "Shell, you're wonderful. And did I mention loyal? And," she added, "did I also mention I'd give a hundred bucks to see it happen?"

The sun was out when Kat carefully moved across campus toward the gymnasium. She'd spent all morning packing her VW before handing over the dormitory keys to Shelley. Now, the skies were a beautiful blue, dotted with white fluffy clouds, and a soft breeze blew her hair back from her face. It felt wonderful. The administration had considered having the graduation ceremony outside because of the large crowds expected, but had changed their minds due to the chance of thunderstorms.

She and David managed to grab a few moments to rehearse their song prior to the ceremony, but as usual, she still found herself nervous. She was determined, however, to put the thought of the parolees out of her mind. This was too special a day to allow thoughts of them to ruin it.

At ten-thirty, the graduates gathered in line,

preparing to come in two by two. As the orchestra began playing *Pomp and Circumstance*, the graduates filed in. Zachary, one of her classmates, held on to her arm as he walked with her; Kat appreciated that. Falling this morning would be disastrous to her ego.

The gym rapidly grew full. Students filled not only the chairs on the center floor, but also took up the lower two rows of the bleachers on each side, and since Kat was to sing, Zach walked her up toward the front and helped her to sit on the bottom row to the left of the stage.

"Thanks, Zach," she whispered. "You're my hero."

"Anything for you, kid," he whispered back, grinning as he went to sit down.

Kat scanned the stage, looking for Shelley. She found her roommate seated by one of the deans, looking extremely nervous. When Shelley's eyes lit on Kat grinning at her, she seemed to relax.

Shelley rose to speak, and Kat, from where she was sitting, watched the faces of the students as they listened. They looked impressed.

As Shelley ended her speech and the thunderous applause began, Kat stood. Seeing Shelley descend the steps and come toward her, she scooted down and motioned to the spot next to her.

"Bravo, Shell!" She hugged her friend fiercely.

"Oh, gosh, I didn't think I could do it."

"But you did, and *beautifully*. Did Gabe and Cynthia make it in time?"

"Yes. See—directly across from us on the third row of the bleachers? Gabe has the camera aimed at us. Cynthia's beside him, trying to take it away from him, but he's not having it."

"So that's Gabriel."

"Yes," Shelley whispered back. "But take my advice and never, ever call him by that name. You'll be sorry. He hates it."

They were still whispering to each other when they noticed the gym had become quiet.

Kat heard a man clear his throat and looked toward the stage. It was Dr Wilson, who was grinning at them.

"I swear I don't know what we'll do next year without you two."

Kat glanced penitently away. As she did, however, a white gown moved in front of her gaze.

"Katlynne, it's time," David said, holding out his hand. He helped her up and escorted her to the stage and up the steps, leading her over to the stool placed in front of the microphones. He appeared the complete gentleman as he helped her to sit. Dr. Sanders, who was leading the orchestra, raised his brows as if waiting on the notice to proceed, and she nodded. The introduction to *The Prayer* filled the air.

Kat looked over the faces of her friends as they sang, touched by their smiles. She'd grown to love each of them dearly during the years she'd been there. By the time the song was over, it was difficult to keep back the tears. She shook her head at the call for an encore, and blew them a kiss instead.

David, however, after bowing over her hand, turned and began bowing to the audience. Kat waited a moment for him to help her down and toward the steps, but he made no move to do it.

It was Dr. Wilson who came over, graciously holding out his arm. She took it, thankful for his help getting her safely across the stage and down the steps. They were on the next to the last step when a loud thump was heard, followed by a few unmistakable chuckles from the students.

Kat closed her eyes as she reached the ground floor.

What Shelley had predicted had happened after all.

She managed to hold her composure together until Dr. Wilson escorted her to where Shelley sat and seated her.

"Thank you, sir."

"Thank *you*, darling Kat."

She watched him return to the stage before she met

Shelley's eyes, remembering her earlier prediction, and Kat looked away quickly, trying not to chuckle along with the other students.

Finally, Shelley leaned over and whispered in her ear.

"Told you."

That did it. Kat was unable to help herself. At Shelley's words, she finally lost the battle. Giggles erupted from her first, then from Shelley, as they tried unsuccessfully to keep quiet.

"Shh," Shelley whispered, finally. "Look at Gabe's face. He's not happy with either of us."

Kat looked up. Cynthia was holding the camera now, and Gabe's face had a distinct expression of disapproval. She managed to control herself as she looked away, but even then, it was difficult.

Two

M *eeting the family...*

As the ceremony ended and caps flew into the air, Kat held hers firmly to her chest. "Not about to let this one out of my sight. I worked too hard for it to lose it now," she muttered toward Shelley, who was hanging on to hers as well. Hugs from students followed in multitudes as Gabe and Cynthia made their way over.

Shelley suddenly cried out with glee. "You're here!" She ran forward and hugged, first Gabe, then Cynthia, grabbing each of them by the arm and dragging them over. "You have to meet my cohort. Kat, my brother Gabe! And Cynthia, this is Kat. She's both my room-mate and my partner in crime."

"I noticed," Cynthia said, laughing.

"So, did I," Gabe added. He didn't sound amused. "I thought of taking you both outside for laughing at the mishap of another student."

Was he serious? Kat met his eyes with an expression of defiance.

"Oh, lighten up, Gabe," Cynthia playfully smacked his shoulder. "I thought they were adorable."

"Of course you did. Anyway, congratulations, girls. I applaud you both. And Katlynne, it's nice to meet you."

"Nice to meet you, too. But nobody calls me Katlynne. It's Kat." Her voice was firm as she glanced up at him, surprised at how far she was forced to crane her neck to see him.

"We feel as if we've known you for years," Cynthia said with a smile. "Please, come and eat lunch with us. You must be hungry."

Katlynne was just about to say yes when she saw a figure retreating toward the doorway.

"Uncle Ted!" she called out. But when he didn't turn back, she hurried after him as fast as her braced legs would allow.

Strong arms caught her about the waist suddenly, before setting her on her feet and turning her to face their owner.

Gabe's firm glance met hers. "I'll get him, Katlynne. Stay here."

Gabe left Kat staring at him as he sprinted across the auditorium toward the older gentleman she indicated. Outside, he caught up with him.

"Sir? Is your name Ted?"

"Yes," was the uncertain answer.

"There's a young lady inside who wishes to see you," Gabe said, "and she'll be very disappointed if I don't bring you back."

Ted's face brightened. "That's my Kat," he grinned.

Gabe heard Kat's squeal of delight from across the auditorium when he approached with Ted. Moving forward, she threw her arms around him. "Uncle Ted, I'm so delighted that you could make it. Everyone, this is Ted Baxter. He and Lorina are my family."

Ted hugged her, lifting her off her feet. "I was a bit late getting in, Kat. I almost didn't find a place to park. Lorina's getting things ready for you and couldn't make it. But she said to tell you to invite Shelley and her family over for supper."

"Tell you what," Cynthia smiled from Ted to Kat.

"If you'll come to lunch with us, we'll come for supper with you. Deal? You can ride with us."

"Deal," Kat nodded, "We'd love having you."

Ted smiled. "I can't stay, but I'll tell Lorina. And Kat, I have a surprise for you in the greenhouse when you get home."

"Really? I can't wait to see it." She hugged him again. "Thank you so much for coming today. And please tell Lorina I missed her." There were tears in her eyes, and Ted leaned down and kissed the top of her head.

"Wouldn't have missed it, sweetheart. We'll see you this afternoon." He winked and was gone.

Shelley leaned forward, whispering in her ear. "I think David wants to see you."

Kat turned. David was smiling, looking as self-assured as ever. If his fall off the stage had bothered him, it wasn't doing so now.

She introduced him to each of them. However, as he met Gabe, his million-dollar smile faded, and he backed up a step.

"Hello," he said, glancing from one to the other. "I... Kat, I'll see you later," he said and left.

His hasty retreat brought a grin to Kat's face. "Give Lauren my love," she called out. When she turned back to face the others, Shelley was glancing up at Gabe with respect.

"Whoa, Gabe," she said, laughing. "How did you do that? I've been trying to scare him off for years. Kat's too nice to do it."

"Did I?" Gabe raised a brow. "My opinion must have shown."

It was all he said.

As Kat rode to the restaurant with them, they stopped to pick up one more, an older gentleman with a big smile and a sense of humor.

"Will's our pilot," Cynthia said, introducing him. "The best in Wyoming."

Will nodded. "Nah. Cynthia just likes me because I fly her to Billings or Sheridan once in a while to shop."

Lunch was great fun. Gabe and Will discussed the ranch at length and told Kat stories about the employees there. It made her long to meet them.

When they had finished lunch, however, Cynthia turned to Kat. "Sweetie, I think I'm going to have to take a while and rest. Would it be all right if we came between four and four-thirty?"

"Sure. That would be fine. If someone could just drop me by my car at school, I can go on home."

"We'll be glad to," Gabe answered as he held out his hand. "Let's get you back, Katlynne," he said.

Kat stood where she was and sent a defiant glance up at him. "Kat," she corrected.

He raised a brow. "Excuse me?"

She lifted her chin. "Call me Kat, or I'll call you Gabriel."

Gabe stepped forward until his face was inches from hers. "Trying to blackmail me, young lady?"

She glared. "Absolutely."

He stared down for a moment, and then threw back his head in laughter. "I'll let you get away with that one. But just this once. Next time, beware."

Katlynne took the hand, her head held high. "Thanks for the warning."

A moment later, he nodded. "You'd do well to remember it."

As they pulled up to her car a few moments later, Gabe turned to Cynthia. "I'll take Katlynne home if you or Will can drive back to the hotel. And if it's all right with you, Katlynne, I'll borrow your car after I take you home and bring it back this evening?"

"It *would* be, but—" Her voice was uncertain.

He turned in the seat and looked back. "But?"

"But I've packed the car to go home, and the passenger seat is full. You can't open the door unless you want to see an avalanche."

"Show me." He opened the door and, waving goodbye to Cynthia, got out of the car. Kat watched as it pulled away, dismayed.

"You might have to strap me on top," she said seriously.

"I see what you mean." He laughed. "Perhaps we can re-pack a bit. Keys?" He reached for the passenger door as she dug into her bag for them.

"Here," she handed the keys to him. "But don't open the passenger door. Stuff will..." she paused as a big pile of underwear tumbled to the ground, adding, "fall out." Her cheeks grew hot with embarrassment.

"You packed this?"

"Yes. I'm not *helpless*."

Gabe reached down and took her chin in his hands, lifting it further so she was forced to face him. He was frowning. "I never said you were, Katlynne. I never even thought it. But you *could* use some lessons on packing."

Kat was embarrassed. All her life, she had worked extra hard to ensure people didn't perceive her as lazy. It had been her biggest fear. Yet she'd fallen into her own trap of trying to prove to him that she worked as hard as anyone else, when it wasn't what he was thinking at all. She started to reach down for the embarrassing pile of bras and panties, but he stopped her with a restraining hand.

"I'll get them," he said firmly. "Go sit down."

Kat remained where she was. Gabe, however, advanced to the front of the car to open the trunk.

"I think we can make this work," he said. "If not, we'll have to take some things back into the dorm."

"We can't."

"Why?"

"Because this was my last load, and I gave my key to Shelley."

Silence.

"And she turned it in," she added.

He swiveled slowly toward her.

"I tried to tell you," she said softly.

Gabe stood up straight and looked down at her. "Yes, you did," he said quietly. "I just knew you must be tired and hoped I could make things easier for you."

Kat responded by averting her gaze.

"Thank you. Sorry."

"Don't be. Just go sit in the driver's seat for a few moments until I can get things moved around." When she looked as if she would argue, he added, "*Now*." He took her hand and led her around to the driver's side, opening the door. "Sit," he ordered.

She exhaled a long sigh and frowned, but she sat. Shelley had described her brother as bossy. After meeting him, Kat decided she was right. Never had she met anyone quite this dictatorial. She watched, scowling as he continued moving stuff into the trunk in the front. A few moments later, the passenger seat was clear. Gabe came to the door and opened it, reaching for her hand.

She ignored it. "I can make it."

Slowly, he brought his head down until his gaze met hers. "You won't." He took her hand in his, raising her to her feet.

Irritated, she let him lead her around to the other side of the car.

"Here. In you go." As she sat down, he leaned forward, finding the seat belt. Bringing it across her, he fastened it snugly.

His presence was overpowering, and she glanced upward. His face was inches from hers. Their eyes met suddenly, and she looked away.

"Thank you."

With a firm nod, he backed out and closed the door, moving around the car. It was when he put the key in the ignition and started it, and all the lights came on, that he paused, looking from one gauge to the next.

"When was the last time you checked your gauges?"

"I don't know." She shook her head. "Is there something that needs attention?"

"Several things."

Within seconds, he was behind the car at the engine. Kat leaned back against the headrest, watching him in the mirror.

"Where's the nearest gas station?" he asked, back in the driver's seat.

"Just down the street. Why?"

"Because you need a few things." He pulled out silently and entered traffic.

"Like what?"

"Like oil. And gas."

"Oh." Her eyes grew wide as she mouthed the word.

He disappeared into the convenience store, and a moment later, came out with two cans of oil and a can of something she didn't recognize.

When he got back in the car and started the engine,

he moved to one of the pumps and filled the tank. "Now," he said, "you should be good to go. But check these things within a month. You should always keep an eye on the oil and the gas tank, Katlynne. According to the sticker on your windshield, your car's due an oil change, but you needed some to get home. Perhaps I can get that done before we go back to Wyoming."

"I can do it. And how much do I owe you? I can't let you service my car, or pay for my gas for nothing." She stopped when she saw him lean toward her, frowning. Shaking her head, she looked down. "It's just not right."

"Now, some directions on where you live? Or do you have it programmed into your phone?"

"No, it's not that far."

Gabe glanced down at her. "How old is your car?" he asked, pulling out into traffic.

"It's a '66 model. Dad bought it used for me when I was sixteen. He tried to buy me a new one. I put up a fuss."

"Why?"

"Because I wanted this one."

"He was looking out for you."

"I know. And, before you try to talk me into buying a new one, *I like* my car."

"I'm not saying you should buy a new one. But

older cars do need maintenance, Katlynne. And I notice your tires are showing wear, quite a bit."

"I noticed the tires. I was just waiting until I got a job after getting out of school."

"What was your major?"

"Biology. And a minor in chemistry and art."

He looked down at her quizzically. "Chemistry and *art*?"

"Well, art is really my first love, but I didn't want to join the ranks of starving artists out there. And I really didn't have a desire to teach it. Dad insisted I'd better major in something I could get a job doing."

"Your dad was a wise man." He was quiet a moment, but spoke again, finally. "Getting back to your car..."

"Must we?"

"Yes," he said firmly. "Let's see if we can get some service done on it tomorrow or Monday. That way, I can go with you."

"Do I need you to go?"

"Yes. You do. Don't think that just because you're little and cute, someone won't take you to the cleaners."

"I..." she averted her gaze. "I never considered myself *either*."

"Well, you are, young lady. *Both*. You can stop

blushing; it's the truth. And someone needs to be with you who has a knowledge of cars when you go in. There aren't a lot of Volkswagens around these days, and not many people who service them, either."

Kat bit her lower lip. For a moment, she said nothing.

He spoke again a moment later. "Do you always react this way when someone tells you you're cute?"

Still, she said nothing until they turned into her neighborhood.

"This is my house."

Gabe pulled into the driveway, noticing Lorina as she came running out.

"Sweets! We've missed you—" She stopped short when she saw that someone other than Kat was driving. Kat smiled and waved at her from the passenger seat and reached for the handle on the door.

Gabe, however, stopped her. "I'll get you, Katlynne."

"But it's my car, and my house, and my driveway. I can do it myself."

"Katlynne." It was one word, but spoken in such a deep tone that she halted. She sat there, fuming, as he got out of the car but unfastened her seat belt.

She listened as he stopped to greet Lorina and introduced himself. "Gabe Ingrahm, ma'am. I'm Shelley's brother from Wyoming. I brought Katlynne home. She's tired, and I thought I'd unload her belongings so she could spend the afternoon resting."

"Oh, do come in, Gabe. That's very sweet of you. I was worried for a moment that something had happened."

Determined not to wait any longer, Kat opened her door. She rushed around the car and into Lorina's arms, enveloping her caretaker in a fierce hug. "Aunt Lorina, I've missed you." Turning to Gabe, she spoke, a defiant tone to her voice. "I never said anything about being tired."

His expression was no less stern than it had been when he got out of the car. Taking her arm and leading her into the house, he spoke in a deep voice. "Are you always this obstinate, young lady?"

"Oh yes," Lorina said, laughing behind them. "I'll get Ted; he can help you unload."

"Thanks, ma'am, but there's no need to disturb him. I don't mind at all. I just need to know where to put things." Lifting Kat off her feet, he carried her into the great room before leaning down to whisper in her ear. "And you, young lady, I'm putting *here*. And I expect you to stay." He turned and set her down with a thud into the brown leather recliner that had once been her father's favorite chair.

Kat scowled back at him, but leaned back into the recliner and pushed the button so the foot rose. Like it or not, she had to admit that it felt good to sit. She'd made trip after trip to the car with her belongings that morning when she got up until it was time to practice with David in the music room.

She glanced down at her braces. Should she take them off? She changed her mind, however. As soon as Gabe was gone, she planned on heading into the kitchen.

He loaded her things into the foyer, stacking them and giving her an occasional glance to see if she was where he'd left her. Her glare back at him didn't seem to improve his humor any.

"Shall I put these things in her room?" he asked politely.

Lorina shook her head. "Thanks, Gabe, but we'll need to go through them first. It was very kind of you to bring her home, and bring it all in. Thank you so much. You all will be coming for supper, right?"

"Yes, ma'am," Gabe answered. "Is there anything we need to bring? There are four of us."

"Nothing at all. And please encourage everyone to come. It's all prepared; all I have to do is heat it." Lorina added, grinning. "We'll see you whenever you get here."

"Perfect. I'll bring Katlynne's car back this afternoon unless she needs it sooner. See you then." He smiled, and then turned to Kat. "Later, young lady. I know you'll do just what you want after I leave, but I advise you to get some rest." Nodding, he turned toward the front door.

Kat watched his retreat through the front window until he wound up his tall frame and got into the car. Lowering the recliner's footrest, she rose and stood at the window until he backed out. Lorina was in the kitchen, humming a tune, but she turned and straightened when Kat wandered in.

"Katlynne," she said, frowning, "what's gotten into you? He was so polite and helpful, and you sat and glared at him the entire time he was here."

"He's bossy and dictatorial and overbearing, that's what." Kat paused as she searched for words. "And he hovers too much. He wouldn't even let me get out of the car in my own driveway."

Lorina tilted her head. "But you did," she said with a wink.

Kat suddenly let out a giggle. "I did, didn't I?" They were both laughing now, and Lorina motioned to the table.

"Have a seat, sweetie. I made you something special."

"Oh, I can't wait." She took one of the little individual cheesecakes with blueberry topping and took a bite. "Mm. My favorite," she said, closing her eyes.

"Would you like to nap this afternoon?" Seeing the look on Kat's face, she grinned. "Just thought I'd ask. Ted took a video of your ceremony this morning so I could see it. He said you sang with David."

"David the peacock?" Kat's eyes twinkled. "I'm sorry. That was ugly of me. But I want to see the video."

"Really?" Lorina looked surprised. "I didn't think you ever liked watching your own performances."

"Oh, I don't care about watching the song. I just want to see David fall off the stage again."

"Katlynne!"

"Sorry. But Shelley and I were making bets on how long it would take." She laughed suddenly. "Don't mind me, Aunt Lorina. I'm just being petty because he chose Lauren instead."

Lorina was watching her thoughtfully. "You know, sweets," she said, "you're used to having three kinds of people in this world around you."

Kat paused. "Oh?"

"There are those who adore you and who really want to help. I know Ted, and I fall into that category. And although people like that are wonderful to have around, they wouldn't necessarily make good partners, because they won't hold you accountable. Then, there are those, like David, who are self-centered and concerned about how others perceive them. They might seem to care as long as others are watching, but when it gets tough, they disappear. That's not what you need in a partner, either."

Kat set her fork down. "Who said I needed a partner?"

Lorina laughed. "Bear with me a little longer, sweetie. What I'm trying to say is that there's a third category: Those who might seem a little strict, but care about you. They might even make you angry, but they're the ones who look out for you and try to help you avoid problems. And those are the ones who make good partners."

"You can't be talking about Gabe."

"Can't I? If I don't miss my guess, he'd make a great match for you. It's obvious he cares what happens to you."

Kat stared at her. "He can't," she said, frowning. "I just met him this morning. And besides that, he's Shelley's brother. I can't get involved with him."

"Why?"

"Because if it went badly, it could ruin my friendship with Shelley. That's too valuable to risk messing up."

"I see." Lorina gave her an indulgent smile. "All right, then. If you're determined not to rest, Ted has a surprise for you in the greenhouse."

"And I'll bet I know just what it is," she exclaimed. Finishing the rest of the cheesecake, she rose from the table and leaned forward, kissing Lorina's cheek. "Thank you, Aunt Lorina. It's so good to be home."

"Even though I give my unsolicited advice?"

Kat grinned. "Your advice is always welcome."

Ted glanced up as she entered the greenhouse. "Kat! It's so good to have you home. I have something to show you."

"And I can't wait to see it." She followed as he led her over to a bench that had all kinds of flowers blooming on it.

"Close your eyes." He said, his own eyes sparkling. Silence was broken by the sound of rustling as she waited. "All right. You can open them."

Kat gasped when she looked at the bloom he held out to her. "The blue rose... oh, my goodness," she exclaimed in delight. "Dad's favorite. How did you do it?"

"I've been working on it for years, Kat, *because* it

was your dad's favorite. I gave up on it for a while after..." he paused, shaking his head, "well, *after*."

Kat knew what he meant. Her eyes filled with tears as she gently touched one of the petals.

"I'm sorry, Kat. I didn't mean to make you cry."

"Oh, you didn't. I'm just so touched that you would keep working on this. It's so beautiful." She handed it back to him, kissing his cheek.

But as she returned to the house, she exhaled a long breath of sadness.

There was no way she could leave them now.

Three

V*isitors...*

Gabe pulled back out on the road, thinking what a stubborn young woman Katlynne was. Had they not been in the presence of Lorina, he might have been tempted to put her over his knee for a swat or two. His face was grim, his mouth a straight line. And yet, he had to admire her determination. She had managed, despite her limitations, despite the loss of her father and all that had happened to her, to graduate from college on time with an additional minor. He knew from Shelley that Katlynne had managed to maintain a 4.0 GPA throughout school, and he admired and respected that immensely.

He hoped she would decide to come home with them for at least the summer. At the same time, he found himself frowning. She'd have to learn to follow a few rules if she came. It was imperative if he was to be responsible for her. There were so many dangers present at the ranch. But how to tame that stubborn streak she seemed to possess? He shook his head.

When he reached the room at the hotel, Cynthia and Shelley were seated on the divan in one of the suites with their heads together.

"You're back," Cynthia said. "Did you get our little gal home safely?"

"Despite herself," he said, sitting down and stretching out his long legs. "I left her sitting in the recliner in the living room, but I'm quite sure she didn't stay there after I left. I met Lorina Baxter. Nice folks. Are they really family?"

Shelley shook her head. "No, but she thinks of them that way."

"I see. She invited us all for supper. Where's Will? Asleep?"

"You guessed it," Shelley grinned.

Cynthia glanced toward the door to the suite. "Do you think we're working him too hard, Gabe?"

He frowned at Cynthia's question. "I do. I'm

trying to get him to take on a different role, still as our pilot, but with less physical stuff and more oversight. Pay would be the same, maybe a little more. Tim could take over more of the physically demanding stuff—and could use a raise, too. But Will's got to decide to make the change first. He loves what he does." He glanced at Shelley. "By the way, Tim has asked me every single day for the last year if I've heard from you."

"How is he?" Shelley asked.

"Tim," he answered, his eyes crinkling at the corners, "is waiting impatiently to see you."

Shelley blushed as Cynthia came back from the fridge with a glass of iced tea, handing it to Gabe.

Gabe nodded. "Thanks. And by the way, Shelley. I found out just before I left the ranch, Ian is back in Big Horn County."

Shelley tilted her head. "Doing what?"

"Sheriff's department. He's a deputy."

"Oh my."

"So watch your speed. He'll stop you for certain if you go over the limit."

Shelley laughed. "I don't speed. You know that."

Cynthia eyed her with amusement. "What Gabe didn't tell you, was he stopped by the house and wanted to know when you'd be home from school."

Shelley groaned. "Oh, dear Lord. The Winslows never give up, do they? Gabe, they still want that section of our land badly, don't they?"

Gabe grinned back at her. "You know they do. But Dad told me once never to get rid of that part of the land, and I'm following his advice. I'm not sure why they want it so badly. They have about the same amount of land we do." He glanced between Shelley and Cynthia. "You both look a little troubled. Anything else going on?"

His scowl increased when both Cynthia and Shelley returned his frown.

"What is it?" He leaned forward.

"You'd better tell him, Shelley," Cynthia said quietly.

Shelley took a deep breath. "Kat's gotten two letters in the mail in the past two weeks from the Department of Corrections. The first one said the men —all four of them, would be brought before the review board for a hearing. They wanted to know if she wished to be there, but she didn't get the first one until she was in the middle of term exams." She sighed. "It was followed by another one a few days ago."

"When is the hearing?" his voice was dark and husky.

"I think it might be scheduled for June 2nd. They know where she is, Gabe, where her bedroom is, where she sleeps." Shelley's voice was trembling. "It's only been four years, and already..." she swallowed hard, unable to continue.

"What else did it say?" Gabe demanded.

"She wasn't going to even let me know about it at first. But I saw it and pressed her. She finally just handed it to me. It said that prisons are overcrowded; the men had been model prisoners. Gave the date and said for her to write if she wanted to be present for the hearing. The nightmares have started again, almost every night, since then. It's almost as bad as last fall when she returned to school. I don't think it's going to help for her to be back in the house again. They'll just get worse."

Gabe leaned back, staring into space at nothing in particular. Fighting the urge to jump in the car again and go back to the house was difficult.

Fury was building inside him. Katlynne needed to be away from this area.

Now.

"Kat?" Lorina called from Kat's bedroom doorway, "Shelley and her family are here."

"Already?" Kat sat up, forcing her legs over the side of the bed. "I'm so sorry. I didn't intend to fall asleep. Please tell them I'll be right down." Still groggy, she pulled on her braces and shoes, and moved toward the mirror. Grabbing her hairbrush, she tugged it through her dark locks to keep it out of her face. What was it Gabe had said earlier about her being little and cute?

She stared back at her dazed reflection. "I don't see it," she murmured, turning toward the door. She stopped at the top of the stairs; instead of riding the stair elevator down, she carefully took hold of the banister. Halfway down, she caught Shelley's attention and waved.

Gabe, when he looked up, instantly looked alarmed and shot toward the stairway. He was halfway up when she stopped and scowled at him.

"Gabe Ingrahm, I know what I'm doing, thank you very much. I do *not* need an escort."

Gabe was not amused. "Why aren't you using the stair elevator?"

Kat glared, her voice sarcastic. "Odd thing, you know. Once in a while, I just get this overwhelming urge to *walk*."

"You can stop being sarcastic, Katlynne Elana; I'm not in the mood to be trifled with. Take my hand."

She didn't move. "How did you know my middle name?"

"Doesn't matter. You can take my hand, or I'll put you over my shoulder and carry you down."

Kat's mouth grew flat as she stared back.

Gabe, however, bent down closer to her ear. "Don't believe me?"

"No, I don't. You wouldn't dare."

But when his hands rested on her waist, she tried backing up a step.

"Katlynne? You have five seconds."

She bit her lip, but finally put her hand in his and let him lead her down.

"Good girl."

As they reached the bottom of the staircase, she pulled free of his hand, moved to her father's recliner and plopped down. She looked up to see Lorina at the doorway, frowning at her and shaking her head.

"Dinner will be ready in about ten minutes," Lorina flashed a smile toward everyone and disappeared back into the kitchen.

"I'm sorry, everyone. My manners stink this afternoon. I fell asleep looking at old Victorian magazines. I should have been down to welcome you. Anyway, I'm glad you're here."

"No, you shouldn't. We all napped. So should you." Cynthia's grin was unconcealed.

Kat knew Lorina's dinner would be splendid. As they finished, however, Cynthia turned toward her, leaning forward. "I've seen some of your artwork, but would you be willing to show us a bit more?"

Kat met her gaze curiously. "Sure, if you really want to see it."

"Take them into the study, sweets," Lorina suggested.

Kat turned. "All right." Glancing at her guests, she rose from the table and moved toward the study. "This was Dad's hideout," she explained, opening the door and reaching in to flip the light switch. "I'm not sure why Lorina wanted me..." She stopped as she looked around the room. "Oh, my."

Not one, not two, but ten of her drawings had been framed and displayed on the walls of the study. She stood there silently, staring from one to the next.

From the doorway, Cynthia looked past her and wandered into the room, admiring them one by one until she had seen them all. Finally, she turned back to Kat.

"Tell me about this one?" she asked, pointing.

Kat stared at it with a gulp. "I didn't know they had framed it." Approaching Cynthia, she stared at the charcoal drawing. Done in dark tones and shadows, it showed her father's hand as it reached down from heaven and her own as it reached upward from earth. "This one was after... Dad died."

Cynthia seemed unable to take her eyes off of it. "Kat," she said as she shook her head slowly, "this is exquisite." She moved to another one. "And this one?"

That one was easier. "This was from a photograph he took of my mom when she was about twenty."

"I thought perhaps it was you. You look so like her."

"Really? Do you think so?"

"She was beautiful. How old were you when you lost her?"

"Two months," Kat explained, "so I've never been able to remember her. She was already ill, and Dad flew in a governess and a nurse to look after us both. The nurse had been exposed to the poliovirus, but she didn't know it when she got here. She came down with polio a few days after she arrived and gave it to both of us. Mom passed away a week later, but I only ended up with residual paralysis that affected my legs." She looked down. "Lorina and Ted moved into the house to care for me, and the nurse and the governess both left shortly after that."

"What a tragedy," Cynthia said quietly. I'm so sorry."

"Come, Katlynne," Gabe said thoughtfully, leading her to the swivel chair behind her father's desk. This time, she didn't argue.

Cynthia, completing the circle of the room, turned to face her.

"Talk to us, Kat. We want to know more about you. A lot of people would be extremely bitter about having such a thing happen."

Kat considered the statement thoughtfully. "Bitterness is pointless. It doesn't do anything but feed on itself. Of course, I'd still love to have my mother with me, but polio taught me lots of things: patience, how to figure out ways to do what I normally couldn't, and determination." She smiled at Gabe. "So, if you think I'm obstinate, that's the reason for it." Her eyes twinkled with merriment.

He was grinning at her. "Ah. So now I know."

Cynthia, however, was leaning against the desk, still admiring the drawings. Resting both hands on the desk, she leaned forward. "Do you," she asked, "have any idea how wonderful these are?"

Kat's eyes widened. "You really think so?" She saw movement from the corner of her eye and turned to see Lorina, standing in the doorway. "Thank you, Aunt Lorina. You did a wonderful job of framing and hanging them."

"Ted did, sweetie. We started this about nine months ago, after you went back to school. They were too precious to not be displayed."

As they filed back into the great room a moment later, Cynthia sat down facing her.

"All right, Kat, I have a proposition for you. We have already discussed this, and we're all in agreement. We would love for you to come back with us, at least for the summer. I know you just graduated from school, and the Baxters would miss you. Do you have employment lined up yet?"

"No. Not yet."

"Well, I realize I'm being selfish, but here it is. I'm writing a book," Cynthia explained, "about the Shoshone People. And I need someone to illustrate it for me. You, Kat, have no idea the amount of talent you have. I've never seen anything like these." She motioned toward the study. "You've not only captured the likeness, but you've also captured the soul." She paused a moment before continuing.

"So, here's my proposal. Please consider coming home with us, at least for the summer. I'll pay you well. I can't tell you the exact amount until I speak to the publishers, but the first thing we'll do is draw up a contract for royalties. They've been after me for some time to do this book." She looked toward the kitchen door as if to make sure Lorina had left the room. "Please consider it?"

Kat followed her gaze toward the kitchen. "I would dearly love to come," she whispered, "but I'm so afraid I'll disappoint them. Please understand."

Cynthia leaned back, clearly disappointed. "I do understand. But if you change your mind for any reason, even after we leave, you can call, and we'll fly you out."

Kat looked away. "It's not just that. I have nightmares, and I'm afraid I might disturb everyone else in the house."

"We know about those, Kat. It's all right." Cynthia's voice was soft. "We were hoping that if you came out west with us for a while, those would stop."

They looked up as Lorina stepped into the room.

"Dessert, anyone? I've made Kat's favorite. Blueberry cheesecake."

Gabe observed Kat as the conversation lightened. Lorina brought in dessert and coffee to them. Shelley and Kat giggled, and Cynthia rolled her eyes as Will told old jokes he knew she'd heard a million times before. She also shared the changes in the ranch that had occurred since Christmas and their plans for the summer. Kat listened, leaning forward to loosen the straps, and kicked her braces to the carpet, revealing one leg that was slightly smaller than the other, and turned inward a little.

Gabe watched her, smiling. "Feel better now?"

"Yes. They get heavy after a while."

As he continued studying her, he noticed her lids were drooping. He wasn't surprised when, a few moments later, he looked over to find her asleep. Rising, he went to find Lorina.

"Yes?" she came forward when she saw him.

"Katlynne's fallen asleep," he explained. "I'll carry her up if you'll show me where her bedroom is."

"Absolutely,' she nodded.

Gently, Gabe scooped Kat up in his arms, cradling her head against his shoulder. She didn't stir.

Lorina quickly grabbed the braces and led him up the stairs. "In here," she whispered, turning on the room lamp that sat on the highboy just inside the door. Gabe followed, lowering Kat onto the pillows and bringing the covers to her chin before striding toward the door.

"Thank you, Gabe. She dreads going to bed so much she frequently falls asleep downstairs, and then Ted either has to carry her up, or we have to awaken her. We've tried to get her to change rooms, but she's refused. Anyway, I appreciate it."

Gabe paused outside the doorway and looked back at the sleeping Kat. "I hope she sleeps well tonight."

"I hope so, too," Lorina whispered, starting down the stairs.

In the great room, Cynthia and Shelley were getting their things together. Lorina, however, caught their attention. "Please," she said, urgency in her voice, "stay for a moment? I'd like to talk with you about Kat."

Cynthia sat back down. "Certainly."

Gabe could tell Lorina was struggling. "I heard you talking earlier about taking her home with you."

"Only if she wants to go," Gabe interjected. "And only—"

He halted as an anguished cry came from upstairs. "Katlynne," he said, taking the stairs three at a time.

When he reached her, her eyes were wide open in

sheer terror. "Katlynne, *Shh.*" He lifted her and cradled her against him, sitting down on the side of the bed. "It's me, Gabe. I won't let anyone hurt you." He continued to speak softly to her until she blinked several times. As if she realized someone was holding her, she gasped and looked into his eyes with alarm. His shirt was tightly seized in her fingers, and she made no move to let it go.

"Gabe?" Her voice was shaky.

"Yes, I'm here, sweetheart," he said, his voice soothing. "It's all right."

But Kat shook her head, closing her eyes once again. "No," she whispered. "It's not all right." After a moment, she spoke again.

"It'll *never* be all right."

Her words clutched at his heart. Gabe looked back toward the doorway. Shelley had silently moved into the room, and Cynthia stood at the door behind Lorina. It was Lorina's face that caught his gaze, so full of deep sorrow. He continued to sit there, holding Kat, until he realized that her breathing was even, and her hands had relaxed and released their hold on his shirt.

He began to lower her down onto the pillows, pausing only when she opened her eyes briefly and realized he was still there. He smiled at her but wasn't sure if she really saw him. When he finally managed to rest her head back down on the pillow, he knew she was asleep.

He moved to the door, resting a comforting hand on Lorina's shoulder.

She shook her head with a sigh. "Would you all please come into the kitchen?"

With one last look toward Kat, Gabe followed.

Four

T *he caretakers...*

Gabe watched as Lorina took a moment to regain composure. Ted stood next to her, his arm resting around her shoulders. When she saw him in the doorway, she took a breath and began.

"We had so hoped Kat would feel at home here... welcome here."

"She feels welcome, sweets," Ted gently corrected her. "What she doesn't feel is safe."

Lorina nodded. "She may not ever feel safe again," she trailed off briefly–and then concentrated her gaze on Gabe and Shelley. "She called when the letter came to let us know about the possible parole. We offered to go with her, but we knew she wouldn't be able to make herself go."

Ted straightened his shoulders. "What my wife is trying to say is, we've been talking about it. If you all really want to take her home with you, we would ask you, even encourage you, to do it."

Lorina nodded. "She loved this house, until the last four years. Since then, it's been like a tomb."

"Lorina and I are willing to move," Ted added, "if Kat wants to sell out. We even thought that if she goes to Wyoming for the summer, we might move back into the pool house until she decides if she wants to keep the house. We could just close it up until then."

"We'd dearly love to take her with us," Gabe said quietly. "But you need to discuss these things with her, and let her come to her own decision. She's very devoted to you both."

"We'll do that," Ted added. "We just wanted to let you know how *we* feel about it. We'll discuss this with her in the morning, and if she decides to go, we can get her ready before you need to leave."

Gabe studied them, deep in thought. "I want to say something, too. I'm just throwing this out here. We have a cabin out at the ranch that's empty and ready to move into. It's quite nice. Cali, our housekeeper, decided to move into the big house, so it's no longer needed. Since it's a good distance from the house, you'd have your privacy. It's just an option for you, for a spot to stay until this is over. If Katlynne comes out west with us, please consider coming as well."

Ted was touched. "Thank you, Gabe. We'll certainly consider it. If these men are released, we may need to. And if so, we'd be glad to pay rent and utilities."

"No need," Gabe shook his head. "The cabin has been there a long time, and I keep the power on, and lights on a timer so it will look as if someone's living there. Katlynne could run over and see you whenever she wanted. And, of course, you would always be welcome at the house."

Later, as they left for the hotel, Shelley turned toward Gabe. "That was so nice of you."

"Are you kidding?" he returned. "I'd kidnap her and bring her home with us if I thought I could get away with it."

Girl's chat...

The clatter of dishes awakened Kat the next morning as Lorina entered her room with a breakfast tray. "Breakfast, Kat."

Kat stretched and yawned. "You're sweet, but you didn't need to do this. I could have come downstairs."

"I know you could, sweetie, but I thought you deserved a treat. I brought up the carafe of coffee so we could have a girl's chat."

Katlynne grinned. "Ah. I've missed those, And I've missed you and Uncle Ted, too. What's he up to this morning?"

"His favorite place in the world. The greenhouse."

Katlynne laughed. "I should have known." She eyed the tray, smiling. "Blueberry scones? Oh, my," she said with delight.

"Yes, and I don't know how much coffee you're drinking these days, but I suspect a lot since you've been studying for exams lately. Anyway, there's plenty. I also brought up hot tea." Lorina pulled a chair up close to the bed.

"I recognize that expression," Kat said, tilting her head. "Something is on your mind. Tell me." When there was silence, she looked down. "It happened again last night, didn't it? I seem to remember Gabe being here when I woke up." She leaned back and sighed.

"I'm so sorry. I was hoping to at least be able to be here a few days before scaring everyone."

"No apologies, sweets. Ted and I know how devoted you are to us. But we also know being in this house is dreadfully hard for you now. We wish it could be different, but you've been through so much here, and we fear it will never be the same for you. And now, with the parole hearing coming up," She spooned some clotted cream on a scone and held it out to Kat, who took it gratefully. "I just fear for you."

Kat didn't reply.

"What I'm trying to say is, Ted and I would feel better about your safety if you went to Wyoming with Shelley and her family, and we don't know how to say it without giving you the impression that we want to get rid of you."

"I would never think that. Never." Kat threw her hands up in the air, frustrated. "I just feel like such a wimp. I should be able to cope with all this better than I am."

"Oh, honey, no. You're not to blame at all." At the shake of Kat's head, she continued. "Besides that, there's more," Lorina's voice brightened. "A lot may happen between now and then, so I don't know if we'll take him up on this or not, but Gabe offered the use of a cabin on their property, at least for the summer."

"Really?" Kat paused with her scone halfway to her mouth.

"Yes. Again, we don't know if we'll do it. We're still talking about it. I know Ted would miss his green-house, but he might be able to put up a small one somewhere near the cabin. If we don't do that, we'll probably move into the pool house for the summer and close up the house until you come back. But I do love the mountains. Ted does too."

"Do you think you could be happy there?"

"Happy?" Lorina took a bite of the scone and sipped her coffee in thought. "Of course. But—the keyword is *needed*." She leaned back. "We've been care-takers here for so long; Ted and I are accustomed to being needed. It would be very hard for us to sit and do nothing. Now, a vacation might be nice."

Kat put her hand over Lorina's. "You will always be needed, Aunt Lorina. This place will stay for a long time. I don't know if you're aware of what Dad put in the will. When I no longer need the house, it will become yours. I don't know what will happen in the future. But I do think it might be... good," she added, stumbling over her words, "for me to get away for a few weeks. And if you could bring yourself to come,

I'd really love for you to be there." Her voice trembled. "No matter what you decide, I want you to be happy." She swallowed hard. "But my question is, will you be okay if I go?" She waited quietly for Lorina's answer before adding, "Because if you're not—"

"Sweets, I'll answer your question with your own words. "We'll miss you. But no matter what you decide, we want you to be happy." Seeing Kat's unsatisfied expression, she added, "And we fear you won't be able to relax another day in this house. We'd both feel better about you if you went."

There was a long pause. Finally, Kat nodded. "All right. I'll go."

The phone rang, and Lorina patted her hand and went to answer it.

"It's Gabe," she said, appearing at the door a few moments later, "He says to get busy. He has an appointment for someone to work on your car at ten-thirty."

"I swear. He is the most—" but she stopped when she saw a shake of Lorina's head.

"Gabe's a good man, sweets, and you'd be wise to appreciate him going with you. Some places would take advantage of you because you're young and pretty. He won't let them do that. Are you finished?"

"I am. And it was delicious. I'll keep the coffee,

though."

"Just leave the cup here, and I'll get it later. I can take the rest of it down, then." Lorina carried the tray to the doorway, but stopped in the hallway and turned back. "Another unsolicited piece of advice, though, sweets?"

Katlynne was sitting on the side of the bed now and paused.

Lorina raised a brow as she spoke. "You can take it for what it's worth, but Gabe doesn't seem like a man you can push too far," she said quietly. "You might want to start watching your mouth a little better."

Kat, her mouth open, watched Lorina go with astonishment written all over her face. Even so, she had the distinct feeling that Lorina was right.

Kat was sitting in the recliner trying to fasten her braces when Gabe arrived at five minutes to nine.

Lorina moved quickly to the door to open it. "Morning, Gabe."

"Morning, Miss Lorina," he nodded, smiling back at her, and then turned to Kat. "Morning, Katlynne Ela—" he stopped. "Kat."

"Morning, Gabriel—" she grinned, her eyes

sparkling, "Gabe."

"Cute." He responded. "Ready to go?"

"No. I'm trying to put 'my feet' on," she said, struggling with her right braced foot, trying to get it into her shoe. "And they've decided to be a pain in the ass today."

"Excuse me?"

She took note of his expression. "Sorry. But it's true."

"Here, let me help."

"You're early," she said.

"Attempting to change the subject? A little. I don't know how far it is, and I don't want us to be late." He paused. "There you go. You're all set."

She lowered the footrest on the recliner as he finished tying her shoe. "Thank you. Can I call you the next time I have trouble?"

"Only if you're in Wyoming." He chuckled.

"Hm." Leaning forward, she pushed herself over to the edge and up from the chair arm. Gabe helped her up.

"Got your keys?"

"Nope. They're in my room, in my purse."

"Stay put. I'll get them."

"No, I can..." But he was already halfway up the stairs.

A moment later, he returned. "I brought you a jacket too. It was hanging on the end of your bed. It's chilly out this morning."

He took her arm as they went to the car, but Kat stopped when she saw it. "What did you do? It looks different."

"Just ran it through the car wash. That's not something many college students have time to do during the weeks around finals. The next one will be on you."

"It looks nice, Gabe. Thank you."

He glanced down from the driver's seat. "Have you thought any more about Wyoming?"

She looked up. "Yes. Lorina wants me to go with you."

"And you?"

"Me? Oh, I want to come. That is, if you all still want me to?"

"Absolutely. It was a unanimous decision. Are the Baxters leaning toward coming?"

"I don't know. We talked about it. They're just worried about the prospect of not being needed. They've been taking care of me—and of the house and gardens and greenhouse since I was two months old. And Ted loves his greenhouse. She asked if it would be okay if he put up a small one, so he'd have a place to putter."

"It would be okay with me if we had a big one," he said, grinning. "I've been thinking about doing that for a long time, but I don't have the time to work on it, and no one else does either. However, that's a big project by itself."

He pulled out onto the busy highway and continued. "Mariah, who does the cooking, is in heaven when she can get fresh vegetables, but her back won't allow her to do outside gardening anymore." He looked down at her. "Like the Baxters, Mariah and Cali have been with us since my earliest memories, and certainly Shelley's. Both are getting on in years now. I was telling the Baxters last night that Cali has moved into the house now and vacated the cabin, which is where I thought they might want to move. I hope they'll take me up on it."

"It would be wonderful to have them close enough to go see," Kat said thoughtfully. "Thank you, Gabe. That's so thoughtful."

"Good Lord. Thoughtful has nothing to do with it. I'm selfish, Katlynne. I want you out there with us, and I want you to be happy while you're there. That's all."

Something in her stirred with excitement. She wasn't aware he was watching her until he spoke again.

"Thoughts, Katlynne?"

She looked up, surprised. "Don't ask me that."

"Why?"

"Because I'd be embarrassed to tell you."

Gabe threw back his head and laughed.

"Your thoughts?" she asked.

"Actually, I *will* share them with you. But later."

"Oh." She decided not to press him. "There's the shop on the right." She studied his face as he pulled into the lot. "I should be able to handle this." She reached for the door handle, surprised when he put a restraining hand across her.

"I don't think so. It would be better to let me." He looked down. "And before we go in, a couple of things so that we're on the same page. This probably isn't the best place to get new tires. And if you're coming home with us, you could probably wait until later to replace them. But I think you'll need a timing belt—unless you remember having it changed at some point?"

Kat shook her head. "I didn't know it had one."

"Then let's get you an oil change and have them do a once-over and see what they recommend. But I know engines pretty well, so I'll know if their recommendations can wait or if they're unreasonable. Although I have to say I'm not completely up on *this* one. You really do need new brakes, however. Yours are sad."

"You're my hero."

"I believe you said that yesterday." He opened the door and sent her in ahead of him.

Kat stood back and listened as he spoke to the men behind the counter. His manner was respectful but impressive, and they seemed to be listening with equal respect.

After standing for a few moments, she sat down in the front lobby, where there were a few chairs, a coffee pot, and a box of donuts. She was eyeing them when he returned and sat down next to her.

"Did you have breakfast, Katlynne?"

She looked up. "Lorina brought up a tray. I had a blueberry scone and coffee."

"That's not enough."

"No, it was plenty. I'm fine."

He chuckled. "There must be a verse in the Bible somewhere that says, "Young ladies shall not live by blueberry scones and coffee alone." He grinned.

"Good grief. I'm sure there isn't."

But he ignored that. "Your car won't be ready until four this afternoon, and Cynthia and Shelley want to meet you for some serious shopping at two if you're up to it. So, before I call a taxi, tell me where you'd like to go for a bite to eat."

"There's a little pizza shop within walking distance that's good."

He looked down at her. "At this hour of the morning? You sure that's what you want?

Kat began counting on her fingers. "Let's see... bread, meat, cheese and vegetables. What's not to love? And it's not too far to walk."

"How far?"

"A couple of blocks, I think. Not far."

"Can you make it? "

Her mouth flattened. "Yes. If you'll stop hovering."

"If not, I can give you a piggyback ride. Or carry you."

"You will not."

He raised a brow. "Try me." Standing, he held out his hand.

Kat sighed. "Gabe Ingrahm, has anyone ever told you you're a bully?" she frowned.

"And you, young lady, has anyone ever told you you're a—" Turning to open the door, he noticed that the men behind the counter were watching them curiously and chuckling. He didn't finish until he got her out the front door and closed it. "Recalcitrant little brat?" He concluded.

"Once or twice," she uttered.

"Your attitude is showing," he said. "All right. Which way?"

"This way," she retorted, tugging on his arm, "and I am *not a brat*."

"Matter of opinion."

Kat stepped off the curb to cross the street when Gabe lifted her off her feet and back to the curb in a single move. A truck honked at her, and the driver scowled through the window as he sped past.

"Oops."

Gabe, too, was scowling down at her. "Did no one teach you to look both ways before crossing the street?" He scolded.

"I didn't see him. And besides that, he was speeding."

"You didn't look, Katlynne. I'm going to hold on to you. No arguments." He looped his arm through hers, holding on.

She rolled her eyes.

"And you can stop that."

A sigh escaped. "Fine." She ignored the look of censorship from him but noticed he had slowed his steps to match her pace. Neither of them spoke until they reached the front door of their destination. It was a small place with a cozy atmosphere, and he took her to a booth in the back.

Once seated, he turned to her.

"I have some questions for you."

"Oh?"

"About your limitations. I know," he held up his hand against her forthcoming protest. "I know you don't feel like you have any, but I'll explain why it's so important that I know them."

"Have it your way," she said, failing to meet his eyes. "You said you'd tell me what you were thinking this morning. Is that it?"

"Yes." He leaned forward on his elbows, looking down into her upturned face. "Katlynne, I've dreaded having this conversation with you, but I must."

Kat met his eyes. "What conversation?"

He continued. "At the ranch, we have a strict set of rules that absolutely must be followed." He paused when the server brought their drinks and set them on the table.

"Ready to order?"

"Katlynne? What's your favorite?" Gabe studied her.

"I like everything."

"Then I recommend the works." The server was writing now.

"Sounds good," Gabe handed him back the menus, and he left.

Five

R*ules...*

Kat kept her eyes on his face as the server left. "Rules. What rules?"

"These have been in place for as long as I can remember. And before Dad made them, he had reasons for each one. So, I've left them. Over the years, almost without exception, every time someone has gotten hurt, it has been because they didn't follow them. But," he studied her face, "disobedience is followed with consequences. And that's what I need to discuss with you."

Her eyes were growing larger. "Consequences?"

"First, let me explain what they are. Let's start with the horses. Do you ride?"

"I did once when I was a kid, but not in a long time. I fell under the horse. Dad wouldn't let me ride after that."

"Were you hurt?"

"No. When I hit the ground, the mare jumped over me. I was terrified she would step on me. She didn't, but it scared Dad."

"I can certainly understand why." His brows raised. "So, you've seen first-hand why you should never ride alone."

"I suppose."

"All right. Another is, never to get near Thunder. He's my stallion, and I'm the only one besides Will and Tim who can ride him safely. Thunder is a huge fellow. Don't ever go near his stall unless I'm with you. Do you understand?"

She nodded. "Yes. I'll bet he's beautiful."

"He is. And very dangerous. The third thing is, never, ever let the horses see you with a whip in your hand. We don't use them on our horses. A lot of our animals are rescues. Will trains them, and they think he's one of them. When he has them ready to ride, all you need are commands. If one—especially Thunder, ever sees you with a whip, he might rear in fright and trample you. He was cruelly treated before he came to us, and it took a long time to get him over his fear. Understood?"

Kat was trying to count on her fingers the rules he had discussed.

"Katlynne?"

"Yes?"

"All right. If you ever want to ride again, you'll need to ask beforehand so we can make sure someone can saddle up the horse for you and go with you. Most of the time, it will probably be me. And don't go out to the barn with carrots or sugar cubes or apples to treat them unless one of us is with you. Do you need to write these down? If you do, we'll go over them again when we get to the ranch. But I want you to know now what they are."

"I think I've got it. And I won't go near the barn anyway."

"Ah. Then that won't be a problem. That's all the ones regarding the horses," he answered.

She stared. "There are more?"

"Yes. Ready?"

"No."

"Too bad. All right. Never go off walking alone. We have parameters set up, and I'll show you where they are when we get there so you'll know how far you can go safely."

She felt her eyes widen. "You mean if I'm walking?"

"Yes, walking. We've had an influx of snakes this year. It's worse than usual. And a lot of them are rattlers. They have dens, and you could walk right into one unless there was someone with you who knew where they tend to be. I'm not trying to scare you, Katlynne," he said gently. "I just want you to stay safe."

She knew she didn't look convinced.

"Even if the Baxters come out, although the cabin is on the property, you need to take the golf cart or the SUV if you go to see them. Cynthia even has a car she'd let you use, as long as you ask permission from someone so they know where you'll be. And don't try to walk it."

"Because of snakes?"

"Because of snakes."

"I see."

"And another. You may need to go into town occasionally to do some shopping. Shelley, Cynthia, or one of us will need to go with you. If the rare occasion does arise that you must go alone, clear it with me first. No one else, just me."

"Got it."

"And another thing. Always take one of the satellite phones with you. Cell phones don't work well for long stretches out there, and if you had a breakdown, there would be no way to get hold of me."

"Is all that really necessary?"

"Absolutely. With your limitations, I can't afford to take a chance on you breaking down miles from home. Stop bristling, little cub. Even if you could walk, it would be way too far. So always take one of the satellite phones. That's probably one of the most important things you'll need to remember. And if you do go into town, make sure someone at the ranch sees to it that you have enough gas before you leave. There aren't gas stations on every corner."

"I do know how to read a gas gauge, believe it or not. And I can fill my own tank." she quipped, sarcasm creeping into her voice. She paused as the server arrived with the pizza and served each of them a piece.

As he left, Gabe looked down at her. "Humor me, Katlynne. Too many for you to remember?"

She nodded. "My head is swimming. What happens if I forget one?"

"I'll make you a list. And we'll go over them again when you get there. Until then, try to remember as many as possible. And you can always ask if you have a question."

"Shelley said you were strict," she said, under her breath.

"I have to be. I'm the responsible party. If someone breaks one, defiantly or otherwise, lives could be at stake."

She didn't say anything for a moment. Finally, putting her fork down on her plate, she looked up at him. "You didn't answer my question."

"I know I didn't. If you forget one, I will remind you. I might lecture you in the process, to imprint on you how important it is that you remember them the next time."

"You still didn't answer. What," she said quietly, "if it happens again?"

Gabe put his own fork down, capturing her hand with his, and leaned forward. "Before I answer that, Katlynne, let me share something with you. I rarely ever discuss this with anyone, but I feel you should know."

She waited, noting the expression of pain that crossed his face.

"When I was fourteen," he began, "we were a wonderfully happy family: Dad, Mom, Shelley, and me. We had those rules then, too. Shelley and I were pretty good about following them, even as kids. But my mother was not. She and Dad should have been in complete agreement, but they weren't. Mother was beautiful, but she was also determined. She could wind Dad around her little finger, and he, for some reason, continually let her get away with things he shouldn't have. She didn't think the rules applied to her."

He was silent for a moment. He was still looking down at her, but Kat felt as if he was looking through her, seeing what had happened all those years ago. She remained silent, waiting until he spoke again.

"Then, one day, she saddled up her horse and went riding without letting anyone know where she was going. No one saw her leave. When she didn't show up at lunch, and no one knew where she was, Dad and Will and the men took off looking for her."

Kat froze at the tension that hovered in the air like a cloud. "What happened?"

Gabe met her eyes once again. "They found her late in the afternoon. She'd jumped a fence and fallen from her horse into a den of rattlers. She'd been dead for hours." His voice became very quiet, and Kat reached out and gently touched his hand, tears trickling down her cheeks. "I'm so sorry, Gabe."

He reached down and gently wiped away a tear. "Thank you, Katlynne. The truth is, even now, I still don't know whether to feel sorrow or anger at what happened. But to answer your question, if you break the rules, you might be subject to discipline."

She didn't meet his eyes. Staring down at her plate, she didn't speak for a long time. "Does this happen a lot at the ranch?"

"I can't even remember the last time it happened. If one of the employees breaks a rule, which never happens, I deal with that on an employer/employee basis. But everyone knows and follows them because they understand their importance. We're a team, Katlynne. It's important that everyone works together. I think I know you well enough to be assured you'll try your best. But you also deserve to know what will happen if you don't."

"Thank you."

"I promise to be as lenient with you as possible. I don't know if that helps any, but," he reached over and lifted her chin, "That's the reason we have rules, and it's also the reason why I enforce them. I watched Dad lose his spirit after Mom died. It was dreadful. We could see him die a little inside every single day. He married Cynthia two years later, and she was wonderful. She was a great wife to him and always good to us. But Dad developed cancer shortly after they were married and died when I was eighteen. We begged Cynthia to stay with us, so she did. She was more of a friend than a stepmother. And she was really good with Shelley."

Kat listened to the respect in his voice, silent for a long time. She thought of the ache in her heart for her own mom and dad and how Gabe must have felt having lost his mom under such tragic circumstances, and then his dad after that. It was sometime later when she said softly, "Gabe, I'll do my best to obey them."

"Good girl. I knew you would."

Six

S *hopping...*

At one forty-five, Gabe called Cynthia and Shelley and told them where he and Kat were eating. She had ravenously finished the pizza on her plate, plus three more pieces.

Looking up, she smiled. "You don't like pizza? Gabe, you didn't eat much. Are you all right?"

"I'm fine, Katlynne. Unlike you, however, I had a decent breakfast."

"Well, the mall has a food court. You can get anything you like there if you get hungry. Or are you going back to the garage?"

"I'll accompany you all," he said, picking up his

phone. "Surely there will be more to do there than sit and look at a box of stale donuts."

Katlynne listened as he called the garage. After a moment, he ended the conversation and turned to her. "They said to give them until five-thirty. I'll go to the mall with you. I may find a few interesting. places." He glanced up, looking past her. "Ahh. I see Shelley and Cynthia. Wait for me. I'll be right back."

She could see him at the counter, paying, and then waving to a car in the parking lot. When he returned, she was standing outside the booth, putting her jacket on and reaching for her bag. "Can I cover the tip?" she asked.

"No. I took care of it already."

Kat frowned. "I didn't intend for you to pay for my lunch."

Gabe stopped at the doorway. "Just say thank you, Katlynne."

She looked up, her cheeks pink. "Thank you," she said quietly. "That was very nice of you." She waved as she saw Cynthia and Shelley approaching.

The mall was busy when they arrived. Kat listened to Cynthia with amusement as she talked about everything she'd like to find.

"And this, ladies," said Gabe, "is where I leave you. Shop until your hearts are content." He winked at Kat as he turned away, and she watched him leave curiously.

"I'm afraid he'll be terribly bored here."

Cynthia laughed. "Gabe? He'll find a way to amuse himself. He'll hit whatever he can in the way of electronics supply stores, boot shops, and bookstores, and then he'll get bored and call to see if we want to meet him for coffee."

Shelley grinned. "Where to, Cynthia? Since you're the one who never gets to shop these days, lead the way."

Cynthia was more than happy to take the lead. "Wyoming," she explained, "is a wonderful place to live, but it requires quite a bit of travel from the ranch to get to good shopping."

But Gabe showed up at four o'clock outside the dress shop on the second level.

"Hey, Gabe," Cynthia said, noticing him standing outside in the hallway, hands jammed into his pockets. "What's up?"

"I'm bored," he said, grinning. "Entertain me."

Kat gave off a giggle. "Why, oh why, am I not surprised?"

"Kat, you're elected," Cynthia looked at her watch. "I'm not finished shopping." With a wave, she and Shelley were gone.

Gabe was leaning over the rail, looking at the food court below. "Anything else besides this available? Like a restaurant?"

"There's a place called Garfinkel's downstairs around the corner. They have a nice selection—and some good desserts, if you like."

"Sold. Come, Katlynne."

She took the hand he held out and looked up at him. "Why do I feel like I've been set up?" she said, raising a brow, "And how did you know where to find us?"

"Because you have," he said, "and because Shelley sent me a text."

"Hm. I thought maybe that was it. Why did she do that?"

"Because I told her to. And because I'm her brother, and she respects me, unlike some other young ladies I've met recently."

Kat shook her head. "And because you threatened her?"

"Within an inch of her life," he said, grinning. "You held out better than I thought you would."

"I'm full of surprises."

"Yes, you are." He said, guiding her toward the escalator. "Do these things give you any trouble?"

"What, escalators? No."

"Just wondered."

"Would you please quit worrying? I can do anything anyone else can do." She scowled. A moment later she looked up, seeing his brows raised. "Well, almost anything."

"Cut me some slack, Katlynne," he said firmly.

They found the entrance to Garfinkel's and were seated quickly. Gabe ushered her into the booth and sat next to her, instead of across from her. She looked up at him curiously as he slid in and put his arm around her shoulders.

"Cynthia and Shelley may decide to join us, although I doubt it," he said. "and besides that, young lady, I'm about to give you a lecture. And I'd rather be close enough that no one else can hear. What would you like to drink?"

"Iced water with lemon, please," she said, her mouth suddenly dry.

Neither of them spoke again until the waiter took their order. "And so help me, Katlynne, if you insist on paying, you'll be in trouble."

"But—"

"*Katlynne.*" It was only one word, but it silenced her. "Answer me this, young lady. Why are you so determined to refuse to let anyone do anything nice for you?"

She looked up into his face, genuinely surprised. "Am I?"

"Absolutely." His voice was low and in full lecture mode now, "Do you feel obligated to pay your own way? Can you not just accept that sometimes others want to do nice things for you?"

When she remained quiet, he said, more gently, "Katlynne. I'm trying to understand you. Are you not used to people being helpful?"

"It's not that," she said quietly.

"Then what are you trying to prove?"

Kat looked up, hurt. "Is that what you think?"

Gabe lifted her chin. "I don't know. You're a puzzle, young lady."

Kat refused to meet his eyes. "My whole life," she said quietly, "especially in the beginning, I was so dependent upon others. I couldn't walk by myself, I couldn't take a bath by myself, I couldn't do *anything* by myself. Then they got me the chair, and I could get around by myself. But we had a two-story house, and I couldn't get up and down the stairs without crawling or asking someone to carry me. Then, one day, I was standing outside the kitchen. I was four or five, and I think I heard Dad and Lorina talking about a stair elevator. I stood at the bottom of the stairs, looking up at all those steps, and thought how wonderful it would be not to have to ask someone for help, or scuff up my shoes crawling up and down. I began saving my allowance for it."

"That sounds like you."

She ignored the remark. "I came to Dad one day with my piggy bank and asked him if that was enough to pay for it. He smiled and said, yes, he thought so. The next thing I knew, there was one installed." A small laugh escaped. "The first day, all I did was ride it up and down. Stop laughing at me."

"Just thinking about you at four years old, offering your piggy bank to pay for a stair elevator. I'm touched, Katlynne. I can almost see you doing that."

"Gabe," she said softly, "it's not that I'm trying to be stubborn. It's just that there have been so many things over the years I've had to be dependent on others to do for me. My whole desire in life was to be able to be self-sufficient. The physical therapists always said, *You can't depend on others all your life. You have to learn how to do things by yourself.*"

"And you did," he said softly.

"I never thought I'd be able to get around well enough to leave home and go to college. To actually be able to walk up to the stage and pick up my own diploma... by myself..." Her eyes were misty, and she found herself suddenly wrapped in his arms.

"I'm so proud of you." His voice dropped. "So, that's where your independent streak comes from."

She frowned. "But I freely admit, it's hard to know where being self-sufficient ends, and where accepting help from others begins."

He put a hand over hers gently. "Katlynne, I hope you'll learn to accept help from me without feeling insulted. There are some things you'll need to let me do for you, and there are some things I'll just want to do for you. I hope you can be gracious and accept them. It's not because I expect anything in return, except maybe a simple thank you."

Kat's mouth was a flat line. "I'll try."

"The second thing is just what I said at the escalator. You've been acquainted with yourself for 23? 24 years?, and I'm only just beginning to get to know you. I'll figure out what you can and can't do eventually, but until then, you'll have to be patient and tell me. Don't get huffy when I ask." He paused. "Learn to let me ask questions about your limitations. No more of this '*I'm not helpless*' stuff from you. Answer my questions, just as you did a minute ago. Tell me stories about how you grew up."

"You really want to hear them?"

"Absolutely."

Kat grinned. "All right. Do you want to hear the

one about being in detention in the seventh grade and two girls in the bathroom who dared me to jump out a second-story window?"

He stared at her. "I can't wait," he said, brows raised. "Where did you land?"

"In the dumpster below."

He was quiet for a few seconds, but turned, quite slowly, to face her. "Were you hurt?"

"No. I was just a little... fragrant. But when I got out, the doors to the building were locked, and I couldn't get back in."

"Good Lord. How did you get home?"

"I walked. It took me a while. But, the thing that irritated me the most was that the school gave me detention for three more days, because I didn't get back to class. No sense of humor at all." At the shake of his head, she shrugged. "It taught me one thing, though."

Gabe was still staring. "I'm afraid to ask."

She grinned. "I'll tell you. Don't accept dares from just anyone." She took in his expression of mirth, adding, "You can stop laughing at me now."

Kat lay on her bed that night, hugging her body pillow, afraid to fall asleep. She knew the dream might recur. But she was also thinking about the day she spent with Gabe; the way he pulled her back when she'd stepped out into the street without looking; how he reached out and brushed away her tears when talking about his own mother's death; his closeness as he ushered her into the booth at Garfinkel's and put his arm around her, lecturing her in that firm voice. Something unfamiliar stirred in her as she thought of his dominance.

But Gabe's lectures hadn't been over for the day. When Cynthia had dropped them off to pick up her car, Kat had opened her purse to get out her debit card. Gabe's voice was firm as he spoke. "Katlynne, I need you to sit down and wait for me. I'm going to insist on talking to the mechanics, and I want to see evidence of what they've done with your car."

Kat looked up in disbelief. "Gabe—"

"Do as I say, please, Katlynne," was all he had said before turning on his heel to approach the desk.

Fuming, she'd gone to sit down, but the only seats available were the same ones she'd taken that morning. The box of donuts was still on the table, and the same two donuts.

So much for finding a seat close enough to hear what was being said. Still, it was difficult to hear all of it. She did catch the words "talk with the mechanic" just before Gabe and the manager disappeared through the door, and it closed behind them.

She was still fuming when he came back in. He'd glanced down at her, raising a brow when he saw her expression. She immediately grabbed the nearest available magazine from the rack and pretended to be interested in it.

As she listened, however, the conversation between Gabe and the manager seemed jovial. Gabe had appeared a moment later next to her and leaned down close to her ear.

"Interested in hunting black boar of Missouri, hm?"

Kat glanced down at the magazine article open on her lap. The headline at the top of the page said, *Landowners in Missouri concerned about the dangers of the black boar.* Her mouth became a straight line. Was it necessary for this man to notice everything?

He took it from her and set it back in the rack, reaching for her hand. "Not a word, young lady. Let's go." Helping her to her feet, he ushered her outside and to the car.

Kat remained quiet as long as she could.

"Aren't you going to tell me how much the bill was?"

Gabe reached into his pocket and pulled it out, handing it to her.

"Seven hundred and sixty?"

"No. See the ones they lined through? They charged for changing the fuel pump and the water pump. Since your car doesn't have a water pump, I questioned them about it and went to look at it. They didn't change either one—it was a mistake and should have been charged to someone else. Your total is at the bottom. Two hundred sixty-five. They did replace the brakes and did an oil change and lube, and replaced the timing belt. This is why I wanted to handle it. I knew if *you* did, not knowing about cars, you might have paid the whole thing without question."

"I did know my car was air-cooled. But wow, that's a big difference. Thank you, Gabe. I'll just write a check to you, then." Her voice was just as determined as *his*.

"Did Cynthia not talk to you?"

"No."

"Get that suspicious note out of your voice, young lady. Cynthia had the idea that, since you're coming out west—"

"To work—"

"To work," he echoed. "She wanted to pay for your auto repair as part of an advance on your pay. If you're not agreeable, you can take it up with her." He pulled his phone out of his pocket and held it out to her. "She's on speed dial 4."

Kat eyed the phone for a moment before shaking her head. "I believe you."

Gabe was staring down at her, his eyes narrowed. They were in the driveway of her home when she noticed that they had stopped.

He shut off the engine and sat there a moment, looking at her before exiting the driver's side and advancing toward hers. She had unfastened her seat belt and had the door open before he reached her. Setting her on her feet, he steadied her with his right arm and smacked her bottom soundly with his left on the way to the door. Her sudden gasp revealed how shocked she was.

"Sweets! Gabe!" Lorina met them inside but stopped when she saw their faces. "Is everything all right?"

"Fine, ma'am. I've brought your little miscreant back. The car is as good as it can be right now. I'll have to use it to get to the hotel, but I'll bring it back tomorrow or sooner if she needs it." He had guided Kat to the recliner and lifted her, setting her down in it firmly.

"Katlynne," he'd nodded to her and left.

Seven

⌒⌒⌒⌒

M *orning...*

At ten-thirty the next morning, Kat glanced out the kitchen window to see Gabe pull into the driveway. Cynthia and Shelley were behind him in the rental. When Kat opened the door, he was standing outside.

"Morning, brat."

She looked up. "Good morning, sir," she said, emphasizing the 'sir' with politeness.

He stood back. "Well, bless my soul," he grinned, his eyes crinkling at the corners. "I think there must be a crack in the universe. I honestly don't know how you meant that, but I'll take it as a polite greeting. I brought your car back. Shelley's with me, and Cynthia followed in the rental. She wants to know if you'll join us for lunch. She wants to discuss preparations for the trip with you."

"I'd love to," she said, again adding, "sir."

Gabe's expression resembled a deer in the headlights, and Kat threw back her head in a fit of giggles.

Gabe followed Kat into the kitchen, waving at Ted. "Morning," he said cheerfully. "We thought we'd kidnap Katlynne for lunch if it's all right. We need to make sure she has what she needs to bring with her for the trip." He glanced down at Kat and grinned. "And you might need a jacket. It's still a bit chilly outside."

Kat nodded. "I'll be right back."

When she returned, she could hear Ted's voice.

"Gabe," Ted said quietly, "about your offer... I've been thinking."

He's about to say no. Kat's face fell with disappointment.

"So have I, sir," Gabe interrupted, excitement in his voice. "Katlynne told me about your greenhouse. I've been wanting one of those set up at the ranch for a long time, but I don't know how to go about planning or building one. But," he held up his hands, "We'd be happy to help someone else put one up if they'd show us what to do." Gabe promptly took Kat's jacket from her, helping her into it. "I'd love to have a vegetable garden too. If you were to come, do you think you could supervise putting one together and grow some vegetables?"

Kat clearly saw the gleam in Ted's eyes. The expression on his face had changed to one of eagerness.

Gabe continued. "When we bring Katlynne back, I'd love to see yours. Perhaps we could make some plans?"

"Certainly," Ted's voice was enthusiastic.

Gabe cocked his head. "I'm sorry, I think I interrupted you when I came in. Was there something you wanted to tell me?"

"No, *no*." Ted was smiling. "Just that Lorina and I are still thinking it over."

"Good." Gabe grinned back. "We really hope you'll decide to come. Ready, Katlynne?"

"Ready." This time, she took his hand willingly. As he helped her into the car, she turned.

"You're good, Gabriel Ingrahm."

"Oh?"

"You do realize he was about to tell you they'd decided not to come."

He smiled at her. "I was afraid of that. But I'm serious about the greenhouse. And Katlynne?"

"Yes?"

"Don't *ever* call me Gabriel again."

Kat relaxed a half hour later as they were sitting in the hotel, munching happily away on Chinese food and talking. Gabe was seated on one of the sofas between Kat and Shelley, and Will and Cynthia relaxed across from them on the other. Kat couldn't help but notice the occasional look of fondness that passed between them.

Cynthia made a rueful face from across from her. "I goofed yesterday, Kat. Gabe and I discussed covering your car expenses as part of an advance on your pay. I meant to talk to you about it while we were shopping, and I forgot. Sorry."

Kat took a breath. Beside her, she could feel Gabe stiffen. "You really don't need to pay me *anything*. You'll be covering my expenses for food and lodging, and that's enough. And I'll be begging you to take me with you to meet people so I can sketch them anyway."

"Kat," Cynthia leaned forward, her expression incredulous. "Listen, sweetie. If the publishers are right, this book may make some money. I wouldn't dream of letting you work for nothing. It would be unthinkable. I can't tell you right now how much it will make, but I do know the amount of the advance they're paying me, and I'll be talking to them as soon as we get home."

"They could wait to pay me until they see how well the book does."

Cynthia leaned back and looked at Gabe.

"I told you how stubborn she is," he said.

"Am not," Kat tossed out.

"All right, let me put it to you this way," Cynthia said. "The food and lodging are just because we want you as our guest for a while. We would do that anyway. But if word got around that the publishers let my illustrator work for nothing, they would never, *ever* be able to get anyone to work for them again. And since you'd be working with me, my reputation in the writing community would be shot. And," she added, "if word got out you a*greed* to work for nothing, you'd be swamped with publishers wanting to pay you just that: nothing."

That brought Kat's eyes up in disbelief as Cynthia continued.

"It's true. It would be a lose-lose situation for both of us. In addition to that, there will be so many illustrations in this book, that you're *almost* going to be a co-author. You'll earn every penny you get." She sighed, leaning forward again. "Please accept my offer, Kat. As soon as I talk to them, we'll know where we stand. But don't throw this away; it can be the making or breaking of your career as an artist."

Kat looked back at her and finally nodded. "Of course, I accept. Thank you."

Cynthia clapped her hands in delight. "Fantastic! I can't wait for us to get started." She bit off a piece of her egg foo young, savoring it. "Okay, on to other things. Are you packed? Do you need any clothes besides what you have? What about art supplies? I'm slipping. I should have thought of this yesterday while we were shopping. Where's the nearest art shop?" She reached into her bag and pulled out a piece of lined paper, handing over a pencil. "Here, you may need to make a list."

"And don't forget your camera," Gabe added. "The weather is cool. We're in a basin between the Bighorn Mountains and the Absaroka Range, where Yellowstone is. And yes, we'll take you to Yellowstone. And what about boots?" he asked.

Kat looked down at her shoes. "I don't have any," she answered, making a face. "It's hard to find boots that will go on over my braces."

Will leaned forward. "We could have Indy make her a pair," he suggested.

"I'm sure he'd be glad to." Gabe nodded. "You'll

like Indy, Katlynne. His mother had polio—and was in an iron lung for over a year. You'll like her, too."

It was later that afternoon when Shelley leaned forward. "And don't forget your inhalers, Kat. For your asthma."

"I just got them filled," Kat said quietly. "I should have enough to last me a few months."

Eight

T ake off...

Tuesday morning, Kat hugged Lorina and Ted goodbye as Gabe put her in the rental car to take her to the airport. Will was checking over the engines and gauges in the plane when they arrived, and filling out necessary papers to leave. Kat's things, along with Shelley's, had been loaded the day before.

"It'll be a long flight, Katlynne. And possibly a bumpy one," Gabe informed her. "I just want you to know what to expect. Did you double-check your list?" He asked again as he lifted her into the plane.

"Of course I did."

Cynthia leaned forward. "If not, we can stop over in Billings and do some shopping."

"Dream on, young lady," Will looked back at her. But Kat noticed he gave her a grin and a wink. Cynthia stuck out her lower lip.

Shelley rolled her eyes. "Did we mention she loves to shop?"

Kat was about to retort with a 'once or twice,' but before she could answer, Will turned back to them. "Everyone strapped in and ready?"

"Ready," they all answered at once. It became very quiet as they watched and waited. Will skillfully brought the plane off the ground, keeping contact with air traffic control.

Kat leaned back in the seat, hoping for a smooth flight.

Gabe had been hoping for a good flight too, but he was to be disappointed. It was anything *but* smooth. They hit a weather system about two hours into the flight, and the girls in the back were turning green before the first half of the flight was over. Gabe nodded to Shell to pass Kat a bag in case she needed it.

She did, within minutes. Shelley followed. Cynthia

was the only one in the back who managed to make it with no nausea at all. But no one complained.

Gabe studied all three ladies as the landing gear touched down, and Will taxied toward the hanger. The truck and the SUV were already there, and Tim was waiting, from the looks of it, impatiently. Tim was at the door to help Cynthia and Shelley down instantly.

Kat's legs were unsteady as she attempted to stand. "Can I just kiss the ground, now?" she whispered, just before she began to heave.

"Sure, sweetheart." Gabe pulled her hair back away from her face with his left hand as he held her around the waist with his right. "I'm sorry. Flights aren't usually this bad."

"Ah, poor baby," Tim tried to steady Shelley, concerned. "Bad trip?"

"Ghastly," Cynthia remarked. "Will, you're fired," she said with a mischievous wink and a grin. "Take your time. I'll walk to the house."

Will, however, just laughed. "Sorry, all of you. Next time we'll try to pick a calmer day to fly."

Ten minutes and several episodes later, however, Kat tried to sit up. Gabe turned her gently, cradling her in his arms. The rest of the luggage loaded, Gabe held Kat in his lap until they reached the house. Her eyes were closed, but she still looked deathly pale.

Cynthia met him just inside the front door. "Josie," she said, "locked herself in Kat's room."

Gabe frowned and nodded. "I'll put Katlynne in mine." Carrying her down the hall, he entered his own room, gently lowering Kat down on his bed. He removed her braces and spread the quilt over her. One last glance at her from the doorway made him smile. She looked extraordinarily tiny in the huge bed.

Silently, he closed it behind him and grimly moved down the hall where Cali was waiting with the key. Mariah, Tim, Cynthia, and Will were also there.

Gabe spoke quietly to them. "All of you, please stay." Taking the key from Cali, he opened it and stepped inside.

A slender, blonde Josie ran to him when she saw him, throwing her arms around his neck, her eyes suddenly pleading. "*Gabe!* Gabe, I'm so glad you're here. They were going to *throw me out*. They—"

But Gabe was rigid. "Get your things together, Josie." His voice was stiff and deep as he untangled her arms from around his neck. "Tim will take you home."

Josie's expression changed, and she put out a pouty lip. "You can't throw me out in the street, Gabe Ingrahm."

His laugh was cynical. "Your home is hardly the street. Either you go of your own accord, or you can be escorted out by police. My patience has reached its end, Josie. I won't hesitate to take out an order of protection against you this time. Out. And by the way, where did you park your car? I'm sure you didn't carry your suitcases all the way from home."

Josie ignored his question and backed away from him, her eyes flashing with anger. "You'll be sorry, Gabe. It'll be your word against mine." Her eyes grew suddenly wide as everyone from the hallway filed in.

Gabe stood firm. "I believe that's *'our word'* against yours. You have ten minutes to get your stuff together. Tim will wait here while you pack." With that, he turned and strode into the hall while everyone else stayed. Tim's arms were crossed, his expression of disgust strong.

Tim stood in the room with his arms folded, waiting for Josie to move. It took a full five minutes before she slowly began to pull her suitcase from the closet and open drawers, stuffing her clothes inside. "I never thought I'd see the day," she said tearfully, "when *my own Gabe* would throw me out of his house."

Cynthia stood there, her mouth a straight line. It was Tim who said firmly, "Gabe has never been yours,

Josie, and you know it. It's time you faced facts. He's just put up with you because of the family's friendship with your parents. Hurry up."

"Gabe has *always* been mine!" she screamed at him. "None of you can change that!" She sat back down on the bed defiantly.

Tim looked at his watch. "You now have five minutes, Josie. Then I'll cart you out of here, and whatever stuff of yours is left will be delivered to your house later in the week."

Josie huffed out a sigh and sat there.

Cali had gone into the bathroom and retrieved the shampoos, conditioners, curling iron, and other toiletries that belonged to her and placed them on the dresser. "No need to go into the bathroom," she said triumphantly. When Josie made no move to pack them, Mariah brought a bag from the kitchen, holding it out. Cali dumped the items into it and handed it to Will.

Gabe was seated on the stool next to the breakfast bar when they escorted Josie out, screaming. "You'll be sorry, Gabe! I won't forget this!"

Gabe didn't look at her as Tim turned her toward the door and pulled her through it firmly.

Hoping the commotion had not awakened Kat, Gabe approached his room to check.

Quietly, he opened the door and peeked in. Kat was lying on her side and had curled up into a little ball. He stood quietly, watching her, thankful that Josie's tirade had not awakened her.

Mariah was in the kitchen by the time he returned. "I'm so sorry about that, Mr. Gabe. She was in there before we knew it, and we couldn't get her out."

"No, Mariah. Not your fault at all. I'm not surprised. I'm just sorry it upset you all and caused extra work. Keep an eye out for her. I'll probably need to talk with her father before long. I worry about what she'll attempt with Katlynne here."

Cali emerged a moment later from Kat's room. "All done, Mr. Gabe," she said, passing the kitchen with a smile. "By the way, the patio door was open."

"Thanks, Cali. When Katlynne wakes up, we'll move her into it. I think the longer she sleeps, the more settled her stomach will be. Shelley, too. I don't think we've had a flight that bumpy in quite some time."

Cynthia came into the kitchen as he finished speaking. "You all are wusses," she said with a grin. "How's Kat? I just checked on Shelley."

At that moment, the front door opened. Tim had returned, Will trailing behind him. "Will found her car behind the house, so we drove it home. Josie is telling her folks all sorts of nonsense." He shook his head, sitting down at the table. "I tried to tell them the truth, but I don't know if I got through. They've raised a demon, Gabe. I doubt that girl has ever been told 'no' in her life. And I get the impression they're afraid of her now."

"Did you speak to Mr. Lowell?"

Tim nodded. "I tried, but I'm not sure I got through for all of Josie's noise."

Gabe eyed him, frowning. "I feel for them, but it's not a problem I can solve. Nor do I want to. I do ask that you all watch for her on the ranch. I don't want her here."

"She still has this notion that you're going to marry her someday." Will scowled. "I wonder who put *that* in her head?"

"I don't know. I suspect it was her mother. I have to say, I pity the man who ends up with her," Gabe said thoughtfully. He looked across at both of them. "The truth is, I'm a little concerned for Katlynne's safety if Josie comes back."

When Kat's voice came from down the hall, Gabe

turned. "Katlynne." He hurried to the door of his room and opened it.

Kat sat up on the side of the bed, bewildered, as Gabe opened the door.

"Feeling better?"

She nodded. "I just didn't know where I was for a moment. And I can't find my AFOs."

Gabe reached down toward the foot of the bed and grabbed them, moving toward her. "I apologize, Katlynne. I should have put them where you could see them. How's the nausea?"

"Much better. How's Shelley?"

"Still lying down. Motion sickness takes a bit to subside." He knelt in front of her and began helping her put her braces on. Suddenly looking up, he frowned. "What?"

"I can do that, you know."

"I know you can. But this is a high bed, and I didn't want you to fall off trying." He moved to the second one. "It's high in your room, too."

She looked around. "Where am I, then?"

"You're in my room. I put you in here because Josie had taken up squatter's rights in yours. We had to move her out."

Kat frowned. "You kicked her out of her room so I could have it?"

"No, Katlynne." He finished tying her shoe and stood to his feet, helping her to the floor. "We kicked her out of *your* room so you could have it."

"I hope I didn't inconvenience anyone."

"She only lives a few miles away. There's no reason for her to be here, period. Do you feel like meeting everyone? Mariah is working on supper, and I think everyone is in the kitchen."

"I'd love to."

As they reached the end of the hall, he turned Kat toward the kitchen. He'd been right. It was full. The table was full of men from the ranch; enjoying Mariah's coffee. "Everyone? Here is our Katlynne." He introduced them, one by one. "These are my right-hand men, Katlynne. Don't know what I'd do without them. Bill and Aaron are still outside with the horses."

"Kat Abramson," she nodded toward them, smiling. "It's nice to meet you."

"Kat will be the illustrator for the new book," Cynthia remarked. "Kat, want to see your room?"

"Please."

She took in a deep breath when she saw it. "Oh my,

Cynthia. This is beautiful. I love the glass doors. And the reading corner."

"If you need a desk for illustrating, I can probably find you one around here somewhere and move it in. Or you can use the kitchen island, or table, if you like. It just wouldn't be private."

"I'm sure the kitchen table would be fine," she grinned. "Besides, privacy is greatly overrated just now."

"Kitchen table it is, then. Mariah will probably like the company. But I'll ask around anyway, just in case anyone knows what happened to the desk. I warn you, though. Everyone in the place will be looking over your shoulder to see what you're drawing."

"I don't mind at all."

"What's up? Kat, how do you like your room?" Shelley poked her head in from the bathroom. She had pulled her hair back into a ponytail. "Mine mirrors it on the other side of the bath. And how's your gut?"

"Still complaining, but much better than it was."

"Mine too."

Gabe was still in the kitchen when Cynthia returned.

"Shelley's up. They're in the bedroom comparing

puke notes. Gabe, didn't we have an artist's desk here somewhere a few years ago from when I came up with the hare-brained idea that I'd illustrate my own books?"

Gabe looked at her blankly. "Yes, but I don't remember where it went. Tim or Cali might know."

Cynthia nodded. "I was just thinking it might be more comfortable for Kat to work on."

"It might indeed. Tim?"

"I'm thinking. In the attic, maybe?"

They were carrying it down the hall by the time Kat and Shelley returned to the kitchen.

"Good south light comes in that window," Mariah pointed to the spot in the corner of the kitchen. "Plenty of room there, and Miss Kat wouldn't have to keep moving her stuff off the table every time we eat."

"This would be wonderful," Kat agreed. "Thank you. Now I'm eager to bring in my supplies."

Gabe smiled at her excited expression. He wanted so much for her to be happy here.

Nine

V *oices...*

The room was dark. There were sounds within the shadows. Whispers of voices speaking to each other penetrated the silence and the darkness. Smells accompanied them; something had been put over her face, and she jerked, trying to avoid it. Hands were holding her; ropes were binding her to something hard. High-pitched laughter in the darkness made her shiver, and cold air touched her flesh. She could hear the sound of material ripping as her gown was cut away from her body, and she heard a man's deep voice say, 'Bring in the old man.'

Kat took a deep breath and let out a scream of sheer terror.

Suddenly, hands were on her, and she heard a familiar voice.

"Shh, sweetheart, wake up and look at me. You're safe."

Kat was struggling. She had both arms crossed over her chest in an effort to cover her naked body. But when she opened her eyes and looked down, she realized her nightgown still covered her. The arms that held her were gentle and strong, and she looked up, seeing Gabe's face.

She stopped struggling and covered her face with her hands. The sound of her weeping filled the room.

"The dream?" he asked softly.

Over Kat's head, Gabe noticed Shelley standing in the doorway to the bath, her face filled with concern. "I've got her," he mouthed. Shelley nodded and turned to go back to bed.

"Katlynne, no one will hurt you. But I'm taking you out to the living room for a while, until you relax and calm down."

"No..." she choked out. "I want to go back to sleep."

But he rose to his feet with her, pulling the throw from the chaise and wrapping it around her.

"No," he said firmly. "If you go back to sleep, you may fall right back into it." He carried her into the kitchen and set her down on the counter. Reaching for a small glass, he poured it full of milk from the fridge.

"Drink."

"No."

"Katlynne, do as I say."

She took it, trembling, but set it down on the counter next to her. Gabe picked it back up and held it to her lips. "You can drink it now, or we can stand here until you do. I think it will wake you up a little more."

She sighed and took a sip, and then another, until the glass was half gone. "Thank you. That's all I want."

"All right." Gabe rinsed out the glass and set it in the sink before gathering her up again.

"Did I awaken everyone in the house?"

"No. The other bedrooms are all in the back of the house. And the men are out in the bunkhouse. Shelley is probably the one closest to you. And me."

Kat yawned. "You're still dressed. You haven't been to bed yet?"

"No, I've been prowling. I take part of the

watches at night, but mine's over now. And I take after Dad; I don't need a lot of sleep. We take turns watching the property. The cattle and horses have to be guarded. We have wild animals roaming the woods. The Shoshone Forest isn't far from here, this side of the mountains." He sat down with her in the recliner by the window, positioning the throw around her.

Sleepy, Kat leaned her head against his chest.

"Talk to me, Katlynne," he said quietly. "Tell me about your dream."

She shook her head. "I can't." She hated the fact that she was trembling.

"All right," he whispered back. "But I'm here to listen. I know sometimes it helps to talk. And tell me one thing. Is it a dream? Or a memory?"

She gulped. "A memory."

"I see." Holding her against him, he tightened his arms around her. "Dad used to sit in this chair, Katlynne. It was his favorite."

"Like the brown recliner at home."

He nodded. "Exactly. Dad didn't sleep much, and when he was up, he'd sit here. I'll show you why in a moment. He even wired up the lights to it so he didn't have to get up and down all the time. See this button?"

Kat leaned forward. "Yes?"

"It turns them off and on. There's something I want to show you. Here. Press it.'

Uncertainly, she did so. A moment later, the room was lit again.

She nodded.

"All right. I'd like you to turn them off again, and then keep your eyes closed for about fifteen seconds. You can count if you want to. Then open them and look out the window. Ready?"

Kat reached over and pressed it again, putting them in darkness, and then began to count. When she reached fifteen, she opened her eyes. In spite of herself, she gasped.

"It's the Milky Way. Oh, Gabe, it's beautiful."

"It is, isn't it? I sometimes wondered if that's why he built this room facing this direction. When Dad couldn't sleep, I often found him in here, gazing at it. Now I find myself doing the same thing. See it?"

Kat squinted, looking at the pattern he'd traced. "I do," she whispered.

Gabe was silent momentarily, before saying quietly, "Whenever you want to, you can turn the light back on."

"Can—can I look at it just a moment longer?"

"As long as you like."

As the moments ticked by in darkness, he reached

over and turned the light back on. Her hand was resting next to the button. Curiously, he looked down, only to see that her eyes were closed; a peaceful expression covered her face.

She was sound asleep.

Gently, he lifted her and rose to his feet. Carrying her back to her room, he put her back to bed and raised the cover to her chin. Then he quietly walked to the doorway, looking back at her.

In the bathroom doorway, Shelley caught his eye. "Is she all right?"

"She's fine," he whispered back. "She fell asleep watching the stars."

"Ahh," Shelley nodded, as if that explained everything. "Night, Gabe."

Ten

n unwelcome visitor...

The sun, coming through the white fluffy curtains, brightened the room the next morning with beautiful natural light. Kat was smiling when she awakened and lay there for a few more moments, very comfortably. She could hear Shelley in the bathroom, showering and singing in a voice that was slightly off-key.

Wiggling her toes, she sat up on the side of the bed, reached for her braces and shoes, and managed to get them on. Gabe was right. The bed was high. As she moved toward the patio, however, she paused, staring at it.

The patio door was open. She could have sworn it was locked the afternoon before.

"Good morning!" Shelley's voice greeted her from the bathroom. "The comforts of home. We still have hot water," she grinned, her eyes sparkling.

"Sounds heavenly." Her face suddenly became serious. "Shelley, did I wake you last night?"

"Only for a second. I came in, but Gabe had you. You don't remember it?"

"Vaguely." A frown creased Kat's brow. "I remember him dragging me to the kitchen and trying to force cold milk down me. And then we sat in the recliner and he showed me the stars." She blushed, realizing how corny that sounded, and grimaced. "I hope I didn't cause him too much trouble."

"What? Are you kidding? A chance to hold a beautiful girl in his arms?"

"Go away."

Shelley laughed. "Anyway, he takes watch at night. He calls it prowling. So, the answer is no. I'm quite sure you were *not* too much trouble. I'm taking the hair dryer into my room so you can have the shower whenever you want."

Kat, by this time, had gathered up the day's clothes and underwear. "Hot shower, here I come," she muttered.

Twenty minutes later, she emerged from the bath. Even thoughts of the parole hearing didn't lower her spirits. They were far away now. And no one there, except Lorina and Ted, knew where she was. Shelley brought back the blow dryer as she finished dressing and handed it to her through the door, and Kat went to work drying her hair and singing.

Mariah's call for breakfast caught her attention, and she grabbed her art supplies and dropped them off at the waiting desk by the south window. She couldn't wait to use it.

They exchanged greetings as they were sitting down at the table, and the men were coming in from outside, talking among themselves. Mariah had the table set and was putting on bowlfuls of eggs, bacon, homemade biscuits, and gravy. She followed up with a pitcher of ice-cold milk.

Kat eyed the table. "Oh my," she exclaimed. "This is a feast."

Mariah, however, only smiled. "Just breakfast, Miss Kat. Supper tonight, now, that'll be a feast. It's the welcome home dinner for you and Shelley."

Gabe came down the hall from the direction of his room. His eyes came to rest on Kat, and grinned at her. She smiled back.

But as the meal progressed, Kat listened. There seemed to be undertones of worry among the men, but she wasn't sure if she was imagining it. She became convinced, however, when the men began to rise, and she heard Tim's quiet voice to Gabe.

"I saw something disturbing outside this morning. You need to see it."

Gabe glanced down at Kat. "Show me," he murmured, following Tim outside.

Outside, Gabe followed Tim around the corner of the house.

"This," Tim said, pointing, "is what I wanted to show you."

Gabe frowned. There were prints in the flower bed outside the patio, small prints, wandering onto the patio outside Shelley's window, and then back into the dirt. Next, they were seen on the patio outside Kat's room, going up to her door as if someone had looked in through the glass door.

Gabe, dismayed, looked into Kat's room. Her door, he could see, was open. "I suppose I'm going to have to forbid Katlynne to leave her door open," he frowned. "I really hate to do that. I don't want her to feel like she's a prisoner here."

"If I were guessing," Tim said, scowling. "I'd say the tracks are Josie's."

"You're right," Gabe finished, "and I'd say they're fresh enough to have been made early this morning."

"I can make a board that will block the door from opening enough for a person to get through. That way, Kat could still open it just enough to allow air in. I'd be happy to make one for Shelley's, too."

"Thanks, Tim. I'd appreciate that."

Tim nodded. "I don't trust Josie, Gabe. I think she's become a bit unhinged."

Gabe gave a slight nod. "I know she's spoiled, but she seems to have no remorse, and she has a sadistic streak."

"I agree. By the way, I saw the sheriff Saturday morning while you were gone. He said Ian's mentioned Shelley several times, and is eager for her to get home from school. Burns said to let you know it."

Gabe stopped what he was doing. "You're serious. Shelley won't go out with him. She doesn't want anything to do with him."

Tim nodded. "I, for one, am glad to hear it."

"I thought we finally got rid of him for good," Gabe said, under his breath.

"Pardon?"

"Nothing."

"Will has some things to show you, too," Tim added. "Bear tracks in the pasture."

"I'll check on it." Gabe watched him go, closing Kat's door. He followed the tracks around the house as he digested the news that Ian was back.

He and Ian had been at odds since the eighth grade. It had started innocently enough, over a girl, but had eventually progressed. It seemed each time Gabe had developed feelings for a girl, Ian had begun chasing her. By the time Ian left to go away to college and moved to Sheridan, Gabe had been thankful. Then, the year Shelley was a senior in high school, Ian had asked her out. She'd sought Gabe's advice when it happened, and he gave her his honest feelings. When Ian called back and she told him she couldn't date him, he exploded over the phone. Shelley hung up on him. But apparently, he'd been thinking of asking her out again.

But it wasn't just that Gabe and Ian had both had a teenage crush on the same girl. There were other things, too, that had happened: a fire at school, in which Ian had implicated Gabe; vandalism at a teacher's house; Gabe had also found himself questioned for that one. There had been no evidence, of course, but the accusations still stung. He left by the front door, muttering under his breath.

"*Get over it, Ingrahm. I'm sure Ian has.*"

Everyone deserved a second chance.

As he tracked Josie's prints around the side of the house, he noticed that they continued around the other side of the front door and around the edge of the large window, the same window he and Kat had looked out last night while observing the Milky Way.

He cursed softly under his breath. Josie had made no effort to hide these, either. It was completely obvious to him that she wanted someone to see them.

The honk of a horn caused him to turn. Jude and Maddie Barrington, from the adjoining ranch, had pulled up into the front yard. Maddie, however, didn't wait; she flew from the car to hug him.

"Where are Kat and Shelley?" she demanded.

Instead of answering, Gabe grinned and opened the front door, waving her inside. Through the arched doorway, he could see Kat dragging out her art supplies.

"Kat!" Maddie shouted with glee, sprinting toward her. "And where's Shelley?"

"I'm in here," Shelley shouted from her room.

Behind Maddie, Jude watched the reunion, grinning back at Gabe. "She's been bugging me incessantly to bring her over, ever since I told her Shelley was home. She wanted to go to Washington for graduation, but we couldn't get away. I hope you recorded the ceremony, because if you didn't, she'll kill me."

Gabe was watching the reunion between the girls, grinning. "I did, but the editing isn't done yet. I'll make you a copy when it's finished."

Shelley had dragged Maddie and Kat into the bedrooms so they could talk without being observed, and Jude's voice interrupted his thoughts.

"Ian's back."

Gabe stared at him. "So I heard."

"I spoke with him yesterday."

"How was he?"

Jude shrugged. "I don't know how else to say it. He seems to have turned over a new leaf."

Gabe frowned. "Time will tell, I suppose." Finding Kat, he grinned at her. "I need to go over the ranch rules with you this afternoon. Can you stay out of trouble until then?"

Kat tilted her head saucily.

"Not a chance," she said.

⁓

The morning was spent catching up, and Kat was relieved to see Maddie so happy. She hadn't seen her friend this happy and relaxed since before she'd left to come to Wyoming early last summer. Jude Barrington had been good to her.

And, he's been good for her.

Kat smiled and waved as Maddie and Jude pulled away in the pickup. He'd been true to his word, and rounded up Maddie before lunch, promising to bring her back before long. Knowing it might upset Maddie if she told her about the upcoming parole hearing, Kat kept silent.

"You didn't mention the parole," Shelley said softly, as they watched the truck turn left and disappear.

Kat shook her head. "I decided not to. This is the first time I've seen her so happy, and I didn't want to spoil it."

Cynthia came down the hall from her study. "Kat? I have the publishing department on the phone. Do you have a minute to talk to them?"

Kat followed, feeling a little queasy. However, by the time she got off the phone, she was amazed. The offer they had made for an advance based on Cynthia's recommendation was generous; so was the percentage of the royalties. They promised to send a contract by the next day for her to sign. When she came back down the hall at the sound of the lunch bell, she was ecstatic.

The atmosphere at lunch, however, brought her back to the present. It was quiet, and Kinsey asked Gabe to accompany him to the barn when it was over.

Kat watched him go and pulled out a large piece of art paper and her new pencil set.

She took her place at the desk and looked out the window, quickly sketching the view of the ranch outside. The birch trees that reached toward the sky were awe-inspiring, and she wistfully pictured how they might look in the fall when they turned such a bright yellow. Would she be here that long? She hoped so.

When she finished sketching the view from her window, however, she became restless. Cynthia was somewhere in the house, and Shelley was nowhere to be seen. Setting her pencils down, she wandered outside onto the front porch. The memory of what Gabe said about telling someone where she was tugged at her, but she'd only be a minute. She wasn't going far.

Outside on the porch, she looked around. She couldn't see Gabe anywhere. She could see some of the men far out in the pastures, working with the horses, but he didn't seem to be among them.

"Hello there," said a strange but friendly voice from behind her. She turned to see a tall, slender girl with long blonde hair smiling at her. "You must be the new illustrator."

Eleven

osie...

Kat looked up. "Hello," she said uncertainly, but smiled when she saw Josie's friendly expression. "Yes, Cynthia did ask me to illustrate her new book. You must be Josie? I'm Kat."

"Do you ride?" Josie wanted to know.

"Not for years," Kat confessed. "The last time I was thrown, so I've stayed away from horses since then."

Josie was eyeing her braces. "What are those?" she asked curiously.

Kat looked down. "They're called AFOs."

"Do they keep you from riding?"

Kat smiled. "I don't think they would, but it doesn't matter. Gabe said not to ride without talking to him first."

"Gabe says a lot of things." Josie waved away her argument. "For instance, he said he would marry me." Josie was laughing. "That went all to bits."

Kat was silent.

"And now it seems he wants to marry *you*. By the way, don't tell him I was here, or he'll ban me from the ranch. I know he gave you *my* bedroom."

Kat frowned at her. "Josie, I'm not discussing Gabe with you."

"Oh, lighten up. Can't you tell when I'm kidding?"

Kat shook her head. "No."

Josie gave off an exasperated sigh. "Let's go see the horses."

Before Kat opened her mouth to object, Josie grasped her arm firmly. Helpless to stop it, Kat was dragged suddenly off the porch and down the hill toward the barn. She looked around again to see if anyone was within calling distance, but saw no one.

"Josie, I can't go down there." But Josie was pulling her along as if she were a beach ball on a riptide. "I have asthma. I can't go near the barn."

Josie slowed at this for a moment. "Really?" she said, brows raised, "You use those pump things?"

"Inhalers, and yes. Josie, *Stop*. Let go of me."

"Stick in the mud." Josie laughed, pulling harder. "I just want you to meet Daisy."

Kat was struggling to stay on her feet. Twice, on uneven ground, she lost her footing and went down on one knee, but Josie paused only long enough to let her get to her feet before tugging again.

Before Kat knew it, she was at the bottom of the hill.

The barn loomed ahead; however, that wasn't what captured her attention. A huge black horse was tied up outside. The horse seemed startled at Josie's noise and movement. Kat could see the uneasiness in those big, beautiful eyes.

Josie shoved Kat up next to the animal and almost under it.

"Kat, meet Daisy," Josie said, stepping back.

It was tense. Kat looked up at the tall creature, whose startled eyes were fixed on her, and began to speak to her. "Hello, pretty girl," she said softly.

The horse blinked. Kat continued, trying to keep her voice calm. It happened slowly, but eventually, the animal brought its head down and gently nudged her shoulder as if being playful.

"Here," Josie said from behind her, "you'll need this."

Kat felt something rub against her back pocket and looked over her shoulder curiously.

But Josie was gone.

"Josie?"

There was no sign of her at all. For a moment, Kat was beginning to wonder if she had fallen asleep and dreamed her up. But Daisy head-butted her, pushing her another step backward and she laughed softly. "I like you too, girl," she reached up again, trying to pet the soft, velvety nose. As if wanting her ears scratched, Daisy leaned closer, obliging her.

It was then she heard the deep voice from behind her.

"Katlynne Elana."

Kat froze. Gabe! His voice wasn't raised, but there was an undertone of warning she dared not ignore. She felt hands grasping her shoulders, pulling her backward. The next thing she knew, Gabe had put himself between her and the horse. When she looked up, she gasped. The forbidding expression on his face let her know in no uncertain terms she was in trouble.

"What are you doing down here, young lady?"

Kat was unable to meet his eyes. How should she answer? Finally, she took a breath. "Meeting Daisy."

"And who," he said, his voice lowered, "told you his name was Daisy?"

Kat opened her mouth to speak, then closed it again.

"Answer me, young lady."

She gulped. "*His* name?"

"Look, Katlynne. I believe you can see that from where you are."

Her eyes followed the direction he indicated, and her cheeks flushed a deep red.

"*Oh.*"

He loosened the reins that tethered the stallion and sent him farther out to pasture with a pat and a command. Then, very slowly, he turned back to face her. "His name, Katlynne, is *Thunder*; and he's my stallion. The very horse I warned you not to go near."

The blush on her cheeks had disappeared now; she could feel it as her face drained of color. "Thunder," she echoed.

"It seems, young lady, you have some explaining to do."

"*Thunder...*" she repeated, backing away from him. Mentally, she was trying to count how many rules she'd already broken, and if what Gabe had told her was true, she knew she was in deep trouble. She licked her lips nervously. "Gabe, I'm sorry..."

"Katlynne." At his commanding voice she met his eyes. He reached down and lifted her chin higher. "Does anyone know you're down here?"

She lowered her eyes. "No. No one except..." She stopped, staring back at the hill Josie had dragged her down. Did she dare tell him Josie had been here? Could she afford *not* to tell him? She took another step backward but lost her balance on the uneven ground, and he reached out and caught her by the waist to steady her. As he did, something moved in her back pocket. His face became even more forbidding, and he turned her around.

His voice seemed to drop another octave. "And what," he demanded, "is *this*?"

Kat looked up to find that he was holding a small riding whip, and gasped in disbelief. She remembered Josie's voice saying, 'You'll need this', and closed her eyes in dismay. "You told me not to trust her," she said in a small voice.

He had heard, however. His face was inches from hers now. "Who, Katlynne?" His hands grasped her shoulders. "Has Josie been here?"

Kat lowered her gaze to the ground between them. How could she refuse to tell him? She had already done the unthinkable, whether she had realized it or not. "I can't tell you..."

ARMS OF COURAGE · 131

"Katlynne. I'm ordering you to tell me." His voice was stern, his face more forbidding than she'd ever seen.

"Katlynne Elana."

She traced the dryness of her lips with her tongue. "Yes?"

"You already know what the consequences are, young lady."

Her hands tightened at her sides. "I just don't want to get anyone in trouble."

"So you prefer to be in trouble, is that it?"

"No." She hung her head.

Gabe had his hands on her waist now, and took a deep breath. "You have five seconds, Katlynne," he said. "I'm waiting."

Kat waited. Mentally, she was counting. She could feel her heart pounding in her chest.

Gabe took a deep breath. "All right. It's time."

She could hear the disappointment in his voice. But she couldn't seem to open her mouth to speak. Gabe reached down and picked her up, tossing her over his shoulder, "I did tell you what I would do."

Gabe took her into an empty stall and sat down on a bench, settling her face down across his lap. "Katlynne, do you understand why I'm going to do this?"

She did know. The rules they had discussed flew through her mind.

"I want to hear you tell me."

The sadness in his voice tore at her heart. "Because no one knew where I was."

"And?"

"Because I got near Thunder."

"Yes," he said grimly, "but I know you didn't realize it was Thunder. The rest of the reasons, Katlynne?"

"It was because of the whip?" she finally managed.

"I know the whip doesn't belong to you. I'm going to give you the benefit of the doubt and say you probably didn't even know it was in your pocket. But you do know, Katlynne, who put it there. And despite my giving you four? five? opportunities, you have completely refused to answer me. That's what you're in trouble for. Do you understand me? And do you understand how terrible it makes me feel to do this?"

She didn't answer.

"And one more question. Is there anything about your disability that should prevent it?"

Kat waited a moment before shaking her head. "No."

Gabe continued lecturing her for a long time about her safety, before he settled her across his knee.

"All right." He was breathing hard; she could hear it. "There will be ten swats, Katlynne, but they'll hurt." His own voice was almost inaudible now. "I warned you." Taking a deep breath, he brought his hand down across her bottom.

Kat tried to remain quiet. The swats didn't hurt all that much. What did hurt was the betrayal in his voice. By the fifth blow, she was crying out. By the eighth, there was complete silence.

"Breathe, sweetheart," he said gently, as if he realized she was holding her breath. "There are only two more."

When she felt the tenth swat, she lay limp across his lap. But it was the thought of disappointing Gabe that hurt the most.

Gabe had dropped the whip at his feet and sat there, his hand resting across her bottom. Then, he lifted her, turning and cradling her in his arms. Kat turned her head into his chest, comforted by being held tightly in his arms.

"I'm sorry, Gabe." The sound of her voice was muffled.

He reached down and turned her chin so that she

had no choice but to look at him. "Katlynne," he said as he moved her hair away from her wet cheeks, "was it worth it not to answer me?"

"No," she shook her head. "*No.*"

He held her a long time, until her breathing became more even, rocking her gently in his arms.

"*Gabe!*" Tim's shout could be heard in the distance, but seemed to be getting closer.

Kat buried her face into Gabe's chest as Tim's voice grew nearer.

Gabe looked up. "In here, Tim."

Tim stopped as he rounded the corner, panting. Seeing Kat in Gabe's lap and the whip on the ground, he cursed under his breath with dismay. "Too late," he said, gasping for air. "Gabe, Josie was here. I saw her dragging Kat down from the porch. Kat was struggling, and went down a couple of times..." he paused, grabbing a breath, "I shouted, but you didn't hear me. I saw you heading toward the barn, but I was in the south pasture, and I couldn't catch Betsy to get on her. I ran as fast as I could. Kat, Gabe... I'm sorry." he was leaning over, his hands braced on his knees, still trying to get his breath.

Gabe handed him the whip. "Dispose of this, will you?"

It was Kat's voice that answered him. "It's not your fault, Tim," she whispered.

Tim shook his head and turned away.

Gabe gathered Kat closer. "Dear *God,* Katlynne..." He closed his eyes as she threw her arms around his neck and held on.

"I should have told you," she said softly. "I won't do that, ever again."

But there was a wheezy sound to her voice, and Gabe noticed it.

When she coughed, he held her back and looked down. "Katlynne?" She was breathing hard, and he was starting to hear a slight crowing sound. She coughed again.

"Asthma," she explained. "It's the hay in the barn."

Gabe rose and ran with her outside and up toward the house. "Where's your inhaler?"

"In the highboy," she answered, coughing. The wheezing was getting louder now.

Seeing Shelley coming out the front door, Gabe shouted for her to bring it. She turned and ran back inside.

But the inhalers were nowhere to be found. *"Cynthia,"* she shouted from the bedroom, "Bring Gabe's supplies! Kat needs an inhaler. I can't find them."

Cynthia was there with the tackle box full of

medical supplies by the time Gabe brought Kat in through the front door, and handed him an inhaler and a stethoscope.

"Stay close with it, I may have to give her some epinephrine if this doesn't work." He pressed the inhaler into Kat's trembling hands and sat down on the sofa with her.

It did work. Within a few short moments, the wheezing was calming.

"I didn't mean to scare you."

Shelley was shaken, her face white. "I couldn't find them, Kat. Any of them. Would you have put one anywhere else?"

Kat looked at her, surprised. "I put two in the dresser, and left two in my make-up case in the bathroom." She whispered.

Shelley turned to go back into her room. A moment later, however, she was back. "There are none in there, either, but your make-up is scattered all over the bathroom. And Gabe, you'll want you to see this. There are tracks." Shelley's face was grim.

Gabe followed, with Kat still in his arms. As he strode to her door, he stopped, looking down. There were dirty footprints leading from the patio door to the dresser, through the bathroom, and into Shelley's room.

Cynthia's voice behind him, spoke. "They have to be Josie's."

He nodded. "She made no attempt to hide these, either."

"She *wanted you* to know it was her?" Cynthia stood behind him, looking with dismay down at the tracks on the light green carpet. "She's crazy."

Kat had stiffened in Gabe's arms, but said nothing.

He sat on the side of her bed, refusing to let her out of his embrace. "Katlynne," he said very softly, "I feel like, on every level today, I have failed you."

But she was shaking her head. "No," she said, fiercely. "You haven't." She reached up and touched his cheek. "I was the one who let you down. I promise, if I ever see her—*ever again*, I'll tell you right then."

Twelve

Exhausted...

Gabe stared down at Kat, still in his arms. She appeared exhausted, physically and mentally, and if he didn't miss his guess, emotionally as well. "Unless you protest terribly, I'm putting you to bed in my room for a while. You need to rest."

She didn't argue, and he took long strides to his room and put her on the bed, removing her braces and setting them next to her in case she awakened and needed them. When he glanced at her again, he wondered how anyone could fall asleep so quickly. She was already out.

Listening to her chest again, he brought the quilt

to her chin and kissed her forehead, staring at her small figure in his big bed for a long time before he quietly walked to the door.

Cynthia had brought the phone to him, but instead of making the call, he tucked it under his arm. "Thanks, Cynthia. I'll take it with me, but I think, rather than call, I'm going over to the Lowell's."

Ten minutes later, he was standing on their doorstep.

It was Josie who answered the door. "Well, well," she smiled, a snide expression on her face. "We don't see you here very often. Did you take the opportunity to teach Kat the rules today?"

Gabe refused to dignify that with an answer, but said instead. "Where is your father?"

"Here, Gabe." Joseph Lowell's voice spoke up from behind him. "I would say it's nice to see you, but the look on your face tells me otherwise. What brings you here?"

"Your daughter's behavior." Gabe was not smiling. He could see Joseph wilt. "We invited a young lady home with Shelley for the summer. Her name is Katlynne. She's going to illustrate Cynthia's next book. But Josie took up residence in her room right before we got there, locked everyone out of the room, and refused to leave. When Tim brought her back yesterday, she had instructions not to come back."

Joseph Lowell nodded. "And did she?"

"This morning, we spotted tracks—Josie's tracks, outside the rooms of both Katlynne and Shelley. After lunch, one of my men spotted her dragging Katlynne from the front porch, down to the barn, and shoving her under Thunder's hooves. Katlynne is very small and was no match for Josie's strength. *And* she's disabled."

"Josie!" Mr. Lowell's face held hurt and surprise. "How could you?"

"I didn't, Dad. I merely led her down there. And I thought I was introducing her to Daisy."

"Josie," Mr. Lowell shook his head. "Do you really expect me to believe that?"

"The next thing she did," Gabe continued, "was to go into Katlynne's room and take her asthma inhalers —all of them—out of her room. When Katlynne had an asthma attack shortly after that, we had to resort to taking one from the emergency kit. If we hadn't had that, I hesitate to think what would have happened."

"Is this true, Josie?" Joseph's face was white.

"He can't prove any of it, Dad. Don't listen to him." Josie's voice was pleading.

"Josie," her father's voice held weariness. "You've

done a lot of stupid things in your time," he said. "But your mother and I can't handle this kind of stuff anymore. We've put up with it all we can."

"Dad?" Josie peered at her father. "What are you saying?"

"I'm saying one more incident, Josie, and you'll have to move out. Your patterns keep repeating themselves. After what happened the last time to another guest of Gabe's, I decided that was it. You showed no remorse at all after it."

He rose to his feet. "And I'll tell you something else. Your mother and I have already spoken to the lawyer. One more incident—just one more, and the lawyer has instructions to cut you off, completely. I'm sorry, but that's the way it is." He turned to Gabe. "Gabe, thank you for telling me. We needed to know. If she causes you any more trouble, call the sheriff. *He* can come and get her. And if you find out that anything happens to her mother or to me, call the lawyer. He'll know what to do."

"*Dad*!" Josie leaned forward, in earnest now. Tears were flowing down her face. "You can't throw me out! Where would I go?"

"You can go back to school, Josie, and get an education. Learn to develop some responsibility, and make something decent of yourself. Your mother and I are extremely disappointed in you." He walked sorrow-fully toward the doorway, looking more tired and aged than Gabe had ever seen him.

Gabe found himself wondering, for once, if Josie's drama was an act or if she was really this disturbed. But she rose and silently left the room, without looking at him.

He knew one thing, however. His heart went out to Joseph Lowell.

Slowly, he rose and left the empty room.

Gabe could see Cynthia's face at the window as he approached the house. As he closed the front door behind him, he sank down on the sofa. "I'm glad I'm not in Joseph's shoes right now."

"I was just saying that about you," Cynthia said. "I'd hate to have to go over there and talk to him about her."

He shook his head. "Tim's right. Joseph's afraid of her. I have no doubt of it." Glancing down the hall, he added, "Has Katlynne awakened?"

"Not yet. I did put my head in and check on her. She seemed to be breathing well."

"I appreciate that." He rose, shaking his head. He'd

brought her out here to keep her safe. But was she? Cracking the door to his room open slightly, he watched as she stirred slightly and turned over to face the window. He moved forward, picking up his stethoscope on the way to the bed, and listened to her chest.

He breathed a sigh of relief. She sounded clear now.

Next, he wandered into the kitchen, where Mariah was busy cooking.

"Steak Diane," she grinned, whispering. "I hope Miss Kat likes it."

"I'm sure she'll love it, Mariah." He smiled and winked. "Who could *not* love your cooking?"

Mariah chuckled.

Cali approached, taking a dishcloth and wiping down the table. "I ran the vacuum in the girls' rooms. Everything all right, Mr. Gabe?"

"Thank you, Cali. And the answer is, I have hopes," he nodded. "It would be to Josie's benefit to stay away from here now."

That was all he said.

The next morning...

It was the next morning when the doorbell rang. Cali reached it first.

"Gabe!" she shouted, as soon as she opened it. He was beside her in an instant, and she moved out of the way. Josie stood quietly outside, waiting for him to speak.

"What do you want, Josie?" he asked, frowning.

"I would like to talk with you," she said, "and with Katlynne, if you don't mind."

Gabe frowned at her. "I do mind. Say what you have to say to me, and I'll decide whether or not you can see Katlynne."

She dropped her gaze. "I just wanted to apologize," she said, "and to give her back these." She handed him a bag, and he opened it and looked inside. "It's the inhalers. She didn't deserve what I did to her yesterday."

"No, she didn't." His frown did not change. "I'll give her your message."

She stood there a moment.

"Is there something else?" His expression was still harsh.

She waited a moment, and then shook her head. "Just... I'm sorry."

Gabe watched her go to her car and get in. When

she backed out of the driveway and drove away, he felt a nudge at his elbow and turned to look down.

"I heard," Kat said, beside him. "She seems sad."

Gabe closed the door and turned to her, raising her chin. "Katlynne," he said, "Only time will tell if she means it. This isn't the first time she's come by to apologize after a stunt. If it's an honest apology, she'll stay away. If not, she'll do her best to gain your forgiveness, until she sees another opportunity to pull something. Understand?"

She nodded. "Yes. I feel sorry for her, that's all."

Gabe lifted her chin a little higher. "I know you do, but that's exactly what she wants. If she can get back into your good graces, she thinks she's got it made."

She looked away. "I suppose so."

The doorbell rang again a half-hour later. This time, Gabe was near enough to answer it. To his surprise, Ian Winslow stood outside the door, wearing a deputy's uniform.

"Hello, Gabe. It's been a long time. How are you? And how's the family?"

Gabe hoped his true feelings didn't show. "Good," he said. "And you? I heard you were back from Sheridan."

"Yep. I transferred back recently. It's good to be home. How's Shelley? I suppose she's home from college." He glanced around, seeing Kat working at her desk. "And who's this little gal? I've never seen her before."

Gabe found his back stiffening, in spite of himself. "Shelley's fine. Katlynne is a friend of hers. They both just graduated."

"She's a cutie."

A silence lay between them, and Ian smiled. "Well, I didn't want to keep you. I just wanted to say hello and let you know I'm back. And," he paused, "if you need anything, please feel free to call. I'll help any way I can."

Gabe nodded. "Thanks. I appreciate that. I can't think of anything at the moment, but if I do, I'll let you know. I'm glad you stopped by. It's good to see you again."

"Sure." Ian waved a hand. "Later, then."

"Later." Gabe watched him go uncertainly. As Ian pulled the sheriff's vehicle out onto the road and turned east, Gabe closed the door and turned to see Kat, sketching at her desk. The light from the window reflected onto the paper, lighting her face, and suddenly, she looked up, giving him a big smile.

Ian was right. She was a cutie, and she had no idea just how adorable she was. He thought about Ian's unexpected visit. There was no mention of the

Winslows wanting the Ingrahm land, and nothing Ian had said should have brought on the protective, jealous feeling that engulfed Gabe, yet he couldn't seem to make it disappear. Perhaps it was remembering what had happened back during their school days.

Gabe shook his head. "You should have let that go a long time ago, Ingrahm," he muttered.

Thirteen

oing over the rules... again

Kat let Gabe take her hand as he led her into his study that afternoon. This time he found her a yellow legal pad and a pen so she could write down what they discussed. Situating her in his large desk chair, he leaned against the desk next to her, and set the bag of inhalers down.

Kat listened as he once again explained the reasons for each one, trying not to concentrate on his closeness. It was disconcerting.

"Katlynne?"

She met his eyes.

"Write these down?

"Oh. Where were we?"

"I think the question is, where are you?"

"Oh. I was just..." Her voice trailed off.

"Repeat them back to me."

She did, but the last two she had not written down. He took the pad and pen from her and added them.

"And for you, Katlynne, there are another two or three."

"More than anyone else?" she scowled.

"Yes. After yesterday's experience, I think these are necessary. First, always be totally honest when I ask you a question. I think you already know that now, but write it down anyway."

Embarrassed, she wrote.

Be honest.

"Second, don't be afraid to scream for help. Mariah, Cali, Cynthia, and Shelley were in the house yesterday morning. They could have stopped Josie from dragging you to the barn and shoving you under Thunder's hooves." He leaned back and crossed his arms. Looking down at her, he continued. "Kat, it's nothing but a miracle that Thunder didn't rear when that happened and trample you."

"He was startled at first," Kat admitted, nodding.

"I know you're fond of him. And he seems fond of

you, too. I've never seen him allow anyone to scratch his ears on their first encounter with him. But it absolutely scared me to death when I came around the barn and saw you so close to him. I could see him trampling you underfoot before I was able to get between you." He was leaning forward now, and very close. "And when I realized you had the whip in your back pocket, it scared me even more."

Kat glanced at the paper, realizing she'd been doodling on it. "I felt something. It was when she said, 'You'll need this'. But when I turned around, she was gone. It was as if she'd just vanished into thin air. I was beginning to think I'd dreamed her up. And I forgot about feeling something in my pocket."

"Thunder is a good judge of character. And he despises Josie, by the way. She's pulled some of her stunts on him in the past, too. He hasn't forgotten."

"What kinds of stunts?"

He leaned slightly closer. "I'll tell you what happened a few years ago."

She met his eyes, nodding, and he continued.

"A college friend of Shelley's came three years ago. It was Thunder that she was riding. He liked her, too. Josie went down to the barn and told Kinsey that I wanted to ride, and asked him to saddle up Thunder, which he did. He thought it was unusual that I didn't come down and saddle him myself, but he did it. Josie waited until Thunder was unattended and put a burr underneath the saddle. And then she coaxed Jenny onto him. She wasn't a hundred yards away when he bucked her off.

"Oh no!" Kat frowned. "Was she all right?"

"She had two fractured ribs and a broken collar bone. She spent several days in the hospital. They had to repair the collar bone in surgery."

Kat closed her eyes, almost feeling Jenny's pain.

"When we found her, she was having difficulty breathing," he continued. "Thunder has been trained never to leave an injured rider, and he was standing by her, not knowing what to do. I reached her first, and when he backed away from me and didn't want to let me on, I knew something was wrong. That's when I found the cocklebur. I'm not talking about a little one; I'm talking about this size."

Kat's eyes widened as he showed her.

"When I removed it, he let me on, but it had damaged his flesh. He took a bit to heal, too. Will flew Jenny to the hospital in Billings. And when she was well enough to travel, he flew her home. Josie, on the other hand, is still congratulating herself."

Kat was shaking her head in disbelief.

"Do you see, Katlynne, why I want her to stay

away from you? This is not the only stunt she's pulled around here. And do you see why I don't rush to accept her back into the house when she comes back and apologizes?"

Kate nodded. "I see... Has she ever done anything like that to Shelley?"

"Yes, but Shelley is older now and can pretty much take care of herself, unlike you. You can't; you're too small. You might outwit her, but you're no match for her size or strength. Yesterday, the only thing you could have done would have been to scream for help. So," he took the pad from her and wrote.

Don't be afraid to scream. "And I'll add the next one, too."

Never trust Josie.

His eye once again caught the bag full of inhalers that Josie had handed him. "And while we're here, I want you to check these. I just don't trust her not to have tampered with them."

Kat reached into it and pulled out one of the inhalers. She frowned and dumped out the rest of them on the desk in front of her. "The protective foil wrappers are missing on all of them," she said, her brow forming a crease.

Gabe leaned forward. "These are the ones you brought with you?"

She nodded. Instinctively taking one in her hand and pushing on the pump, she sighed. Nothing happened, and she turned to him. "It's empty."

Gabe reached over and tested each one, in turn, as Kat watched his face go from forbidding to utterly furious. Every one of them was empty. "I'll contact Dr. Graves and get several more for you. He's the one I call when I need supplies for the ranch. And I want you to keep at least one of them with you constantly."

Kat nodded her head, meeting his eyes. "I'm not afraid of her," she said, repeating what she had said the day before and trying to look as brave as possible.

Gabe reached down and lifted her chin gently.

"You should be, Katlynne," he said. *"You should be."*

"Kat?"

Kat looked up from her sketching to see Cynthia approaching. "Yes?"

"When would you like to go for our first visit to the Shoshone?"

"Now?" Kat knew her expression was eager.

Cynthia laughed. "Well, I was thinking about

tomorrow, if it's all right with Gabe. I think he's wanting to go. Shelley? Want to join us?"

"I don't know," Shelley said thoughtfully. "I was considering going riding with Tim."

"As long as Tim's with you, I won't worry," Gabe stuck his head into the living room.

"Ahh. Then I think Shell will *not be going* with us tomorrow." Cynthia laughed. "After all, what female could pass up a chance to go riding with a gorgeous hunk like Tim?" Shelley was blushing now, and Cynthia laughed. "Sorry, Shelley. Gabe, what time do you want to leave in the morning?"

"I should know by early in the morning. I'd rather you not go by yourselves, but I know you'll need to do it a lot in the next few months and I won't always be able to go with you. Right now, though, I have some projects to ask Indy about. And I thought I'd talk to him about measuring Katlynne for some boots that might fit her braces while we're there."

"The place we're going is right on the edge of the reservation," Cynthia explained. "It's really not all that far. Indy would be a great one to draw. He has this craggy face. You'll love him. And his mother has such wonderful eyes. They just sparkle when she talks. And when she smiles, she looks like she's sixteen again."

"How old *is* she?"

Gabe looked down thoughtfully. "I'm guessing early seventies, but I'm not completely sure. She's a delightful lady, and full of stories. And Cynthia's right. You'll love Indy."

"An interesting name, Indy."

"His name is Indiana," Cynthia explained. "He's the best boot maker alive, in *my* not-so-humble opinion."

"Can't wait!" Kat said, her expression full of excitement.

The next day was exciting. As Cynthia had said, Indy was just on the edge of the reservation. Gabe took her arm and brought her into Indy's shop, putting her in front of him.

"Indy, meet Katlynne," he said, grinning.

Cynthia smiled. "She's illustrating the book on the Shoshone. Is it all right if she sketches you?"

Kat watched as the man with the tanned, weathered, and craggy face came forward, holding out his hand. He flashed a wide smile, showing a full set of white teeth.

"Sure. Hello there, Miss Katlynne. And how are you?"

"Hello, sir, and I'm fine. And I hear you're the best bootmaker alive?" She grinned back.

Indy's glance took in her braces. He looked back at her face quizzically. "AFOs?"

"Yes, how did you know what they're called?"

"My mother wears them. She was a polio survivor. But surely you're too young for that?"

At the ranch, Tim was leaning back in the saddle and watching Shelley as she chatted about how good it was to be home. Her long blonde hair hung loosely down her back in waves, blowing gently in the breeze, and her cheeks were pink. He thought she had grown even more beautiful during the past year away.

"Tim? You're not listening," she turned to him, scowling.

"I'm admiring your beauty and desiring you intensely."

"Right," she drawled. "You're being facetious."

"Somewhat. The truth is, I've missed you this year."

"Why don't you call me Shell like everyone else?"

"Because I like the name Shelley. It fits you. And by the way, Gabe hardly ever calls you Shell. Shell is the little brat I've known since she was a tomboy. Shelley, on the other hand, is a gorgeous young woman."

"You're being silly."

"I'm never silly."

"Of course you are."

Tim scowled down at her. "Keep it up, young lady."

"And you'll what?" she teased.

"I don't really think you want to find out."

Shelley's eyes widened. Changing the subject, she looked at him from under her long lashes. "You've changed this year too, you know."

"How so?"

"You've become more... hmm, I'm not exactly sure how to say this."

"Respectfully, Shelley. *Respectfully*." His brows were raised.

Shelley grinned, and bubbled with laughter.

"Go on," he said, "I've become more *what*?"

"Bossy," she said, sending her horse into a canter.

He caught up with her within seconds. "I'll hold you accountable for that remark," he said, grinning. "So, remember that before you let your mouth run away with you." He winked.

She grinned at him. "Sure, I will." She laughed, sarcasm and playfulness both in her eyes.

"Brat." Tim chuckled. Riding up next to her, he reached an arm out and brought her over in front of him on the saddle.

"What are you doing?" She looked back at him incredulously.

"Helping you remember," he said. Turning her in the saddle slightly, he gave her three sound swats. "There. Maybe that will help.

"Ouch!" Shelley scowled at him, rubbing the offended spot. "You're mean."

"Not at all," he grinned. "I warned you to be respectful. Is it my fault you ignored me?" He pulled her back against his chest and brought Digby, his stallion, to a canter. Whistling to her horse, he started back toward the barn. "I need to get back," he said in Shelley's ear. "Gabe will be back soon, and I still have a few things that need to be done."

Shelley nodded. "Thank you for taking me riding. It's been fun." She turned back, smiling into his eyes.

"Yes," he said, grinning back, his eyes lingering on her face, "it has." He pulled up near the barn and brought Shelley down to the ground with him in a swift move. Turning her to face him, he leaned down and kissed the top of her head. "Come, young lady. I'll walk you up to the house."

Fourteen

C *oncerns...*

Gabe listened carefully to the conversation between Kat and Indy's mother that afternoon while Cynthia recorded it, and took meticulous notes. Leanna talked about post-polio syndrome, and how it had affected her with new weaknesses she hadn't had before. But it was obvious her spirit was good. Gabe frowned at the thought of Kat being plagued with new challenges after working so hard to overcome the ones she'd had. He was silent during the trip home. Kat hadn't spoken either.

Shelley and Tim were just approaching the house,

laughing and talking to each other, as Cynthia got out of the car with her recorder and notebook.

"Hey, guys!" she grinned. "Have a good ride?"

"Excellent," Tim said, grinning. "How was your afternoon?"

"Mine was productive," Cynthia added, glancing toward Gabe and Kat. "I think Kat's was too. I haven't seen her sketches yet."

Kat waited until everyone was inside before she reached forward to open the door. Gabe, however, reached forward and took her arm.

"Wait for me, sweetheart," he said quietly.

A few seconds later he was opening her door. He paused, focusing on her face, but she couldn't seem to meet his gaze.

He reached for her hand. "Come with me for a moment."

She glanced down at the large hand that held hers, expecting him to lead her to the front door of the house. Instead, he led her down the walkway and around to the side. She walked quietly beside him until they came to a little cove near the back with a few trees and a small teakwood bench. Sitting down, Gabe lifted her into his lap and put his hands around her waist.

"Tell me more about the possibility of you having post-polio syndrome. I was just thinking, on the way home, and wondering if there was anything I could do to make things easier for you; to lighten your load, or keep you from expending too much energy."

"Gabe," she said softly, putting a hand up to his cheek, "you can't protect me from everything. The best thing you can do for me is to let me do what I can. I can't live in dread every day. If I let myself do that, I will have allowed it to rob me of all the good years I have yet to enjoy. Don't you see?"

He smiled. "And what do you hope to enjoy in the coming years?"

"Lots," she announced. "I want to backpack around Australia on my honeymoon. I want to go to New Zealand and watch them shear sheep. I want to go to England and see the moors, and Scotland and see the highlands... and Ireland, and Germany. I want—"

"Whoa. To backpack in Australia on your honeymoon? Where did you come up with that idea?" his look was incredulous.

"It just occurred to me. Don't interrupt. And I want to climb the Eiffel Tower—"

"The Eiffel Tower has elevators," he said, brows raised.

"Indulge me," she said. "I also want to climb Denali, and—"

Gabe was laughing now. "Your husband will have

to be either a wuss and let you walk all over him in order to do what you want, or a very strong man and work overtime to keep you in check."

"I hadn't thought of that. I certainly don't want a wuss."

"Rascal," he said with a grin. "So, we've established that you need a strong man who's willing to take you in hand?"

She glanced down at the buttons on his shirt. "I don't know that I want that, either."

"But what you want and what you need may be two different things. The question is, will you be willing to let him guide you in what he thinks is best?"

She was quiet for a few seconds. "Perhaps? That might be a challenge."

He hugged her tightly, chuckling. "What am I going to do with you?"

"I don't know," she said, shrugging.

Kat wasn't sure exactly when it happened, but their faces were close now. She lifted her mouth as he lowered his. What was happening here? A shot of adrenalin moved through her as he planted a kiss on her forehead, then her nose, then moved to her mouth.

She'd desperately waited for this kiss. She felt her eyes widen as he took possession of her mouth, exploring, tasting.

But it was over in an instant. Gabe lifted her to her feet, and with a playful smack to her bottom, he led her toward the front of the house. "You're a mess, Katlynne Abramson," he said, "has anyone told you that? And... so help me, if you say once or twice—"

"You'll what?" She grinned. "And you, Gabe, are a..." She looked up to see his brows raised, as if in a playful threat. "Nothing," she finished, pulling free and trying to get ahead of him.

She was unsuccessful. Two seconds later, he took hold of her and picked her up, throwing her over his shoulder and laughing when she squealed.

"Put me down."

"When I'm ready." Carrying her into the house, he set her down in the kitchen at her desk. "Now, brat. Get to work."

"I can't. My stuff is in the car."

"Sit tight. I'll get it."

Kat looked at the clock as he brought her supplies to her. It was four-thirty. Greeting Mariah, she realized she had plenty of time before supper. She scanned through the images on her camera, then looked through the sketches that she had done of Indy. They weren't bad, she decided, but they lacked 'soul'. Pulling out her art paper, she went to work.

She finished three of them before supper, and

showed them to Cynthia when she was satisfied. "Which ones do you like?"

"Oh my, Kat," Cynthia looked from one to the other. "I can't decide. These are awesome. I probably need to finish my notes to decide which ones go together the best."

Kat nodded, smiling. "I'm glad you like them."

"I don't just like them. I *love* them. And by the way, the publisher sent the contract for you to sign this afternoon while we were gone."

Gabe heard Mariah's call from the kitchen for supper and turned. Cynthia went to grab the two-way radio and called for the men to come in. Within fifteen minutes they were seated at the table. Gabe sat and reached down, touching Kat's arm, and she grinned up at him.

Cynthia smiled from across the table. "Gabe, I can't wait for you to see the drawings of Indy and Leanna. You'll be blown away." Gabe smiled as she continued. "I still have some work to do on my notes, though. I'm supposed to contact the editor with my first chapter by June 2nd."

"You're a day late," Tim said, laughing, "but hopefully not a dollar short."

Gabe began to speak, but when he saw Kat's face, he stopped. She had frozen. He touched her shoulder gently.

"Katlynne?"

She sat unmoving until he leaned forward. "Katlynne? What is it?"

She blinked, and met his eyes, her own full of fear. "Has anyone heard from Lorina and Ted?"

Gabe rose immediately to his feet, taking her hand. "We'll be right back," he said to the others, leading her into the living room. He picked up the phone and dialed the cell number Ted had given him, heaving a sigh of relief when Lorina's friendly voice answered. He pressed it into Kat's hand.

"Lorina," Kat was so relieved, tears sprang to her eyes. "Are you and Uncle Ted all right? Have you seen or heard anything unusual?"

Lorina answered. "We're fine here, sweets. Ted and I have closed up the house and moved to a hotel for a day or two. There was a notification from the Department of Corrections." There was an uncomfortable pause.

"*And?*" Kat's knuckles, gripping the phone, were white.

"Sweets," Lorina's voice was soft, as if she was trying to find the kindest way to speak. "Their parole was *approved.*"

Kat was staring out the window at nothing as Gabe took the phone from her hands.

"Lorina," he tried to keep the concern out of his voice. "I want you and Ted to get away from there. I can send Will for you tomorrow, if you can be ready to leave the day after. The cabin here is ready for you, anytime."

"Oh, Gabe. We appreciate it, but we think we'll be all right for a few days. Maybe by the end of next week we can be ready? And don't ask Will to come all the way here. We can book a flight to Billings, and perhaps he could just meet us there. The police do know where we are, and they'll contact us if anything happens to the house. Hold on, let me put Ted on the phone."

Kat listened quietly as Gabe tried to coax them into coming sooner. But when he hung up the phone, he had been unsuccessful. He reached out and gathered her into his arms. Quietly, she leaned against his chest, saying nothing. Tears slid out from under closed lashes.

"They'll be fine, sweetheart. They're at a hotel, and the police know where they are. And if anything happens at the house—"

"I don't care about the house." Her voice was forceful. "I just want them to be safe."

Gabe turned her to face him. "What I was going to say was, if anything did happen, or the alarm went off for any reason, they'll contact Lorina and Ted to make sure they're safe." He continued to hold her closely for a long time. Finally, he held her away from him and studied her. "Are you all right?"

She nodded. "I guess so." She met his eyes squarely. "You... knew about the parole, didn't you?"

"I did, sweetheart. That's why I wanted so badly to bring you home with us. I didn't want you there when the results were decided." He brought her close again. "Katlynne, I would give everything I have to keep you safe."

She nodded, turning her head into his chest. "I know."

"Can you finish eating?"

Kat hesitated. "Mariah's been working on it all day. I need to try. And the others are probably worried about us."

Cynthia prodded the others into conversation as Gabe brought Kat back to the table.

"Lorina and Ted are fine," she said.

Gabe knew she was making an effort at a smile and

added, "They've moved into a hotel until they're ready to come."

"Fantastic," Will nodded. "I can go get them any time."

"Thanks, Will," Gabe nodded. "I did tell them that. But they're both determined to wait a week or so. And you may only have to go to Billings to pick them up."

Will smiled. "Ah. I can do that too."

Gabe observed Kat as she glanced at Shelley and heard the whispered words, "They're free."

"Oh, Kat. I'm sorry," Shelley whispered back, shaking her head.

The rest of the group made casual conversation during the rest of the meal, but Kat ended up just pushing around what was left of the food on her plate. Finally, she glanced up at Gabe and excused herself, disappearing into her room.

Shelley watched her go, glancing up at her brother.

"Check on her," he suggested.

Shelley found Kat leaning back against the head-board on her bed. She was clutching a pillow to her and staring across the room.

"Hey, Shelley," she said as Shelley sat down on the end of the bed.

"Hey, Kat."

Kat squeezed the pillow more tightly. "I should have made myself go to the hearing," she said quietly. "Perhaps it might have mattered."

"Perhaps," Shelley answered quietly, "and perhaps not."

"Suppose they do it to someone else... and suppose I could have prevented it..." Kat closed her eyes, tears forming without permission.

"It wouldn't have made any difference. You have no control over that, and you have to stop blaming yourself for everything that happens. It wasn't just a matter of assault. They caused your father's d—" Shelley's voice cut off abruptly. She couldn't get the word out.

"Death," Kat finished for her flatly.

They sat in silence for a long period of time. Kat finally spoke. "Gabe knew about the hearing. What else does he know?"

Shelley turned to her. "Honestly?"

"Please."

"He knows what I told him, I guess. After we began rooming together, I explained it to them. I told both of them about the break-in and the assault. And about your dad's death. I don't think I've ever seen Gabe so angry. He admires your heart and your determination, and even though he refers to it as stubbornness, he admires your brave spirit."

"Trust me, I am anything but brave right now. Shelley, there's something I haven't told anyone," Kat's voice was muffled. "There are some things about that night that I still don't remember. It's as if I've blocked them out."

"Have you remembered anything else since then?"

"*Yes.*" Kat raised her eyes. "Once in a while, especially after a nightmare, something surfaces." She closed her eyes. "The thing that I keep remembering now, I can't exactly place the hissing sound. In my nightmares, it happens constantly. But they all start with that sound. I hear it in all of them now."

"I'll never understand why they held your father responsible. It was a jury trial, after all," Shelley added.

Kat sat up straight suddenly. "The jurors! I wonder if those men plan to go after the jurors, too."

"I'm sure the possibility of that has occurred to the police."

Kat leaned her head on her hand. "I hope so. I feel as if some of this is my fault."

"But you were in shock. There's probably no way

you could have remembered everything. I'm sure they realize that."

Kat's expression was doubtful. "Oh gosh. I hope so, Shelley."

Fifteen

The coming night...

Gabe expected that the nightmares would return that night. He stayed in the great room so he could reach her at her first sound of distress. Staring outside, he thought of the conversation he had with Shelley just after Kat fell asleep. She didn't tell him all that was said, but enough to rekindle his anger, considering all Kat had been through.

When the anguished cry came, he ran for her room. Shelley had just come through the bathroom door as Gabe reached her bedside and began speaking softly.

"Katlynne, it's the dream, babe. I'm here. No one can hurt you."

Kat had opened her eyes, but when she focused on him, she rolled over on her left side and covered her face, weeping. Gabe gathered her up, sheets and all, and lifted her, carrying her into the great room. Sitting down on the large recliner with her, he rocked her gently.

"Oh, Gabe," she whispered. "Thank you for waking me. It was awful this time."

"Katlynne, I'll say this once again, sweetheart. I want you to feel as if you can talk to me."

"I can't," she said sorrowfully, "I can't. Oh, Gabe, I just feel..." she paused abruptly, then added, "damaged."

"No, sweetheart," he said, bringing her closer. "No. You're the most innocent young lady on the face of the earth. Nothing can change that. You have every right in the world to despise those men. But don't allow yourself to feel that they have changed your worth., or your purity. Nothing can lower either of those things."

"But I don't feel that way."

"Then you need to try to see yourself the way everyone else does."

"It's not only that. It's the disability, too."

"What disability?"

Kat met his eyes, not believing what she heard.

"To me, sweetheart, what you have are limitations. You have so many *abilities*," his voice was firm now, "that they far, far, outweigh any 'disabilities' you may perceive yourself as having. Do you have limitations? Yes, you do. More than a few. But don't get into the mindset of wrapping yourself up in a labeled word. Do you understand what I'm saying?"

"Yes, but—"

"No buts. I do *not* want you to think of yourself as 'damaged' or imperfect in any way. *Ever*. To me, and to everyone else, you're *perfect*."

This time, Kat leaned voluntarily into his arms and buried her face into his chest. His arms closed around her, enfolding, comforting.

"Thank you, Gabe," she whispered.

"Don't thank me, sweetheart." he said, over her head. "*Believe* me."

He sat there, holding her, until she relaxed in his arms, and then looked down. She was getting sleepy again; he could see her eyelids beginning to droop.

"Do you feel like going back to bed yet?"

Kat hesitated. "Would it be all right if I looked at the Milky Way again?"

Gabe, grinning, moved his arm so that she could

reach the button on the arm of the recliner. "Absolute-ly." He watched as she reached out and pressed it to turn the lights in the room off.

He sat there, enjoying the feel of her in his arms. She was so adorable, this beautiful young woman. It was hard not to lean down and bring her lips to his. Finally, he spoke into the darkness. "The stars are addicting, aren't they?"

When Kat didn't answer, he reached down and turned on the lights. She was sound asleep.

But now, she was smiling.

A cool breeze...

The morning breeze in Kat's room gently blew her hair back from her face as she opened her eyes and glanced toward the patio door. It was opened only a few inches, blocked by the length of wood Tim had placed in the track.

"Shelley?"

"Morning. Your door is opened a little. I thought you'd enjoy the fresh air." Shelley stuck her head in from the bathroom. "It was about time to wake you, anyway. Breakfast will be ready soon."

Kat stretched and yawned. "Thanks. It feels so nice. Was I really loud last night?"

"Not at all. I had just gotten up to use the bathroom, or I might not have heard you. Gabe was already in here when I came into your room." Shelley moved closer and sat down on the edge of the bed. "You might not have noticed this, Kat, but it's obvious to me. I'm getting the impression that Gabe..." She stopped.

Kat swiveled slowly, turning to her. "You're doing it again. Spit it out, girlfriend."

Shelley laughed, before lowering her voice to a whisper. "Gabe is very, *very* fond of you."

Kat blinked, and stared at her. "I think you've lost your mind."

Shelley rose. "Do you?" She grinned as she went back into the bath. "We'll see."

Gabe listened intently to the conversation revolving around the table during breakfast.

"We saw brown bear tracks on the other side of the barn this morning. The calves are all accounted for, but there was a commotion during the night."

Gabe frowned. "You're sure they were brown and not grizzly."

"Positive."

Gabe nodded. When he looked over and realized Kat was watching him, he softened his expression. She was listening with wide eyes, and he reached over and put a gentle hand on her shoulder.

"Gabe? Phone call," Cynthia peeked around the corner, and he rose quickly.

"I'll take it in the great room." Giving Kat a wink, he disappeared.

"It's Lorina," Cynthia whispered, handing him the phone.

Gabe kept his voice low as he took the phone. "Lorina? Is everything all right?"

Her voice had a tremulous tone to it when she spoke. "We're fine. What about Kat?"

"She's all right, other than a few nightmares," he answered solemnly, "What's happening there?"

"Gabe, we got a call at the hotel from the police during the night. Someone broke into the house and set the alarm off."

"Are you all right? Did they do any damage to the house?"

"We're fine, Gabe. Please stress that to Kat when you tell her. As for the house, nothing was touched except," her voice trembled, "except Kat's bedroom. They drew a picture of a girl's body on the bedspread."

His hand tightened on the phone. "Go on."

"It was a drawing of a naked girl, tied, and lying face down... with stripes across her back all the way down her body. They also drew a whip next to her body, and a note that said, "We'll be back.""

"Fingerprints? *Anything?*" The fury in Gabe's voice was evident.

"They said they didn't find any. We only know what they described to us. They told us not to go near the house yet."

"Do they have an address for the parolees?"

"I don't know. They didn't tell us. They did say that they would contact us again when they had more information."

"Did they tell you not to leave town?"

"No... but we need to be able to get back into the house and clean the room up before we leave."

Gabe was scowling into the phone.

Lorina's voice was quiet. "They're trying to keep it off the news. So far, they've been successful, but it's only been a few hours."

Ted's voice spoke into the phone. "Gabe?"

"Hello, Ted. I'm sorry," Gabe replied, trying to keep the frustration out of his voice. "I'm just trying to figure out how to relay all this to Katlynne without frightening the daylights out of her. But she deserves to know what happened." He looked back toward the kitchen, only to see Kat standing in the archway between the kitchen and the great room, her face white. "I have to go," he said quietly. "Let me know when Will can come and pick you up, or where to meet you. I'll call you back this evening." He ended the call with a 'Stay safe' and turned to the doorway.

Kat was trembling; that was easy enough to see. Her eyes were wide and a lighter blue than usual. "What's happened?" she demanded.

Gabe sat down in the recliner and patted his thigh. "Come here, sweetheart. Ted and Lorina are all right. But I have something to tell you."

* * *

Kat gulped when he told her. Gabe had taken her by the waist and set her in his lap, holding her tightly in his arms. He hoped the warmth from his body would nullify the sudden cold that had seemed to envelop her. He grabbed the throw from the side of the chair and wrapped it around her, watching her face as her expression changed, slowly, from fear to anger.

"How dare they." She sat up, her shoulders straight, her eyes blazing. "How *dare they*!"

"Katlynne?" Gabe's tone was surprised as he gazed

down at her. Then he brought her closer, hugging her tightly. "That's my brave girl."

Kat could feel his comfort. She also felt the depth of his warmth seeping through into her bones, instilling her with courage. The urge to bury her face in his chest and throw her arms about his neck was overwhelming, but she was determined not to do it.

Finally, Gabe allowed her to sit up, but had his right hand around her waist, and the left around her shoulders, with a firm grasp on her. With a soft, deep voice, he leaned forward, saying into her ear, "All of us will do everything in our power to keep you safe from harm, sweetheart. Hear me?"

"Yes," she said, "I believe that with all my heart."

Kat's courage waxed and waned as the day passed. She wanted so much for the Baxters to be here, out of harm's way. At times, her anger got the better of her, and she had to stop her artwork to do something else. When she calmed, however, she found herself moving back to the desk once again.

Gabe was encouraging. "They want to come as soon as they can get the house cleaned up, Katlynne.

Until then, I guess we'll just have to be patient. No one but the police and us know where they are."

Kat spent the day drawing more sketches of Leanna and Indy, but there was one of Gabe in there, too. He, along with Tim, spent the day wandering back and forth from the pastures to the house to check on things, and Kat noticed. She noticed, too, that Tim kept a close eye on

Shelley, who was staying close by. More than once, she looked up from her drawing to see Gabe watching her, and caught an encouraging smile and a wink from him.

She found herself staring at Gabe as he stood just inside the great room, speaking to Tim.

Comparing him to the sketch she'd finished, she let her mind wander. That mouth had planted more than a few kisses on her forehead since she'd arrived, and one or two brief ones on her mouth; she treasured those.

A real kiss, though?

Gabe suddenly grinned at her from across the room, and Kat suddenly realized she'd been staring at his mouth. Her cheeks suddenly felt hot, and she knew they were a distinct shade of dark pink. She looked away, embarrassed.

She heard Tim's chuckle as he turned to Gabe. In a quiet voice, he said, "I believe someone is keeping an eye on you, too." With that, he turned toward the front door.

Kat watched him, her mouth open. What surprised her the most, however, was the response she heard from Gabe.

"I hope so," he remarked. "I certainly hope so."

"Kat? Phone call for you." Cynthia called from the great room. As Kat approached her, she mouthed, "A man."

Kat immediately glanced up at Gabe. "Who would be calling me here?" she asked as she rose. "Uncle Ted?"

Cynthia handed her the phone, but shook her head. "It doesn't sound like Mr. Baxter," she whispered.

Gabe scowled, watching Kat's face. "I don't know, sweetheart. Do you want me to take it for you? Or to listen in?"

Without hesitation, she nodded. "Listen, please." Taking the phone, she fought to keep her voice from trembling. "Hello?"

A friendly voice answered. "Hello, Katlynne. You don't know me yet. My name is Ian Winslow. I'm an old friend of Gabe's, from the sheriff's department. I was just wondering if you'd be interested in joining me for dinner this Friday. There's a little place in Red Bull that serves an excellent steak."

Kat looked up at Gabe, frowning.

"Do you want to go?" His whisper was quiet.

"No," she mouthed the word.

"Then, don't."

She thought it over a moment, brought back to the present by Ian's voice.

"Katlynne?"

"Yes. It sounds lovely, Ian, but I'm unable to make any plans right now. Thank you so much for asking."

There was a bit of disappointment in his voice when he answered, but he still sounded friendly. "All right. Perhaps another time. Have a great day."

"Thank you. You, too." She hung up the phone and turned to Gabe. "I haven't even met him. How did he know I was here?"

Gabe turned her to face him. "I confess. He came by yesterday morning and saw you working at your desk, sweetheart. He asked about you, then."

She tilted her head. "But you didn't introduce me. Why not?"

"No. I can't give you an answer as to why. I

suppose if I were honest, I'd admit I'm jealous. Should I have?"

"Probably."

He stared at her. "I see. Would you have liked meeting him?"

She hesitated before answering. "No." There was another pause. "But, if I'd have met him when he was here, at least I'd have been able to form an opinion of him. That would have been better than a phone call just coming out of the blue from someone I don't know."

"Ah. Good point. My apologies, then."

She grinned and pressed a hand to his cheek. "You're forgiven," she said, moving back to her desk. But she couldn't manage to keep the smile from her face.

Sixteen

few days later...

Gabe had finally heaved a sigh of relief when the Baxters decided to come. As he turned toward the great room the next morning, he found Tim standing in the arched doorway, his hands jammed into his pockets.

"What is it?"

Tim turned to face him. "Has it occurred to you..."

"That we haven't seen hide nor hair of Josie for the past few days? Yes. She doesn't usually give up this easily."

Tim nodded. "I may drive by her house this afternoon and see if her car is there. Just out of curiosity."

"It might have something to do with the fact that her father threatened to cut her out of the will, but I don't know."

Tim's brows shot up. "Really? No kidding. I didn't think he had it in him." He scowled down at his boots. "Still..."

"I know. It would be more like her to think she could get around that. When she's quiet like this, it makes me suspicious that she's up to something sinister." He nodded toward Tim. "Let me know if you see her car. Will's taking the Cessna to go to Billings this afternoon to pick up the Baxters. I'll be relieved to get them here. And I'm taking Katlynne over to see Indy, but we won't be gone long. Her boots are ready."

Tim nodded, putting on his hat, and disappeared through the front door. "I won't be gone long either."

Gabe went to find Kat. She was sitting on Shelley's chaise lounge with her feet propped up, chatting. He could tell by the sparkle in her eyes that she was excited. She waved at him when he stuck his head in.

Gabe looked down at Kat. "Hey, brat. Ready to get your boots?"

"Yes!" she said, bringing her feet down and grinning. "And who told you it was okay to call me a brat?"

"Behave, young lady. Or I won't let you go."

"Sure, sure. Threaten me. I know your tactics." She grinned as she passed him.

"No respect," he said, with a wink, as Shelley giggled.

Taking her out to the SUV, he carefully tucked her into her seat belt. But as he circled the drive and pulled out into the road, he rested his hand over hers.

"Katlynne, I'll take you down to see Lorina and Ted this afternoon when we get home. But don't forget the rules."

"Ah, the rules. They never end."

"Yes, sweetheart, the rules. I don't want you going over to the cabin alone unless you clear it with me first, every time. Even then, I want you to take the golf cart or the SUV. And if you do, take the satellite phone with you."

"Even to the cabin?"

"Even then." He nodded, his voice firm. "It's out of sight of the house, and you could have trouble with the vehicle. And it's too far for you to walk. Understood?"

Kat sighed. "Understood."

"Good girl."

He pulled up outside Indy's shop and reached over and grasped her hand, squeezing it, before exiting the car. "Be right there."

Kat reached for her sketchpad and pencils as he opened the door and unfastened her seat belt.

"Hello there, Gabe. Hello, young lady. Ready to see what I have for you?"

"I *am*." She grinned at him. "And I can't wait."

With a wide grin, he motioned toward the boots he'd set on the counter.

Kat gasped when she saw them: a pair of deerskin boots with rawhide straps in the front and rabbit fur showing at the top. Gabe lifted her and set her on the counter.

"Oh, Indy," she breathed, "they're beautiful. How can I ever thank you?" Her eyes were wide as he brought them over, and she touched the soft doeskin and the rabbit fur. "They're so soft."

"Feel inside, too." Indy's grin was infectious. He watched as she slid her hand inside them. She could feel the firm lining, but there was also a layer of soft rabbit fur inside that she could wiggle her toes against.

"Are they..."

"Yes. I measured your braces the last time you were here so I could duplicate their size for the inside of the boots. They're reinforced, so you should be able to put them on without wearing your braces, and still have the support you need. I'm not recommending you go without the AFOs all the time, but on days when you want to wear the boots, they should be sufficient for you."

Gabe removed her braces, while Indy held a boot so that she could slide her foot into it. The other followed. Kat looked down, surprised that they looked the same size. "The right one," he explained, "has a slight bit of padding added to it, so the differences in your sizes won't be noticeable. And they should be a bit lighter than the braces."

"Oh, Indy," she looked up with tears in her eyes. "How can I ever..."

He leaned back, crossing his arms. "Just wear them, sweetheart," he said simply, grinning. "That will be thanks enough."

Gabe lifted her down to stand on her feet. She walked a few steps and then turned, feeling how comfortable they were. They were hinged at the ankles so they didn't throw her knees forward with each step. Kat walked over to Indy and threw her arms around his neck. "Thank you, Indy. So much!" She kissed his rough, weathered cheek.

"Here, here," Gabe laughed. "He gets a kiss, and I don't?"

She lifted her chin. "He made my boots."

"Keep an eye on him, Kat. He's a jealous one,"

Indy said, laughing. Kat, turning toward Gabe, threw her arms up and kissed his cheek.

"Ah. That's better," he teased.

"That's for bringing me to pick them up."

Gabe raised a brow. "I see. What do I owe you, Indy?"

Indy leaned against his workbench, folding his arms across his chest. "Gabe," he said, "it's like this. It isn't often I get to do something like this for such a delightful and appreciative young lady." He smiled at Kat. "Consider this a labor of love. I enjoyed every minute of making them. And besides that, the book Cynthia and Kat are doing for my people is payment enough." Once again, he turned and looked down at Kat. "My mother and my wife both said to give you their love. Mother had a doctor's appointment in town today, so they aren't here."

"Please, give them mine, too?" Kat asked, as Gabe gathered her braces and ushered her toward the car.

"I will," Indy waved goodbye to them, calling as Gabe put her in the car, "And Gabe, I'm working on your order, but it's not quite finished yet."

"Great," Gabe waved back, "just call me when they're done, and I'll be back. And when Shelley sees these, she's probably going to want a pair just like them. But I'll have to insist on paying you for those."

"Can do."

Kat waved at him again from the window as she and Gabe pulled away. Then she brought her feet up and rested them on the dash, admiring the boots again.

"Hey, sweetheart, don't get dirt and gravel on my dash," he scolded playfully.

She smacked him on the shoulder with her small fist, and he caught her hand. When she pulled back, he didn't let go. A few moments later, he still held her hand in his.

"Sit still and behave," he grinned toward her.

"Bossy," she grumbled.

"Am I now? Would you like to find out just how bossy I can be?"

"No." she tossed her head and grinned as he chuckled quietly.

But he still refused to let go of her hand.

The plane was in front of the hangar as they pulled into the driveway. Gabe watched Kat's excitement as she leaned forward.

"They're back!"

"Looks like it." He made her wait, however, until

Will arrived with them at the house before letting her loose to give them a welcoming hug.

"Lorina!" Kat hurried over as fast as she could manage.

"Sweets!" Lorina's arms were around her in an instant.

Ted's hug was next. "How's my girl?" he asked.

"Good!" She glanced from one to the other of them. "I'm so pleased you're here at last!"

"I'll help get your things out and loaded into the jeep," Gabe informed them. "I checked on the cabin this morning, and it looked like everything was ready for you. I'll need to show you the alarm system and how to work the generator in case the power goes out. And a few other things." He waited until the ladies were inside before turning to Ted. "Any difficulties getting away?"

"No," Ted said, setting down another suitcase. "But I must tell you, we heaved a sigh of relief when we felt the plane lift off. We're still concerned for Kat, but we're so glad she's here. She looks good, Gabe. She looks as if she feels well, and her eyes seem to have a sparkle we haven't seen for a while."

Gabe smiled. "Thanks, Ted. I'm glad to hear you say that. And glad to have you two here, too."

Ted looked toward the house. "How are the nightmares?"

Gabe followed his gaze. "There have been some, but Shelley seems to think they're slacking off a little. By the way, you can start picking out the plans and supplies for the greenhouse at any time. Kinsey, Terry, and I will help set it up. You can direct the project and let us do the heavy stuff."

Gabe took Lorina, Ted, Kat, and Cali to the cabin when they finished tea. There was time for a quick tour of the house before they left. Mariah made them promise to come back for meals until they were able to get some groceries in the cabin.

"There is food there," Gabe turned to Lorina on the way, "but it might not be what you're used to cooking, so I want you to look and see what's in the pantry, and if there's anything in the fridge. And we'll leave you the jeep so you can drive back and forth. Or the golf cart, whichever you prefer."

"Did you leave my car at the house?" Kat asked curiously.

"We did, Kat. We locked it in the garage and took a

taxi to the hotel and the airport. I guess we could have driven it out here and saved Will a trip to Billings."

"Katlynne can use one of our vehicles if she needs one." Gabe answered, "and save wear and tear on hers. And trust me, Will would rather fly than eat. He didn't mind in the slightest coming to get you."

He pulled the jeep up in front of the cabin. "And here it is, folks."

Lorina let out a gasp of surprise. "Oh, it's charming," she said in delight. "I love it already."

Cali laughed. "Don't go on about it too much, now. I might decide to move back in." After unlocking it, she turned, handing Lorina her key. "Here you go. Welcome to your new home."

Gabe lifted Kat down and helped her to the sidewalk, then turned to go around the back of the jeep for the luggage. "Stay on the walkway, sweetheart. The ground is a little uneven."

She looked down. He was right. Cali and Lorina had gone inside, and she followed. She, too, took a deep breath when she saw the inside. It was cozy and welcoming.

Cali was in official tour guide mode as she led them from room to room.

"Oh my," Lorina was touched. "I love this, and you are all so sweet."

"Now, don't you cry." Cali grinned. "There's more to see." She turned, leading the way to the staircase that led to the loft, with a landing halfway up. "Watch your head. It's close here. This was my favorite place, but I'm getting too old to take advantage of it, so I really couldn't enjoy it as much as I used to. The big house is easier for me to get around in now."

Kat stopped at the top of the stairs, looking at the loft with excitement almost equal to Lorina's. The late afternoon sun was shining through the window, lighting the whole room. It held a few bookcases and a desk that stood in front of a large window. There was a reading area in the corner next to it, set up with a lamp.

"I see why you loved it so," Kat said, looking around. "This is wonderful."

"Yes," Cali nodded, "You two enjoy the view, while I go down to check on the men."

When Cali was gone, Lorina turned toward Kat; her smile replaced with concern. "I know you're full of questions, sweets," she said.

"I am," Kat said, swiveling around in the desk chair, "but I'd like you to get settled first. What do you think? Can you be happy here?"

"With the cabin? It's wonderful. I think I love it better than the pool house, or the house. Are *you* happy? That's what I want to know."

"I am. I'd love to come over and spend some time here tomorrow helping you get settled."

"Well, I don't think it'll take long," Lorina admitted, "We really didn't bring a lot. Ted did bring a few things from the greenhouse. But we'd love to have you come and spend some time."

Kat leaned forward. "Did he bring the blue rose?"

"He did sweets. I'm not sure what shape it's in after the flight, but if anyone can keep it going, he can."

Cali brought up tea, and they sat a few moments before footsteps were heard on the stairs.

Gabe was ducking his head to clear it. "Sorry we took so long. Ted and I have been picking out the spot for the greenhouse." He looked around the loft, grinning. "I love this loft. I watched Dad build it," he said quietly, and then added, "I handed him a few tools here and there. I think I was four or five." He grinned. "Well, since we have everything unloaded, I guess we need to get back over for supper. Mariah should have it ready any minute now."

Kat stood to her feet, and Gabe held out his hand to her, leading her down the staircase. "This is a tricky case. You have to watch your head pretty closely coming down."

Kat's head cleared easily, but Lorina had to duck

on the way down. Cali was out in the jeep with the windows down when they exited the front door, smiling and enjoying the breeze from the back seat. She looked up toward Gabe. "I just saw Josie drive pull in the driveway, Gabe. When she saw me sitting here, she turned around and left."

He frowned and looked in the direction she indicated. "She's probably curious about what's going on. Thanks for telling me."

Seventeen

orgetting...

Gabe put an arm on Kat's shoulder the next morning when everyone was leaving the breakfast table. "I know you'll probably want to go and spend some time with the Baxters today, sweetheart," he said into her ear. "I'll take you over and come back and get you whenever you're ready."

Kat looked up into his face. "Thank you. I'd love that."

Cynthia had left to go to her studio, and Shelley, to her room. The men had already left, and Mariah was clearing the table. Gabe took her arm and led her into the empty great room. Leaning down, he asked quietly, "Did you look over the rules last night, as I suggested?"

Her sudden quiet gasp told him she had not.

"Go and do it now, then," he frowned. "I'll call the Baxters to check on them, and I have some things to do here this morning. After I speak to them, I'll let you know what time to be ready. I'll come to your room and let you know. By the way, you look adorable this morning."

She gave him a scowl as she moved toward her room. But once inside, she closed the door and began to look for the yellow legal sheet that she had written them down on. Checking the book on the bedside table, then the little occasional table next to the reading area, she straightened. Where had she put them?

When Gabe put his head in a few moments later, she looked up.

"I can't find them," she said, holding up her empty hands.

"Here." He set the yellow tablet down and tapped on the top drawer of her dresser. "I found them in the kitchen a day or two ago." He raised a brow. "I wondered how long it would take you to look for them."

❧

Kat waved goodbye to Gabe as he left her at Lorina's that morning.

"Ahem. Was that a kiss I witnessed?" Lorina teased.

"Just a forehead kiss," Kat tried to wave it away.

"Excuse me?" Lorina's grin was infectious. "How many people does he go around kissing on the forehead?"

Kat grinned. "It had better only be me."

"My point, indeed. I'm telling you, sweets, there's something very sexy about a forehead kiss."

"Oh, but I think you're wrong," this time, Kat's sentence cut her off, "He's just being nice."

"Hm. Have it your way. But one of these days, don't be surprised if that kiss is on your mouth."

Kat only grinned. She wasn't about to tell Lorina about Gabe's kiss a few days earlier, even if it had been brief.

Lorina turned. "Come on in, sweets. I'm getting used to using the kitchen. I love this place. Coffee?"

"Please. Where's Uncle Ted?"

"He's outside in the back, planning out the greenhouse. I swear, I've never seen that man so excited. This one's going to be quite a bit bigger than the one we had at home. Ted is like a kid again." She grinned. She walked toward the back door and opened it, calling to her husband. "Fifteen minutes, sweets!"

Kat grinned at the sound of Lorina's voice, calling to him. They had been married almost forty years and were still so affectionate to one another. Kat hoped that one day she might have that kind of love in her own life.

"So, Kat," she said, grinning, "What have you been up to this morning?"

Groaning, Kat rolled her eyes. "Memorizing rules."

"Ranch rules?"

"Yes."

"Gabe gave us a list of things we needed to watch for and to do. They all sounded reasonable to Ted and me. And he mentioned things like the snakes out here."

"But I seem to have more rules than anyone else," she muttered.

"Ah, but remember sweets, he's the one responsible for ensuring your safety. And I gather he takes his responsibilities quite seriously."

"Well, that's certainly true. But I don't want to talk about Gabe, or me, or ranch rules. Please, Lorina, tell me what happened at the house before you left."

"Yes, absolutely. But I want to wait until we can go up into the loft, just the two of us. Ted's so worried that it will upset me; he's trying to avoid the subject, and I guess I'm doing it around him for the same reason."

Listening to their excited chatter all through lunch, Kat smiled at their happy expressions. She wanted so much for them to love it here.

As Ted wandered back outside, Lorina made coffee and carried it upstairs with the warm brownies she'd just taken from the oven. Setting them down on the table between the soft comfy chairs in the reading area, she and Kat made themselves comfortable.

"Okay, honey," she said, her expression serious. "Now we can talk. I feel like you have every right to know what's been going on."

Kat nodded. "Thank you. I feel like Gabe was watering it down because he didn't want me to worry."

"He probably gave you the facts, but he might not have given you all the details. Is that what you're saying?"

"Exactly." Kat sighed. "The picture of what they drew on my bedspread the night they came into the house... could you draw it for me?"

Lorina stared at her for a long time before nodding. Going to the desk, she pulled out a piece of paper and a pencil and began to draw. When she finished, she handed it over.

Kat took it, staring at it with apprehension.

A likeness of a girl's body lying face down, with her wrists and ankles tied to the posters of the bed. A multitude of stripes went from her back to her lower thighs, and the whip was drawn laid across her thighs just above her knees. On the space between her spread ankles were the words, "We'll be back." With an arrow that pointed upward.

"This," Lorina frowned, "is what they drew. The police insisted on taking it with them as evidence. I tried to talk them out of it. They said the best they could do was promise they wouldn't let the press get hold of it."

Kat's face felt as if it drained of color. "Oh, my."

Lorina continued. "The police do have our cell numbers, and Gabe's landline number. They promised to let us know if anything else happened. If I have any advice for you at all, it would be to try very hard to obey the ranch rules to the letter. Gabe would never forgive himself if anything happened to you; you know that."

"I know." Kat nodded, her voice barely audible.

∾

Later that afternoon...

"Kat, I have a surprise for you."

Kat looked up at the sound of Cynthia's voice. "A surprise?"

"Yes. Tomorrow, we have an appointment to go see a doctor." Cynthia's excitement was palpable, and Kat tilted her head.

"Is this for the book?"

"Yes. You'll love this woman. I've met her only once. She left the reservation to go to medical school and came back to work with her own people on the reservation. She's quite a lady. But we'll have to leave really early in the morning. It'll take a few hours to get there."

"Is Gabe going with us?" The question was out before Kat realized it, and her face flushed suddenly. Cynthia, however, didn't seem to notice.

"No, he can't go this time. It'll just be you and me. Girl's day out." Cynthia grinned, moving around to see what Kat was working on. "Ah, Will," she said. "I love the way you've captured his expression. He has the most beautiful eyes." As if she realized Kat was staring at her, she covered her face. "I didn't say that," she said, "and *you* didn't hear it." But when she moved her hands, her cheeks were a lovely shade of pink.

Kat grinned. "Not a word," she said. "Actually, I was wondering if I did his eyes justice," she frowned. "I was thinking of re-doing it."

"No, no—this one is perfect, trust me," Cynthia smiled. "But... if you, by chance, do decide to sketch it again, could I possibly... have this one?"

Katlynne took the corner of the paper and tugged gently, removing it carefully from the pad. "All yours," she said, handing it over.

Cynthia stared at the likeness as a look of fondness settled across her face. She continued looking at it as she moved down the hall toward her bedroom and studio.

"Oh my," Kat said, watching her go. She leaned down and began absent-mindedly drawing the outline of a face. But a few moments later, she realized that it was not Will's face, but Gabe's, who stared back at her. His expression, however, was not smiling, but stern. She frowned. Finishing it, she flipped over the page and began again, concentrating on doing Will's face again.

She was just finishing it up when she heard foot-steps and looked up. Gabe was standing over her, looking over Will's image, and Kat jumped. She leaned back slightly to allow him to see it better.

He leaned down, pulling up a chair. "I'm blown away by your talent," he said, his eyes crinkling at the corners. "You are an amazing young lady."

Surprised, she met his gaze, and smiled. "Thank you." She continued to look into his eyes and suddenly blushed.

He grinned at her and leaned over, kissing the top of her head, and when he leaned back to look into her eyes again, Kat barely prevented a gasp from escaping. There was a fondness there, too, that she hadn't noticed before.

Gabe, as if realizing his expression gave him away, put his arm around her for a quick hug, and stood to his feet. "Cynthia says you need to go over to the reservation for an interview tomorrow," he said. "I wish I could go with you, but I can't. But don't forget to take the satellite phone with you. And I would really appreciate a call every few hours to check in."

"Yes, of course."

Gently, he tilted her chin up to look at him. After a second or two of silence, he added, "You're precious to me, Katlynne," he said softly. "I'd be lost if anything happened to you."

"Because," Kat gulped, "you're responsible... for me?"

"No," his gaze into her eyes was unbroken. "Just because."

Then, he turned on his heel and was gone.

Gabe found himself breathing hard as he strode down the hill toward the barn, telling himself to get control. He could not give away what he felt for her, not yet. She had to be able to feel safe here. He took another deep breath, remembering the adoring gaze she had returned. There had been no fear there. What *was* it he had seen in her eyes, then?

Desire? He didn't know, but never before had he allowed himself to feel so deeply about a young woman. He slowed, when he heard Tim's voice from behind him.

"I've seen that look before, you know."

Gabe stopped abruptly, waiting for Tim to catch up, and raised a brow. "Oh? On me?"

"No." Tim was scowling as well. "On *me.*" He kicked at the dirt with the toe of his boot. "I swear, Gabe, I can't get Shelley out of my mind. She's the last face I see when I close my eyes at night and the first I see when I open them in the morning. It's killing me. I've never in my life felt so little control over my emotions."

They had reached the barn, and Gabe leaned against the wall, looking back up toward the house. After a moment, he released a deep breath, nodding.

Tim began to move away. "Well, I just thought you should know," he said, looking Gabe in the eye. "If you have a problem with that, I need to know it now."

Gabe, in his own world, suddenly realized what Tim was saying. "What?"

"I said," Tim stared at him, "your sister has stolen my heart. Big time. If that's a problem for you, I need to know it. Now."

Gabe stared back. "Honestly?"

"Honestly. Hello, earth to Gabe. Are you there?"

Gabe was grinning now. "The truth is, Tim, I think neither of you could possibly do better. You're perfect for each other."

"I hope to marry her soon."

"Ah." Gabe nodded.

Tim scowled up at the house as well. "I know she has more education than I do, but..."

Gabe studied him. "Tim, I swear, sometimes you are such an idiot. Shelley may have the education that enables her to teach in a certain field. But you, my friend, are capable of doing *anything*. You could set up your own woodworking shop if you wanted; you could be an electrician. You have enough skills to do a thousand things. I'd be sick if I thought I was about to lose you here at the ranch. I'd never find anyone who could fill your slot."

Tim, considering Gabe's words, grinned suddenly. "Really. So, can I get a raise, then?"

Both of them laughed.

Gabe nodded. "I'm working on it, buddy."

"I'm kidding. You pay me well." Tim repositioned his hat and started out toward the pasture. "And speaking of work, I'd better get busy."

Gabe nodded. Standing alone outside the barn, he stared toward the house. He had calmed down, but each time he thought of Kat's adoring eyes, and the way she had gazed back into his, his heart picked up speed.

He shook his head, scolding himself. "Get a grip," he muttered under his breath.

Eighteen

*D*ay trip...

It was early when Cynthia knocked on Kat's door the next morning.

"Kat? Time to wake up, sweetie."

Slowly, Kat's eyes fluttered open. She pulled herself up and dragged her legs over the side.

"I'm awake."

"Mariah is fixing your breakfast."

It was ten minutes before Kat entered the kitchen, dressed. "Good morning," she smiled, as Mariah set two plates of omelets and toast on the table. "Oh, Mariah, thank you," she said softly. "It's so sweet of you to get up this early."

"Nonsense. Can't let you two go off without a good breakfast in you."

Cynthia grinned. "I'm not sure what time we'll be back this afternoon. If you could just save us a plate, we can warm it up in the microwave when we get back." Turning to Kat, she said, "Please don't let me go off without the sat phone. I very nearly forgot it the last time. Gabe followed me out to the car with it." She leaned forward. "He was not amused."

"Uh-oh."

"Uh-oh is right," Gabe's voice said, behind them. It caused both of them to jump. Kat realized he had the phone in his hands. "I didn't want to take any chances on you forgetting this," he grinned.

Cynthia laughed as she took it from him, handing it to Kat. "Here, sweetie. I'm making you responsible for getting it in the car, since I didn't so well with that last time."

Gabe nodded. "I've told Katlynne, I want you two to check in every few hours today." He continued, putting a hand on Kat's shoulder. "I'll feel much better about you both if I know where you are. Cynthia, you'll have to show her how to use it."

"I will." She turned to Kat. "It's a royal pain," she said, grinning, "but it's better than nothing if you have car trouble."

From the archway, Will spoke. "The car's full of gas. You should have enough to get you there, but you'll need to fill up before you start home."

"Thanks, Will." Cynthia rose to her feet, handing her finished plate back to Mariah. "Take your time, Kat. I'll go get my recorder."

Kat took another bite or two, said a polite thank you to Mariah, and then rose. Gathering the satchel that contained her art supplies, she checked to make sure they were all there. She was about to begin moving her things to the car, when he stopped her.

"Whoa, sweetheart. I'll get these for you." Gabe took her things from her hands, carrying them for her.

Will was walking Cynthia to the car when they approached, and grinned at her. "You girls be careful out there. We'll be waiting when you get back."

Gabe nodded. "And call when you get there safely."

Kat sent a mischievous glance his way. "Does that mean if we have a wreck, we don't have to call?" When Gabe stopped and stared at her with a brow raised, she laughed. "Oops. I didn't think so."

"Brat."

Cynthia was already in the driver's seat when he opened the door for Kat and put the phone and the satchel behind her seat. He fastened her seatbelt and planted a kiss on her forehead, grinning. "See you this afternoon," he said, and waved at Cynthia. "Be safe, you two."

"Wow," Cynthia grinned when she backed out of the driveway. Kat looked up, and she continued. "That man is smitten with you, Kat."

Kat glanced back at the house. She could see the two men, still standing on the front porch. "Do you really think so?"

"I don't think. I *know*." Cynthia looked over at her. She smiled. "He wasn't taking any chances on you leaving the satellite phone, either, I noticed."

"What did he say when you left without it before?" Kat asked curiously.

"Oh, Gabe didn't really say anything. He just handed it to me through the car window and scowled at me. I apologized profusely. But he passed the message along to Will, because when I got back, he gave me a stern and lengthy lecture." Cynthia was pulling out onto the gravel road that passed the cabin. Ted and Lorina must be asleep; the lights weren't yet on.

"Will actually gave you a lecture?" she said, turning back to Cynthia.

Cynthia rolled her eyes, pulling out onto the highway. "Will thinks he's my guardian now, for some reason. Yes, he dragged me back into his study and lectured me for over an hour. So I'm not actually free from being held accountable; it's just that Will is the one who demands it now. And I can't say I mind the idea of it all that much. But the truth is, I hate the actual lectures. Will seems like a teddy bear, but when he's irritated with me, he lets me know it in no uncertain terms. I think he must have written the book on lecturing." She became quiet for a few moments, and when she spoke again, her voice was serious.

"I'm not sure when it happened, exactly. For a while, I was sort of an untouchable, I guess because I'm older, and technically Gabe's stepmom. But a few years ago, things changed. Will started being very stern with me when I became close to breaking the rules. One night, I got home later than I had planned. It was because I had been stopped for speeding, and the officer gave me a ticket. I didn't take the time to call because I was already running late, and Will was waiting frantically when I got home, and demanded to know why I was late. When I told him about the ticket, he took my hand and led me back into his study and gave me a hefty lecture, and said the next time I got a ticket for speeding, he was going to put me over his knee." She was quiet, thinking for a moment. "I think that was about a little over two years ago. I was so surprised, I just sat there with my mouth open."

"Wow..." There was surprise in Kat's voice, too.

"I know. I'm having trouble being honest with myself and deciding whether I hate that..." she paused, "or I like it. There's something very sexy about being cared for to the extent that a man will demand accountability of you to keep you safe, even if it means getting in trouble once in a while. But at the same time, I'm a big girl, and I should be able to do this by myself. A bit of advice, though," she said, grinning.

"I'll take any advice I can get."

Cynthia nodded. "I wouldn't go off and leave the satellite phone, *ever*, if I were *you*. Gabe is strict about that. I know sometimes it's just hard to remember everything. I'm actually the newest person to the ranch, and I still have trouble remembering what to do and what not to."

"What about the men that work here? Do they ever forget?"

Cynthia chewed her lower lip thoughtfully. "If they do, Gabe's never mentioned it. I know there was one fellow who only worked here a short time and was fired. Will mentioned to me that he had a problem following instructions. Gabe never mentioned it, though. The rest of the men were here long before I came."

Kat, frowning, couldn't refrain from asking. "What was Gabe's father like?"

"Nathan was a good man, Kat. He loved me—as much as it was possible for him to. But he was still heartbroken over losing Gabe's mother. I don't think he ever truly got over her loss. If she were alive, I swear, I think I'd wring her neck." Anger had crept into her voice, and Kat was surprised at the strength behind it. She listened quietly, waiting for Cynthia to speak again.

"She had such a wonderful man, and she treated him like dirt. And when she acted stupidly and self-ishly, and caused her own death, she caused the death of his precious heart as well." She was quiet for another long moment before continuing. "I think Nathan was finally beginning to be able to really love me when the cancer showed up. The last several months we had were wonderful. It was as if he suddenly woke up and realized that he had someone who cared about him. After he died, I was so angry for such a long time. I kept asking myself *why*. Why couldn't he have realized what we had before then? We could have had years instead of just a few months of that deep, enduring love. So much of our time together seemed as if it had been wasted..."

"Gabe said that you were wonderful," Kat said softly.

"Did he? He and Shelley were wonderful, too. I can't say enough good things about either of them." Cynthia was smiling now. "And I was delighted when they asked me to stay. Gabe always seemed like a responsible and mature young man, but he's far too serious, in my opinion. I have to tell you, Kat, I've seen him smile more since you've been here than he had in..." she paused, "well, forever."

"Really?" Kat looked up, surprised. "I drew a picture of him yesterday evening, and wasn't paying much attention to what I was doing. And his face, when I finished, was so stern, I just folded it over and didn't show it to anyone. I thought perhaps I was bringing out the stern side in him, the worried side."

Cynthia laughed. "Oh, no, sweetie. You should have known him before he met you. I'm serious. I'll have to take a look at the sketch when it gets a little lighter. Anyway, Kat, I said all that to say this: I'm so glad you're here. Not just for my benefit, even though it is fantastic having you as my illustrator. It's wonderful seeing Shelley relaxed and happy, and although I think Tim is a big part of that, I think you

are too. And Gabe... well, I've never seen him so atten-
tive to anyone, or smile so much." She laughed. "I'm
not sure any of us are ever going to allow you to go
home."

Kat grinned, in spite of herself. "Thank you.
Hearing those words is wonderful."

When Cynthia changed the subject and began
talking about their plans for the day, Kat leaned back
in her seat and relaxed, asking occasional questions.
Cynthia was a wealth of information about the
Shoshone people, and Kat was amazed.

They stopped for coffee at a small place that was
open for breakfast an hour later. Kat was relieved; she
was getting sleepy, and the hot coffee helped her to
perk up a bit.

By ten, they had arrived.

"We'll go somewhere for lunch when we're
finished, but right now, we'd better give Gabe a call
and let him know we're here all in one piece." Cynthia
reached behind the passenger seat and pulled out the
satellite phone. Setting it up on the dash, she opened it
and began to aim the antenna, trying to find an open
area through the trees. A few minutes later, she finally
looked up.

"Ah. Found it. Here." She dialed the number and
handed the phone to Kat. The connection was not the

greatest, and there were long pauses between each phrase. But Gabe had answered the phone, and was quite pleased she'd called.

"Good girl," he'd said. "Have a good day, and give me a call around lunchtime." It wasn't a request, Kat realized. It was a command.

"All right," she'd said. "Bye, Gabe."

"Bye, sweetheart," he'd answered. She could almost see his smile as she hung up.

"I heard," Cynthia chuckled. "Got your sketchpad and your camera?"

"In the back seat. Just a second."

They entered the small building through the waiting room. There were quite a few people in it when they entered; most of them were children, but a few adults too; a man and woman with a tiny little sick child were sitting across from them. The little girl was leaning over with her head in her mother's lap, her eyes closed. She looked terribly pale.

Cynthia and Kat approached the window to speak to the receptionist. "We're here to see Dr. Locklear," she murmured. "I'm Cynthia Ingrahm and this is Katlynne Abramson."

"She'll see you shortly," there was a smile from the receptionist.

Little by little, the waiting room emptied. When

their names were called, they stopped by the window.

"Excuse me," Kat leaned forward. "The little child that's sick?"

"Her appointment is after yours, Miss Abramson."

"No, no," Kat frowned. "Please go ahead and take her. We can wait."

The receptionist smiled. "We can do that. That would make you the last appointment before lunch. You might have more time with Dr. Locklear."

Kat nodded as they went to sit down. The child and her parents were called, and disappeared through the door. Kat watched the receptionist as she answered the phone and looked up records, showing a myriad of expressions. Pulling out her pad, she began to sketch. After doing a few simple sketches, she finished the last detailed one.

At eleven, the door opened. Kat looked up to see a lovely young woman standing at the door. She spoke as Cynthia and Kat stood to their feet.

"Hello, Cynthia, it's nice to see you again—and Katlynne?" she held out her hand in greeting. "Dove Locklear. Please come in."

Cynthia led the way, and Kat dropped off the sketch she had done to the receptionist, smiling, and followed.

Cynthia set up the recorder and set it on the desk,

explaining the book and asking permission for sketches to be done as they talked, and a few photos.

Kat was fascinated by Dove's expressions as she explained how she had been ill as a child and they had been forced to travel long distances to see a physician. This area needed more medical care: more nurses, doctors, hospitals. Her dream was that there would be a new hospital in the area someday.

Kat took a snapshot of the wistful look on her face as she stared out the window, talking about the possibility of a hospital. At present, however, a lot of her care was for people who had little or no money, and finding funds to build a hospital would be difficult. "Sometimes," she laughed, "I get paid with chickens and huckleberry pies—and oh my goodness, how I love that. Better than money." She turned suddenly serious. "But my main concern is that there will never be enough funds to build a hospital here, and my people need it so badly.". She had gone to college, and then medical school in Denver. "And I can't tell you how wonderful it was to get back home to my own area, and my own people," she grinned. "Big cities are just not for me."

Kat's sketches and photos drew her attention more than once. When the interview was over, Kat showed her one of them, and offered to send her one.

"Your receptionist has such wonderful expressions, too," Cynthia said with a smile. "Do you think she would allow us to use one of Kat's sketches of her in the book?"

Dove grinned. "We can ask on the way out," her eyes twinkled. "Heather is a Godsend. I didn't know what I would do when I first opened up without a receptionist. But she moved back here with her husband and needed a job. Before that, she worked as a receptionist in a huge office back east. She's bailed me out on more than one occasion with her meticulous record-keeping."

It was one-thirty before they left the office, stopping by to see Heather on the way out. Cynthia stayed long enough to ask a few questions and get some information. Heather was delighted, and ended up making a copy of the sketch and giving it back so Kat would have it.

"When are you supposed to call Gabe again?" Cynthia asked as they got back into the car.

Kat looked at her blankly. "I'm not sure. I think he said something about lunchtime?"

Kat reached into the floorboard and retrieved the

phone. "Better do it now. I don't want to take a chance on making him peeved. He might think twice about letting us go by ourselves again." Her eyes were twinkling, but there was a hint of seriousness to her voice.

But Gabe sounded delighted to hear Kat's voice when she called. He hung up, telling her to make sure and call back at three, or before, if they left earlier to begin their trip home. "I don't want you out after dark," he said firmly, "Those roads can get pretty deserted. Tell Cynthia that."

"I heard," Cynthia said from where she sat, grinning. "But we do hope to do a tiny bit of shopping while we're here."

Gabe's voice sounded half-kidding, half-serious as he answered. "Ok, but if you're not back by dark, I'll sic Will on you."

"Oh, gosh," Cynthia answered, dismayed. "Anything but that. We'll be back."

"Thought so," was his answer as he hung up the phone.

"I *hate* Will's lectures," she said, closing the phone and putting it back down. "We'll have to get our shopping done quickly."

She pulled up in front of a little place called the *Luna Café*, where the rustic décor was quite appealing. Kat, when she got out, took her supplies in with her, hoping she could get some sketches of the workers, and the décor.

As they were seated, a small woman who looked to be in her mid-fifties came over to greet them. "Cynthia!" she said, her grin wide. "I haven't seen you since you were here with Gabe. Such a hunk. How's he doing, anyway? And how dare he not come with you."

Cynthia grinned, and turned toward Kat. "Gabe couldn't come today. Kat, this is Hannah. Hannah, Katlynne Abramson, the illustrator for my new book. Would you mind terribly if she sketches you?"

"Me?" Hannah laughed, turning to Kat, and fluffed her hair. "Sure, if you're not afraid of breaking your pencil." She threw back her head and laughed at her own joke. "I know you'll want to know what the special is."

"Absolutely," Cynthia answered. "Got anything with huckleberries?" She looked at Kat and winked.

"Ah. I recommend the huckleberry salmon burger. With huckleberry tea? And how about some huckleberry pie for dessert?"

"With huckleberry ice cream on top? Sounds great to me," Cynthia was laughing now.

"Make that double," Kat added, grinning.

Hannah giggled and wandered into the kitchen.

"I like her," Kat said, a huge grin on her face, as she began to sketch.

Cynthia nodded. "She loves to flirt with Gabe. It embarrasses him, and she knows it, so she really hams it up."

"I do *not*," Hannah was back with their tea. "He's just so serious, I can't resist it. Shame it's not the other way around," She laughed and disappeared again.

Lunch was delightful. Kat set the sketchbook aside as they ate. "You mentioned shopping? Where do you go?"

"There are some native shops around here that we like to visit. But we don't get over here that often. Some of them I think you'll really like."

They left the café a half-hour later, satisfied and eager to shop. Kat had given Hannah a sketch of herself— one of two she had done. But as they left, she and Cynthia dropped off her supplies in the car, and turned right into the little row of shops.

Kat was delighted. The first shop they came to featured locally made beaded jewelry. She bought a necklace for Shelley, and a pair of earrings each, for Cali and Mariah. As they continued shopping, she found a cup and saucer for Lorina, and a magnifying glass with a wooden handle for Ted to use in the greenhouse. For Gabe, she bought a hand-carved wooden pen, and a compass for Will. For each of the men, she picked up another little trinket she thought they would like.

Cynthia laughed. "You're spending your entire advance from the book, Kat."

But Kat shook her head. "I'm really not. I brought some funds with me, and this is the first place I've really been to buy anything."

"I know. That's probably the only thing about where we live. Of course, we'll be taking a run up to Yellowstone one of these days, and you can do some shopping there. It's the souvenir capital of the west."

"And I can't wait."

Suddenly, her grin turned to dismay as Cynthia gasped. "Oh! Kat, it's almost five o'clock. What time were you supposed to call Gabe back?"

Kat felt her stomach drop. "Three," she said, meeting Cynthia's wide eyes.

"Let's go. Need for me to carry anything? Here, put some of this stuff in my big bag. We can sort it out later."

Kat dropped several things into it, and they hurried as quickly as they could the three blocks back to the car. Kat was dragging her feet by the time they reached it. She dropped her packages into the back seat while Cynthia pulled out the phone and adjusted the antenna.

"I'll make this call, Kat," she said. "I don't want Gabe to yell at *you*. No..." she said, as Kat began to protest, "I should have been watching. Or set the alarm on my phone." She punched in the number and waited for an answer.

"Where are you?" Gabe's voice was stern. Kat could hear it from where she sat.

"Gabe, this is *my* fault. We were shopping and forgot to watch the time." Cynthia's voice was apologetic but strong. "If you have to blame someone, it should be me." She ignored the shake of Kat's head. "We're still here—we haven't left yet."

There was a pause. "I've been trying to call. Where's Katlynne?"

Cynthia answered. "She's right here. Don't yell at her, Gabe. It's not her fault." She handed over the phone to Kat's waiting hand.

"Hello?" Kat's voice was full of trepidation. She'd seen Gabe upset with her once. She wasn't eager to see it again.

"Katlynne, are you all right?"

"Yes, sir. I'm sorry we're late with the call."

"Not *just* late, Katlynne. Two hours late. I was worried."

"I know. I'm sorry. Cynthia is wrong. It's really my fault."

"The blame lies with both of you, sweetheart." His voice was still stern. "Have you filled up the tank yet?"

"No, we're just about to do that," Cynthia answered from where she was sitting. "Then we'll be on the road."

"All right." His voice, after a pause, still sounded full of anger. "Call me in an hour and let me know where you are. And every hour after that."

Cynthia took the phone back. "Will do."

"And stop along the way and get something to eat for supper, but don't waste any time. Will and I will be waiting for you when you get home. And don't speed." He hung up the phone.

"Oh, gosh," Cynthia said as she pushed in the antenna and closed the case. "We're in trouble, Kat."

Kat's eyes were wide as she looked in the direction of the sun. If it took as long to get home as it did to get here, they would indeed be getting home in the dark.

It took only a few moments to put fuel in the car. The little convenience store had a choice of hot dogs and egg rolls, so Kat went in and got some, along with a drink, for them to take with them.

"Thanks. This will save a little time, anyway. And I think my salmon burger has run out on me."

Kat pulled back the wrapper on the hot dog and handed it over.

"Don't tell Gabe we were eating and driving at the same time, by the way. He feels about that like he does driving and talking on the cell phone. Don't lie if he asks, but..."

"Got it."

They said little on the way home. Kat called at seven, eight, and again at nine to check in. But each time, Cynthia had to pull off the road to find the satellite with the antenna so they could make the call.

Gabe's voice sounded worried. "Hi, sweetheart. Where are you now?"

"Cynthia said we just passed Indy's house about five minutes ago."

"All right. Any problems?"

"No, sir."

"Katlynne, I consider you as responsible as Cynthia. Do you understand me?"

Kat waited a long moment before answering.

"Katlynne?"

"I understand."

"All right. We'll see you when you get home. Call if you have any problems." And he was gone.

Kat put the phone back in the case and closed it.

"I'm so sorry," Cynthia's voice was penitent.

"He's right, Cynthia. Now that I think of it, I don't believe I even told you we were supposed to call back at three. And I should have been watching too. I was having so much fun shopping..." she paused. "But that's no excuse."

"Well, I should have, too. I know how long it takes to make the trip over, and I should have realized it would be dark before we got home. Anyway," she shook her head. "it's too late now." She sighed. "But—we did get what we went for, and I want you to know, I'm extremely pleased with how the book is coming along."

Kat nodded but didn't speak. All she could think of was Gabe's forbidding voice. She hoped he and Will weren't outside standing in the driveway when they got home.

They were, however. Gabe was at the passenger door as soon as Cynthia pulled up and turned off the head-lights; Will, was on the driver's side. Both had been standing with their hands jammed into their pockets, pacing.

"Gosh. Those faces." In the dark, Cynthia shut off the engine. Will had her door open before she had gotten the key out of the ignition. Gabe had Kat's open and her seat belt off. "Hand me the phone, sweetheart."

She picked it up by the handle and handed it to him. He took her hand firmly, helping her out of the car.

"Come with me, young lady."

Kat did as she was told, her eyes downcast. Gabe led her through the hallway into his room, then into his study, and closed the door. Walking over to his desk chair, he took her by the waist and lifted her into his lap so that his face was just inches from hers. He took both of her wrists in his left hand, and with his right, tilted her chin upward so she had no choice but to look at him.

"Look at me, Katlynne."

There were already tears in her eyes, but she managed to obey.

"What do you think I should do with you?"

"I... don't know."

"What were you supposed to do at three o'clock?"

"Call you back..." it was a whisper.

"That's correct. And you didn't call until when?"

"Five

"Because?"

"We were out shopping."

"Did it occur to either of you to check the time, Katlynne?"

She looked down, but he again raised her chin so she had to look into his eyes. "Katlynne? Answer me."

Gabe watched her carefully, waiting for her answer.

"No, sir," she said. "It wasn't Cynthia's fault, Gabe. It was mine."

"What was so important that you shopping for?" His eyes were so stern she had trouble meeting them.

"Gifts."

Gabe was shocked. "*Gifts*?" he frowned. "For whom?"

"Shell, and..."

"And?"

"Mariah and Cali... and you and Will... and Lorina and Ted... and—and Tim, and... the men."

Gabe stared at her. "You bought gifts for everyone?"

She nodded, looking away.

Gabe released her chin and put his hands on her shoulders.

"There was no excuse," she whispered.

"No, sweetheart. None." Suddenly, he gathered her up into his embrace and held her tightly to his chest. "Katlynne."

"I'm sorry, sir. I didn't mean to disappoint you."

"We were so worried, sweetheart. The dark is a terrible time to be driving out in some of these areas. You could have hit a moose, or an elk. And if you'd had a flat tire, or engine trouble, you could have been sitting for hours in the dark on the side of the road. I could imagine any number of things happening to you."

Kat's pent-up worry let go; she was weeping now.

Gabe sat, holding her tightly. "Shh," he said quietly, stroking her back and shoulders gently. He held her a long time before suddenly realizing the room was quiet.

He looked down. The girl in his arms had calmed. Her breathing was even now; her face buried in his chest. And she was asleep.

He rose silently and carried her gently down the hall to her room. Pulling her covers back, he laid her down in her clothes and situated her head on her pillow before removing the boots Indy had made.

Tears still glittered on her lashes, and Gabe gently pushed her hair back. He brought the covers up to her chin before kissing her forehead, and stood there a moment longer, watching her sleep.

He couldn't help himself. He leaned down once more and very lightly kissed her mouth, before turning toward the door and leaving the room.

Nineteen

orgiven...

FWhen Kat opened her eyes the next morning, she looked around the room, dazed. She didn't remember going to bed last night. She sat up on the side, realizing how badly she needed to get to the bathroom, and looked down to see she was still fully clothed.

Noticing the boots Indy had made beside the bed, she slipped into them and moved quickly to the bath.

What had happened? The last thing she remembered was sitting in Gabe's lap, and listening to his lecture. She frowned.

Dropping her clothes onto the bathroom floor, she

turned on the shower and got in, sitting on the bench. Trying to clear her head was another story. Somewhere in the back of her mind, she had dreamed that she was being carried to her room and put to bed. The dream had ended with someone kissing her ever so gently on the mouth before leaving the room.

Her eyes flew open wide. Was it really a dream? If so, it certainly was wonderful. Kat smiled as she remembered it. Surely, it was just a dream. Somehow, though, she had indeed ended up back in her own bed, her boots off, and her covers pulled up to her chin. She had awakened like that this morning, fully dressed.

Wondering how she would ever be able to face him, she finished up her hair and showered and dried off. When she looked in the mirror, her cheeks were a shade of deep red. She glanced up at the clock in the bathroom. It was early yet.

If she had gone to sleep while Gabe was lecturing her, she now realized that he probably wasn't finished with her yet. Her eyes grew wide at that thought. She wondered how Cynthia had managed through Will's certain lecture. Vowing to be more careful on their upcoming trips, she shook her head.

With only the towel wrapped around her and the boots on her feet, she entered her bedroom gingerly and locked the door. She'd just taken some of her lacy underwear from the highboy when she heard the knock at the door, and gasped.

"Katlynne?" It was Gabe's voice. Kat gazed at the doorknob as if it would bite her.

"I'm not dressed yet. Give me just a minute, please?"

"All right. I'll wait."

Hurriedly, she pulled on the underwear and clothes and dragged a brush through her hair. Then she opened the door.

"Yes, sir?"

"I brought your things in from the car," he said, his arms full of bags. 'Good grief, you're almost as bad as Cynthia when it comes to shopping." He brought them into the room, his shoulders filling the doorway. She stepped back, watching him.

"You look cute this morning. As usual."

She looked up uncertainly, "Thank you."

His brows raised, watching her, and waiting.

"I don't remember how I got to bed last night," she said, lowering her gaze. "I was afraid you might not be... finished with me."

"I'm not. Come with me." He held out his hand.

Kat stared at it for several seconds before reluctantly resting hers in it, allowing him to lead her back down the hall to his study.

She froze as he closed the door between the study and the bedroom. This time he sat down in one of the corner chairs, and put her in his lap. He lifted her chin, forcing her to look at him.

Kat moistened her lips nervously. "Are you, um…"

"If you're asking if I'm about to discipline you," he finished the sentence for her, "the answer is no. Not this time, sweetheart. Next time, however, you won't get off so lightly. But I did want to talk with you a little more."

Kat met his gaze, nodding.

"This area, Katlynne, is full of elk and moose. I don't know if you've ever seen an elk up close?"

She shook her head. "Aren't they like deer?"

"They look much like deer, but are quite a bit larger. Because of their height, if you hit one, it's easy for them to come flying through the windshield toward you. Moose are even bigger. And if they aren't looking toward the headlights, you won't see them at all. That's why I worry so about you being on the road at night. I realize Cynthia was driving, and while she's used to watching for them, she can't see them at night any better than you could. And the reason I asked you to call me at three, was because I knew the trip would take hours, and you'd run out of light if you waited longer. I was hoping I could get you two headed back in time to get you back before dark. I wasn't just trying to be mean, or bossy. Do you understand?"

"Yes, sir."

He reached down, gently moving his thumb across her cheek, and smiled. 'I was trying to explain it to you last night, but you fell asleep. *So*, young lady," he said. "This is why it's so important to obey me when I give you instructions to do something. There is always a reason, Katlynne. I never give orders just to feel important, or to test you. I give them because I *expect* you to obey, and to keep you safe. Understood?"

"Yes, sir."

He leaned forward, kissing her forehead. "Good girl," he said, setting her on her feet and sending her toward the door with a gentle nudge. "I think Mariah should be fixing breakfast about now."

Mariah was indeed setting the table when they approached the kitchen. "Good morning. Coffee, Kat? Gabe?"

"Please," Kat answered. A moment later, she glanced up at Gabe. "I think I'll go get the bags," she whispered. Going into her room, she dug through the bags for the things she had chosen. A few moments later, she was back at the table.

Gabe grinned at the excitement in her eyes as she returned, her arms laden down with packages. "Tell me, sweetheart, what did you buy for yourself, yesterday?"

She looked at him, puzzled.

"You didn't, did you? You bought for everyone else, but not for you." He was smiling.

"Oh, but I can't tell you how exciting it was to get to go, and be part of Cynthia's project. It was a wonderful gift."

Gabe only reached over and hugged her as the others began arriving at the table. Kat watched as Cynthia sat down in the chair across from her. She was beaming this morning.

As he finished asking the blessing on the food, Gabe looked up. "Katlynne has some surprises for us," he said, smiling down at her. She rose and took the bags, one by one, delivering them to each person. At the end, she dropped a small bag by Cynthia's plate.

"For me? You shouldn't have done that."

Gabe watched as Cynthia opened it, grinning.

Inside was a coffee mug with a mug that said 'Author' on the side, and a fancy quill pen.

"I sneaked and bought it when you weren't looking."

Everyone seemed delighted with the gifts they'd received, including Gabe. When she returned to sit, he put his arm around her and squeezed her shoulders. In his other hand, he held the pen, carved with an eagle, admiring it. He smiled, and brought her closer for a hug. "Thank you, sweetheart," he said, finally.

It was later that morning that Cynthia came into the kitchen where Kat was sketching. "I want to see what you did yesterday," she said eagerly, pulling over a chair.

Kat backed up several pages, coming across the folded paper that held Gabe's face first.

"Is that the one of Gabe you were telling me about?"

"Yes."

"Do you mind if I see it?"

Kat unfolded it, and Cynthia studied it for a few seconds.

"Ah. I saw that face last night," she nodded at the stern expression Kat had drawn.

"Me too," Kat said ruefully. Looking around the room, she whispered, "Are you all right?"

"Fine," Cynthia grinned. "Will was up lecturing me until late last night. But other than feeling sleep-deprived, I'm fine."

"Well, I'm glad. He looked furious when we pulled up. I've never seen him look like that before."

Cynthia glanced down at the drawing of Heather, the receptionist. "Oh, Kat. This is spectacular. She looks as if she could speak."

"I worked on it a little more." She turned the next page, showing the one Heather had given back, and then one of Dove Locklear.

"This one," Cynthia said, taking a deep breath, "is fabulous."

"This is the one I drew while she was so wistfully talking about the possibility of building a hospital," Kat explained, shaking her head. "I wish there was some way to help with that." She turned the page. There were a couple more of Dr. Locklear, and then she came to the one of Hannah. Cynthia bubbled with laughter when she saw it. "Hannah is such a hoot. I like that girl."

"Wait. There's one I missed." She flipped back

through the pages until she found the one she'd drawn of Will a few days earlier.

Cynthia gasped when she saw it. She clasped her hands together, and whispered. "I think I love that man."

Kat grinned at her. "I thought so," she whispered back.

Twenty

D rawings...

"Katlynne." Gabe approached her the next morning as she was working at her desk, and sat down. "If you'd like to go over and see Lorina and Ted, today might be a good day for it. And Cynthia says the stuff she needs to do on the book is related to the writing. She says you're ahead of her with your sketches." He grinned and put an arm around her, squeezing her in a big hug. She was in the process of drawing Tim, leaning back with his arms crossed. He looked as if he was attempting to be stern, but his eyes were giving him away.

"That's a good one," he chuckled. "So typical. Who else have you done?"

Kat flipped back to the beginning, showing him Mariah, Cali, the pictures of Heather, and Dr. Locklear. The last one was Hannah, at which he groaned.

"Oh my. Hannah is a character," he said.

"She says you're a hunk." Kat gave a soft giggle.

"Who else is there?"

Kat turned over to the next character. Will's face stared back at them. But when she flipped back to the previous page, he noticed the folded one. "Who's that?"

She paused as he unfolded it, and his own stern face was unveiled.

"Wow. Am I always that forbidding?" He frowned.

"Not always," Kat answered, grinning. "That must have been a day when I was in trouble."

"Hm. You have, however, been in that state your fair share since being here, haven't you?" He traced his thumb across her lower lip. Then, he shook his head. "Sometime soon, sweetheart, we need to talk."

"Do we?"

"Yes. But later."

Kat looked down, trying not to show disappointment. Her eyes lowered to the image she'd drawn of him a few days ago, and she nodded. "All right."

Gabe lifted her chin until she met his eyes again, and leaned down once more, giving her a light kiss on the mouth. Then he turned, and disappeared into the great room to make the phone call.

Kat sat there, gazing at Gabe's face that stared back at her from her tablet. Those eyes... the eyes she'd perceived as angry stared back at her. Now, somehow, they looked different. She thought of what Cynthia had said yesterday; he was so full of responsibility from the cares the world had placed on him. She wondered what he'd started to say, and could still feel the kiss he'd planted on her mouth. Each time he touched her, he sent a light jolt of electricity through her. Even when he put his hand under her chin to stare into her eyes, she felt it.

Suddenly, a thrill made its way through her. Her eyes lit with fondness as she continued to gaze downward.

"Sweetheart?" His voice caused her to look up.

"Yes?"

He was grinning. "Lorina would like us both to be there at eleven-thirty for lunch. Can you be ready by then?"

She found herself grinning back. "Yes. I can't wait."

"That's my girl," he said, his eyes twinkling. And he was gone.

Kat turned the paper over to a new page, and began drawing once again, smiling. as she sketched in his face once more. Thirty minutes later, the face that stared back at her from her tablet had a completely different expression. His eyes were crinkling at the corners, and his mouth was turned up in the fondness of a smile.

After lunch, Gabe spent the afternoon helping Ted assemble more of the greenhouse as Kat and Lorina caught up on old times inside. When he came back in to get her, they said goodbye.

He was silent until they reached the house. As he unfastened her seat belt, he turned and knelt. "Climb on."

She stared at him. "You're kidding."

"Nope. I haven't given anyone a piggy-back ride since Shelley was small. Hop on."

Kat did as he said, and he trotted with her around the side of the house, listening to her laugh.

Once again, he put her in his lap in the small cove.

"I love this area," she said softly, looking around. A few flowers dotted the grass, but not many.

"I'm glad," Gabe said, smiling down into her face. "It only has one drawback. It's only visible from Cynthia's rooms and study, and from Will's. Originally, those rooms belonged to my parents. I can't see it from my room, nor can anyone else. It's not even visible from the great room. So, I have to ask you not to come out here unless someone knows where you are."

She waited a moment. "Is that what you wanted to talk to me about?"

"No."

Gabe studied her face as she waited.

A moment later, she spoke. "Gabe? Is something wrong?"

"No, sweetheart, no. What I wanted to talk to you about was..." he leaned down and kissed her mouth lightly. "*This.*"

Her eyes were wide now, and Gabe frowned. "I need to know if that makes you feel the least bit uncomfortable."

She blinked.

"If it does, I want you to tell me. Now," he added.

"You mean," Kat leaned forward, her chin tilted upward, and kissed him back, also lightly. "This? Or," she did it again, for a moment longer and a bit more firmly. "*This?*"

"Exactly," he said, grinning now.

Kat reached out, putting her arms around his neck, and leaned her head on his chest. "Not in the slightest," she answered softly.

"You're sure?" he said, putting his arms around her and holding her to him.

"What it makes me feel," she said softly, "is cared for."

Gabe held her back from him. "Look at me, Katlynne," he said, staring down into her face. "I have a confession to make."

Her eyes grew wider. "You're going to tell me you're an axe murderer," she said, tilting her head. When he raised a brow, she added, "No?"

"No. I'm serious. Be quiet and listen."

"All right. I'm listening." When she leaned back in his arms, he began. "Several years ago, when Shelley first got to know you, she began bringing home videos of your concerts and plays, because she went to them and was so impressed. That was when I first became interested in you. But I thought no one could be as adorable as you. After all, I was seeing your best side, wasn't I?"

She turned her head this way and that. "I don't have a best side."

"Behave. But when you two began rooming together at school, and she talked about you all the time, I began thinking that perhaps you really were the real thing. We decided—all of us—that we'd like to have you come for a summer. That was last year. Cynthia, Shelley, and I discussed it at length."

"She did ask me last year," Kat admitted, "but I couldn't bring myself to leave Lorina and Ted all summer." She lowered her eyes to the collar of his shirt. "It was a lousy decision. By the time I came back to school in the fall, I was having nightmares every night. Poor Shelley." He put his finger under her chin, raising it, and she shivered slightly.

"That's what she told us. But this year, when I saw you come into the graduation ceremony, young lady, you took my breath away. I had accidentally captured you with the camera, walking in, and I couldn't seem to keep it off you. When Cynthia and I walked across the gym floor to meet you, I was already smitten."

"You're kidding. Right?"

"I don't say things I don't mean." His voice was firm. "Katlynne, what I'm trying to say is..."

"Yes?"

He took a deep breath. "The way I felt about you

then has multiplied so many times over." His voice was deep and husky: "I fell for you that day, and since then, my feelings have grown." He traced the contour of her mouth with his thumb, gently, "Katlynne, I don't know how else to say it, but I keep growing fonder of you every single day."

She looked up mischievously. "So now, you can actually tolerate me?"

"*Tolerate* you?" he chuckled.

She nodded.

"Be serious, young lady."

Kat's gaze up into his eyes became serious suddenly. "Oh, *Gabe*," she whispered. "I care very deeply for you, too."

Gabe took her face in his hands and brought his own down to hers. Slowly, but with determination, he took possession of her mouth, exploring it. Tasting her sweetness, he felt her trembling as he demanded her submission.

"Oh, Gabe." She lowered her face into his neck, melting into him when he released her, "I feel as if my soul belongs to you when you do that."

"I believe I should keep you right here. Forever."

Kat snuggled closer. "It makes me happy, being right *here*."

"In my arms?"

"Oh, *yes*," she whispered.

Gabe sat there, holding her tightly, for what seemed an eternity. Suddenly, he heard Cynthia's patio door sliding back, and her voice saying,

"Suppertime, you two lovebirds."

He said softly into Kat's ear, "Sounds like it's time for me to let you up, sweetheart. As much as I hate to." Tossing her over his shoulder, he rose.

"Dammit," Kat said softly, trying to wiggle out of his arms. Gabe gave her a light smack on the bottom, and she jumped.

"Ouch. Gabe Ingrahm, stop it!" she scolded playfully.

"Not a chance," he tossed back, planting another, firmer smack. "You need to add swearing to the list I gave you."

"Ow! Put me down!"

"When you ask nicely," he retorted.

"Please? Sir?"

"Ah. That's better," he grinned. Bringing her back to her feet outside the front door, he turned her to face it. "Now, you can go in," he laughed, opening the door and sending her in with another firm swat. "Just behave yourself."

Kat turned back to him, glaring, but hurried to the table before he could swat her again. He was giving her a warning look, however, as she sat down. Cynthia, across the table, winked at her.

"How was your visit to see Ted and Lorina?"

"Good," he and Kat both replied at the same time, and laughed. Gabe added, "Would you like to visit the hardware store with us the day after tomorrow? Ted wants to stock up on greenhouse supplies, and Lorina wants to get some groceries. I figured you know the owner, Kimbird, is Shoshone."

"You know, I had forgotten that." Cynthia's eyes sparkled.

"And he has quite a story behind him."

"Really? I didn't know *that*. If you're asking if Kat and I want to go, the answer is a resounding yes."

Kat was grinning now. But Gabe looked down at her with a playful scowl. "Katlynne's been a brat. I'm not sure I'm going to let her go."

"I have not!"

"Have too."

"Ahem," came from Will, sitting next to Cynthia, on the other side of the table, and Gabe laughed.

Gabe bowed his head to say the blessing, and at the same time, firmly took Kat's hand in his. She couldn't help but smile, when he squeezed it firmly, finishing the prayer. He winked at her and grinned.

"A body could starve to death in this house," Will muttered.

"Not you," Mariah grinned at him, "that'd take you quite some time."

Will gave her a look of mock horror. "No respect," he said. But a few moments later, he looked back at Gabe. "Plane needs a couple of new gauges, Gabe. I figured I'd take tomorrow and put them on. I already have them."

"Have at it. Need anything else?"

The phone rang, and Mariah went to answer it.

Gabe scowled. "How do they always know we're eating supper?" he said, beginning to rise.

When Mariah appeared in the archway, she looked pale. "Phone, Mr. Gabe. Sheriff's department."

A hush descended over the table as everyone listened, trying to hear Gabe's side of the conversation. Kat was among them.

Kat's heart quickened as she heard his voice.

"When? And where?" There was an intensity to Gabe's voice. "I see. What was her name?"

Then there was silence, and through the archway, Gabe turned to land his gaze directly on her.

"I see," he said, his mouth flat. "Thanks for letting me know."

As he moved back into the kitchen, Cynthia frowned. "Something's wrong."

Gabe rubbed the back of his neck. "The prisoners missed their parole meetings," he said. "And there's been a series of murders. The first one was a week ago. A woman."

Kat's gaze flew to his. "I heard you ask for a name."

Gabe took a breath before answering, and moved to her, putting an arm around her shoulders. "Her name was Claire Saunders. She lived in Seattle."

Kat's quick intake of air caused everyone at the table to turn to her. But her eyes were fixed on Gabe when she spoke. "Claire," she halted, "was…" She turned her gaze toward Shelley.

"Yes, sweetheart," Gabe confirmed. "She was a juror in their trial."

Twenty-One

*ews...*

Will looked up. "And the rest of their victims?"

"Between here and Seattle. The rest of them don't seem related to the trial. One was the owner of a convenience store. One owned a gas station in Oregon, Then another convenience store employee in Idaho. The law thinks they might be headed this way. That's why they called."

No one spoke throughout the remainder of the meal. Kat, too, was silent as she sat there, pushing food around on her plate. It wasn't until the meal was over that she glanced up.

"Ted and Lorina," she said, "we need to go check

on them."

Gabe rose from the table, nodding. "On our way. Katlynne, stay here. Tim, be on guard, you and Kinsey. Will, bring your firearm."

"Please," Kat's voice was pleading, "can I go with you?"

Gabe leaned down. "No, sweetheart," he said. "But we'll probably bring them back with us."

It took only a few moments to confirm both Ted and Lorina were all right; convincing them to come to the house took a moment longer. Lorina didn't want to leave; Ted insisted it would be safer, and finally didn't give her a choice. Will offered his rooms to them, assuring them he wouldn't be using them for a day or two.

Gabe stopped in front of the house, and helped Ted take the packed suitcases from the trunk. Tim met him as he approached the door.

Gabe nodded at Tim. "See anything?"

Tim shook his head. "Not yet. I do want to talk with you when you get a chance."

"Sure. Where are the girls? Let me check on them first."

"Cynthia's in her study with Mariah and Cali. Shelley and Kat are in their rooms."

Gabe strode to Kat's bedroom, opening the door. She opened her eyes at his entrance, and he knelt by the head of her bed. "We brought them back with us, sweetheart. They're here now."

"Can I see them?"

"I think they're already in Will's room. But if they come back out, I'll send Lorina in to see you. Where is your .380?"

"In my boot, next to the bed. I can get to it if I need to."

"All right. Can you sleep in here, or would you rather use my room?"

"I'll be fine in here. Besides, I don't want to leave Shelley by herself at this end of the house."

Gabe checked the door and made sure the block of wood Tim had made was in place, and the patio door was locked. Kat stirred momentarily, turning on her right side and curling up into a ball. Gabe leaned down and kissed her temple, whispering, "Goodnight, sweetheart. I'm leaving your door open just a crack." When she nodded, he left the room.

Tim was just coming from Shelley's room with a grim expression, having tucked her in as well. Both of them went to the great room.

"What is it, Tim?"

"Someone's been watching the house. We found tracks in the mud at the edge of the woods. Kinsey noticed them first. They came from the west."

Kinsey appeared at the door just then.

"Everything all right outside?"

"Yep. Everyone's up. We're all prowling. None of us can sleep, but you guys might as well grab some while you can," Kinsey looked from one to the other. "We took turns getting a few winks this afternoon."

Tim shook his head. "No. I doubt any of us could sleep either."

"I think I'll stay close by. Katlynne's really unsettled right now. I don't want to be too far away, and if she has a nightmare, *no* one will sleep."

But Kinsey ordered them to get some rest. "I'll take over watching the house. If I run out of steam, I'll call you." With that, he disappeared.

Gabe checked on Kat once again before making the rounds outside the house. As he came back inside, he sat down in the great room in the well-worn recliner. He hadn't realized he'd closed his eyes until the phone rang. Will grabbed it, checking the caller ID. He turned to Gabe, handing it over. "I think it's Mrs. Lowell, but she's hysterical."

Gabe took it. "Mrs. Lowell? Please, can you slow down a bit?" After a moment, he shook his head. "I'll be right there," he said. Shoving the phone into its cradle, he headed toward the door. "Something's happened to Joseph. Will, stay here and keep an eye on the girls." Next, he reached Tim on the radio. "I need you to go with me to the Lowell's. Meet me at the car."

Gabe took one last look at Kat before he ran for the front door, wishing he didn't feel as if he had to leave. What in the world was going on at the Lowell house? And where was Josie?

Tim was already in the driver's seat of the pickup when he reached the car. They stopped at the base of the hill where the sheriff's SUV was sitting and explained the situation. It was not Burns tonight, but Ian, who was on duty.

Tim rolled down his window. "I'm glad to see you. Mrs. Lowell called in hysterics. We're on our way over to see what's going on. Can you come?"

Ian nodded. "Lead the way; I'll be right behind you. I'll give Burns a shout, too."

Gabe leaned forward. "She's saying something about Joseph and blood. Someone from the sheriff's department needs to be there."

Tim guided the truck out onto the highway and sped up, passing the Winslow land and hurrying into the Lowell driveway just beyond it.

Burns wasn't far behind them. Mrs. Lowell answered the door, but she was still hysterical. They entered to find Joseph, beaten and bruised and almost unconscious, lying on the living room floor. He was bleeding profusely from his mouth, but managed to look up as Gabe knelt down beside him.

"Joseph? What happened?"

"Josie…" it was recognizable, although it was just a whisper. "Stop Josie."

Tim and Gabe exchanged glances at that, and Burns called for an ambulance as Ian and Tim rose to go and look through the rest of the house. There were several things that represented signs of struggle: a room lamp knocked over, the blood on the floor surrounding Joseph, and blood on the door facing near the hallway.

"Where is Josie?" Gabe asked. He looked up at Mrs. Lowell, but her head was buried in her hands. He doubted he would get an intelligible answer from her. All he could understand from her was the word 'blood' over and over. He began to check Joseph for broken bones.

"Mr. Lowell?" Gabe tried to gain the older man's

focus. Joseph opened his eyes and brought them to Gabe's face. "Where's Josie?" he asked quietly.

Joseph shook his head. "Took... watch out for K..." He closed his eyes briefly and opened them again, staring straight at Gabe. "Kat," he said, before he was again unconscious.

"Katlynne," Gabe echoed, turning to Burns.

Gabe pulled his phone from his pocket, dialing the house. "Will, are Katlynne and Shelley all right?" When Will answered in the affirmative, he relaxed. "I'll be home as soon as possible. The ambulance is coming for Joseph."

At that, Mrs. Lowell began screaming again. Ian, back in the room, put his arms around her, and spoke softly. Gabe watched, but it was Kat's face that remained in front of his mind, asleep in her bed at home. Once, he heard "Josie" escape Mrs. Lowell's lips, but when he gently asked about Josie, she again began babbling incoherently. Ian shook his head.

Burns returned from checking out the rest of the house. "Nothing looks out of place," he said, "except in here."

Ian glanced over at him. "What about Josie's room?"

Burns nodded, frowning, "Her bed hasn't been

slept in. I did find her cell phone and her laptop. They're lying on her dresser."

"I'll get them," Ian said solemnly.

Kat, restless, tossed and turned in her bed. Was there someone in the room? She managed to open her eyes just a peep, but could only see the sliver of light from the doorway. Suddenly, an ominous feeling crept over her, and a shadow blocked out the light from the hall. She heard a sound, faint, but there, by her patio door. She tried to turn and see what caused it, but she couldn't. Then, suddenly, she realized it.

Someone was standing next to her bed.

Kat, in terror, opened her eyes to see a big figure leaning over her. She opened her mouth to scream, but instantly, a strange-smelling cloth was clapped over her nose and mouth. She reached up, scratching and clawing. With her right hand she tried reaching down to her boot for her weapon, but the harder she tried, the weaker she became...

Until she had no strength left.

Shelley, lying helplessly on the ground next to the woods, looked up through slits at the two men who stood over her. She'd been taken from her room in the darkness, not by the men who now stared down at her, but by another, who had left her there to go back to the house. Groggy, she still knew what was happening. The high-pitched laugh from one of the men suddenly triggered something Kat had said, and she knew who they were. One was Billy Raine, and the other was Tommy Miller. But where was Don Heraldson? Suddenly, she knew.

He was going back for Kat.

Footsteps approached, and Shelley heard a voice.

"Piece of cake. I've got her," Heraldson said to Raine and Miller. He had flung Kat, dressed only in her nightgown, over his shoulder and now turned toward the woods.

Raine reached out to slide a hand down Kat's legs, his eyes gleaming, but Heraldson slapped his hand away. "Don't touch her. She's *mine*." Then he turned toward the third man with them. "And I swear, Tommy, if you laugh, *I'll kill you*."

"I wasn't gonna laugh." A sour look made its way over Miller's face, but no one could see it in the darkness.

No one but Shelley.

Kat heard voices talking to each other. What were they saying? She couldn't tell where she was; she only knew she was cold, and felt sick. *But the voices...*

She knew those voices. They were the same voices she had heard for the first time, four years ago; the same voices that she heard again and again, in her nightmares. She couldn't prevent the shiver that traveled through her body, nor the fear that accompanied it.

Where was she? She seemed to be over someone's shoulder, being carried. The cold night air seemed to bite at her body. Hands were holding her upper legs. She wanted to scream, but could only emit a small whimper.

"Don't tell me she's awake again!" a voice said. "Tommy, drug her again—and do it right this time,"

"I didn't do it last time," Tommy Miller retorted. "You did."

Kat tried to protest, but the cloth was clapped over her face for a second time and held there. Despite her struggle, she felt reality easing away from her again.

Twenty-Two

*S*irens...

In the distance, the sound of an ambulance announced its approach, and Gabe's shoulders slumped with relief. Joseph's pulse was regular, but he was still unconscious.

Gabe helped them get Joseph into the ambulance, and left.

"Burns," he said to the sheriff, "Katlynne may be in danger. We need to go check on her."

"Go home. We'll finish up here. I'll send Ian back to your place later."

Gabe nodded and hurried toward the car. Tim beat him to it, and had the engine running before he got there. Neither of them spoke as they took off for home.

They both ran for the house as soon as they pulled up. Will met them in the great room.

"Everything all right at the Lowell place?"

"No, but I'll explain later. What about here?"

"Fine. I checked on the girls a few minutes ago. Kat and Shelley were both asleep."

Gabe walked toward Kat's door and peeked in. But a strange feeling descended over him as he opened it. He stared for a moment, disbelief on his face. When he flipped on the light, he gasped.

Her bed was empty.

Kat's boots were still next to the bed. Instinctively, he reached into the right boot where she'd been keeping the Walther .380 he'd given her. It was still there. There was no sign of struggle, but the patio door was open. There was a slight smell of chloroform lingering in the room. The piece of wood Tim had made to block the door was out on the floor. Footprints dotted the patio, large footprints that could belong only to a man.

Gabe roared with fury and frustration as the realization hit.

Will, in shock, leaned on the door frame for a

second. "Oh, dear God," he choked out a gasp. "She was just here, Gabe, I swear!"

"I believe you. Get Kinsey. I need him to track these prints, now!"

"Right." Will ran from the room.

"This way," Heraldson growled as they crossed the Winslow property and approached the land belonging to the Lowells. "We're going back to get the Lowell girl. We can't let her live. She knows too much." He turned toward the woods where they'd left Josie gagged and bound. "And drug this one again, too," he motioned to Kat. "She's waking up, and I don't like it."

Josie was lying where they'd left her, and Heraldson watched as Billy reached down and pulled Josie to her feet roughly, tossing her over his shoulder and carrying her in the same manner as the other girls.

As they turned to go back down to the house, Shelley began to heave. Heraldson turned to see her as she began to vomit down the back of Tommy's pants and boots. Tommy was fuming.

This time, it was Heraldson's turn to laugh. He approached the back of the house and kicked in the back door, entering. Listening for the screams of Mrs. Lowell, he was pleased when only silence met his ears.

Good. He carried Kat down the hallway and looked into the living room, expecting to see Josie's father. When he saw the blood on the carpet and realized the old man was gone, he frowned. The lights were still on. Someone had been here and taken both the man and woman away. He wondered when they'd be back. Walking into the bedroom, he threw Kat onto the bed and went to the front room window to look out. The Lowell's car was still there.

"Where do you want *her*?" Shelley's captor stopped in the hallway.

Heraldson looked at Shelley. "I don't care. Consider her your *get out of jail free* card." Then, he glanced back at the room where he'd dropped Kat. "I really hoped that one would remember what I did to her, but after us drugging her so many times, she may never wake up."

The three men suddenly began to laugh as they congratulated themselves.

"Enjoy yourselves," Heraldson said. "Do what you want, but do it fast. Whoever took the old man and his wife may be back. I'm going to work on the judge's daughter. I've waited a long time for this day."

* * *

Gabe glanced toward Will and Cynthia as they discovered Shelley was also missing. Cynthia was trying to keep from weeping with frustration, and Will was obviously racked with guilt due to the missing girls.

"Stay and guard the house, Will. We'll be back. And call the sheriff."

Kinsey made his way, running at top speed to where Gabe and Tim were waiting. "Three of them. One set goes to Shelley's bedroom, then Katlynne's; same person, both times. Got a grasp on it now," he said, "Let's roll."

Relieved, Gabe nodded. "Let's."

Fifteen minutes later, they had approached Josie's house. Kinsey had stopped only once, when he spotted emesis on the ground. "Someone threw up. One of the girls, carried over the shoulder," he'd said, moving on.

They approached the back of the house silently.

Tommy had just taken off his belt to secure Shelley to the bed when he heard Billy's call from the living room.

"Tommy, this one's giving me trouble."

Rolling his eyes, he moved back to the living room, where Josie was holding a baseball bat and lunging.

Billy was holding his groin and had backed up to protect himself, a look of agony on his face.

Tommy took one look, surveying the scene, and turned, going back into the bedroom. Whatever happened to Raine, he deserved it.

But as he reached the bedroom, he stopped, staring.

The bed was empty.

Swearing, he looked desperately around the room. The curtains were fluttering, and he ran to the window.

It was open. The night breeze met his face.

There was no sign of the blonde.

Fighting the urge to run, he sat down on the bed and began to curse. "Heraldson's gonna kill me for lettin' her get away," he muttered. Billy's screams again came from the living room, and he thought of Billy, cowering from Josie due to the baseball bat. Heraldson would likely kill Billy, too, for letting a female get the best of him.

Heraldson turned on his heel and strode back into the room where he'd thrown Kat, shutting the door behind him. She hadn't moved. He approached the closet, and looked inside, a moment later emerging with several belts and some long scarves.

They would work nicely. Stopping at the bed, he looked Kat over with an evil smile, and began tying her wrists and ankles to the four posters. When he finished, he stood back. A huge smile worked its way across his face as he took out his knife.

Thinking better of it, however, he put the knife back in its holster and pulled out his belt, wrapping it around his hand. Then, he began to laugh harshly at her helplessness. Now, he could do whatever he wished with her, and she had no choice but to take it. Glancing at the belt in his hand, he continued laughing.

Her skin wouldn't be this smooth for long.

Slowly, he raised his hand, preparing to strike.

Twenty-Three

P *repared to strike...*

The blow never landed. Instead, the belt was now around his neck, being pulled tighter. He reached up, trying to call for his buddies, but was unable to make a sound. His grasp on the belt around his neck grew weaker and weaker, and he fell to his knees. His hands dropped to his sides, and a moment later, he fell forward to the floor.

Gabe stood there, his hands grasping the belt and fighting the overwhelming urge to go ahead and kill him. This was Heraldson; he knew their names now. His hands ached to choke the remaining life from the man at his feet. Instead, he took another of the belts and fastened Heraldson's hands behind his back. The check for weapons revealed a Smith & Wesson and a knife.

It didn't take long to secure Heraldson before moving to Kat to release her. Her breathing was shallow, and he listened, concerned. Carefully, he released her and wrapped her in the quilt from the bed.

Kinsey's voice from the living room caught his attention, and Gabe dragged Heraldson out into the hall, unwilling to leave him in the room with Kat. As he reached the hall, he met Tim, who was pulling Miller out at the same time.

"Where's Shelley?" Gabe demanded.

"She must have escaped. The window's open."

Kinsey had entered the living room, but it did not go as easily for him. Billy Raine managed to whirl back and slice Kinsey's left arm with his knife. The two men were face to face now; Kinsey managed to evade the knife blade that repeatedly caused him to stagger backward. It was then that Raine brought a firearm from his boot and aimed, his finger on the trigger.

Gabe shot it out of his hand.

Screaming profanities, Billy turned away from Kinsey and toward Gabe.

Kinsey, meanwhile, eased up behind him and hit

him on top of the head with the butt of his weapon. Billy Raine dropped like a stone.

"Kinsey, you all right?" Securing Heraldson's arms and feet under pieces of heavy furniture, Gabe picked up a strip of material that lay on the floor and wrapped it around Kinsey's arm. "This looks like a piece from someone's shirt. I'll wrap it, but the wound will need to be cleaned when it stops bleeding. I need to get Katlynne. I'll be right back."

"I'm all right," Kinsey replied, staring at his arm. "Stay with her."

Gabe nodded and disappeared back into the room where Kat lay. She was still deeply asleep. When he returned to the living room, Tim was holding up a small bottle and a cloth.

"I found this inside Raine's right pants pocket."

Gabe brought it up and sniffed the cloth from a distance, growling. "Chloroform. I thought I recognized the smell in Katlynne's room. At least now we know what the girls have been subjected to."

The sound of a siren interrupted them. Sheriff Burns put his head in through the front door a moment later. "Two more deputies on the way: Jason and Ian. I gave the orders as soon as Will called."

"Here," Jason said from the doorway, Ian behind him.

Raine swore as Ian and Burns handcuffed him and put him into the back of the car. He was screaming and demanding to see a doctor. Approaching Heraldson, Jason jumped back as a kick with both legs nearly knocked him over. Nothing but glares passed between them until Jason began reading him his rights. Ian moved to Miller to make sure he was secured. Satisfied, he then managed to help Jason transfer Heraldson toward the car while Burns, inside, searched the house.

They had Heraldson in the car, and Ian was securing him to the vehicle when it happened. Jason was striding back toward the house when a shout came from outside suddenly, and Jason and Burns ran back toward the vehicle to check.

Ian was holding his head and squinting as he leaned against the side of the car. "Heraldson got away," he said grimly, "even with the cuffs on. I'm sorry."

Burns ran forward. In the moonlight he could see Heraldson's retreating figure. Firing over the prisoner's head with an order to stop produced no results. As the sheriff began to pursue him, however, Kinsey stopped him.

"I wouldn't pursue him, Sheriff," he warned. "Rattlers are thick out there. You'll need to wait for first light."

Disgusted, Burns nodded. "All right. Miller's next, then."

But as he walked into the living room, Tommy Miller, who had managed to loosen the belts that tied his hands and feet, raised above the back of the sofa and fired.

Burns ducked just in time as the bullet splintered the door frame. At that very second, a blast pierced the air, and Miller dropped with a thud as blood began pouring from his chest.

Jason stood at the edge of the kitchen, his Glock in his hand. "Sorry, Sheriff. I was afraid for a second you'd been hit."

"Didn't someone check them for weapons? I swear."

"I did," Gabe answered. "I found two on Heraldson; Tim found two on Miller. Is it possible we didn't find them all?"

Burns moved forward to where Miller lay. "Anyway, thanks. He'd have got me." Burns approached Miller and reached down to check for a pulse; at first it was thready, and then it was gone.

Tommy Miller was dead.

There was a long silence in the room when Burns finally sat back on his heels.

"This will end the string of crimes *this* man's

committed," he said, finally. As Ian entered, still holding a hand to his head, Burns glanced up. "How's your head?"

"It's all right. My fault. I should have known his history."

"Soon as we're finished, Jason will take you to the clinic. I'll take the others back to the ranch."

Kat was still in a deep, drug-induced sleep. Gently, Gabe rubbed the red marks on her ankles and wrists, attempting to smooth them away.

"Katlynne? Wake up, sweetheart," he whispered, moving her into his lap. Her pulse was regular, but a little slow. He rocked her gently in his arms.

Suddenly, he heard another voice, a female's voice this time. He rose with Kat in his arms, and strode into the hallway.

"I heard it," Tim's voice interrupted him. "It's Shelley."

"I'm in here."

Gabe, with Kat still in his arms, followed Tim as they both hurried toward the second bedroom. A delicate hand was waving from under the bed. Tim dropped to his knees.

"Sweetheart? How long have you been down there?"

"Since we arrived. I knew they were going to drug me again, and if they did, I might never wake up." She reached for Tim as he lifted her out from under the bed and into his arms.

"But the window was open."

"Yes," she said quietly, "I knew I couldn't run, but if I could get the window open, perhaps they'd think I did. It would give me a little more time to wake up."

"You," Tim said, brushing her hair back from her eyes, "are such a smart girl."

"Thank you," she said, giving him a weak smile. "Remember that."

Sheriff Burns turned to Gabe as he dropped them off in front of the house. "You do realize they'll need a doctor's exam, and it has to be done in a certain window of time."

"I know. Does it matter which doctor?"

"No. I suppose not. You have someone in mind?"

"As a matter of fact," said Gabe, "I do. I'll let you know."

The phone call took only a few minutes. When Gabe hung up, he turned to Cynthia.

"Dove Locklear is waiting for us to come get her. Will? Are you up to flying right now?"

"Absolutely. Cynthia, do you want to go, since you know her?"

"Yes. I'll get my sweater."

"Excellent. Be safe," was all Gabe said. He looked down at Kat again, fighting the fury that was building within him. She was still asleep, but responding some now. He continued speaking to her and rubbing her back, giving very light slaps to her cheeks to try to stimulate her.

Shelley was completely awake now, "I heard Heraldson say that they had drugged Kat three times," she said quietly.

Gabe stared at her before looking away, teeth clenched. If he hadn't reached the room at the exact moment...

When the door opened, Kinsey looked in. "Heraldson's still out there somewhere," he said, scowling. "And I just saw Will taking off with Cynthia."

"To go pick up a doctor from the reservation."

Kinsey nodded. "Ah. I'll bet I know who it is, too."

～

Gabe looked at the clock as he felt it, a sudden alert sensation. Not wanting to awaken anyone else in the great room, he rose and went to check on Kat and Shelley, sleeping soundly in his room. What had he heard, then?

Coming back down the hall, he ducked into the bath between the rooms and peeked into Kat's usual bedroom.

He spotted Heraldson immediately, trying to get into Kat's room.

Moving quietly to Tim, he put a hand on his shoulder and motioned silence. Tim was on his feet in an instant.

"You take the back—I'll take the front," Gabe whispered, heading around the side of the house. As he rounded the corner, Gabe could see Tim approaching from the back of the house. He moved outward so that he and Tim would be at right angles to the man at Kat's door. Gabe couldn't see from his viewpoint whether or not Heraldson held a weapon. But one thing he could see: Heraldson's hands were free; somehow, he'd managed to rid himself of the handcuffs. Gabe only knew he'd removed the gun and knife from Heraldson at the house. Tim moved forward, silent as a ghost.

They watched, both of them approaching, as

Heraldson pulled something from his pocket. Both had a weapon trained on him. But it wasn't a gun he had reached for.

They both heard a click, watching as a flame appeared from the lighter. Leisurely, he put a cigarette to his lips, lighting it. Gabe could see Heraldson clearly now. With both hands busy, they both took the opportunity to put a gun to his head.

"I wouldn't move if I were you." Gabe's growl stopped his movement, and the cigarette fell to the ground.

Heraldson's hands rose upward as he swore. Gabe continued to hold his weapon still, and Tim called for Terry and Kinsey on the radio to bring rope. Within seconds, they were both there and had Heraldson on the ground.

None of them were sure exactly when it happened. As Kinsey had almost finished tying his hands behind his back, the prisoner managed to get his right boot raised to his hand and reached back, grabbing a weapon from his boot. He fired, grazing Terry's right shoulder. Before they could grab him again, he was on his feet and was sprinting toward the woods.

Gabe was after him in a heartbeat, firing over his head. Heraldson fired back; Gabe fired again. This time, a shout of pain was heard, and Gabe followed the sound. Tim paused long enough to check Terry's shoulder and followed, but as he reached the wood, he saw neither of them. Kinsey caught up with him a moment later. A brief light from his flashlight found the tracks.

"Follow me." He advanced, going ahead about fifteen feet, then again turned on his light. He went several feet deeper into the woods and caught up with Gabe.

"It's my fault." Gabe's voice was grim. "This could have been over if I'd gotten him."

"Well, you may *have* gotten him." Kinsey's flashlight was trailing a dark stain on the ground toward the woods. "Blood. Not a lot, but enough to indicate he's injured. Left side." He leaned down. "He's dragging his left leg. Look."

"Shall we pursue?"

Kinsey was quiet a moment. "I know you want me to tell you yes, Gabe. But he'll keep going until he *can't*. And when he can't, he'll hide out and wait until we show up. Then he'll shoot." He turned toward Gabe. "If it were me, I'd let him go until first light. At least then we'll have the advantage of sight. He'll keep trying to move, but he won't get far. The weaker he gets, the less of a fight he'll put up when we do find him. What's your thought? Should we call the sheriff back again?"

Gabe studied him thoughtfully. "Ian's injured. Jason and Burns have both been up all night. I'm willing to go after him at first light, but if we don't find him by seven, I say call them. Who knows, he might just give up the fight and surrender. And Kinsey, the doctor needs a look at your arm."

"Sounds like a plan. I'll be ready to head after him at first light."

Will and Cynthia returned with Dove Locklear a few moments later. Gabe met her at the door as she entered. "I can't tell you how much I appreciate your coming," he said quietly.

"No," she said ferociously, "I would have been hurt if you hadn't contacted me. This family is very important to me. Where's Kat?"

Cynthia interrupted the conversation. "I'll move Shelley into my room so you can see them separately." She didn't give either of them a chance to answer before disappearing toward the back of the house.

Gabe led her down the hall. "Katlynne and Shelley have both been in my room. A good thing; we caught the man responsible for her kidnapping trying to get into her room this morning before you got here. We gave chase, but he got away. Shelley was almost awake when we got there, but Kat was drugged pretty heavily. I found the bottle of chloroform in the pocket of one of the men."

The anger in her expression surprised him, but she managed to control it, nodding to him.

"I'll see what I can do. If I can't awaken her, I might need to stay a while. Heather could reschedule my patients for the day. I'll examine Shelley first, but I want to see Kat for a few seconds now."

Gabe nodded. "I'll go in with you for a minute. I was about ready to check on her when you got here." He moved in ahead of her and approached the bed. "Katlynne? Can you wake up a minute, sweetheart?"

In answer, Kat whimpered and rolled to one side, away from them.

Dove listened to her chest and watched her for a few moments, checking her reflexes. "She'll be all right. Everything sounds normal. She's just extremely sleepy. I'll see Shelley first, and then I'll be back."

∿

Kat looked up at the gentle knock at the door. Gabe had gotten Kat a clean nightgown from her dresser and helped her pull it on over her head. She seemed a little more alert now.

"Hi, Kat." Dove held out her hand, and Kat reached to take it.

"Thank you, Dr. Locklear, so much, for allowing us to drag you out in the middle of the..."

"What?" Dove interrupted her, "For you, Kat, I would do anything." She sat down on the edge of the bed as Gabe got to his feet to leave the room.

But Dove put up a hand to stop him. "Cynthia explained to me what had happened—at least what she knew, but I'm afraid it wasn't much. I'm so sorry this has happened. Could you tell me a little more about what happened?"

Gabe closed the door again, and told her about the chloroform, and that Kat had been drugged several times with it, according to Shelley. He explained what he'd found when they got to the house, and the complaints that Kat had about where she was hurting. Kat listened, her eyes wide, as if she were hearing it for the first time. He also explained that they needed a physician's report filled out for the sheriff's department, and that he knew Kat and Shelley would feel more comfortable with her there to do the exam.

"I'm honored that you thought of me," she said, turning to Kat. Kat, before I touch you, I'd like for you to tell me anything that you might remember."

Gabe nodded, taking that as his cue to leave. "Katlynne, I'll be right outside if you need me."

At the gentleness of his words, Kat felt the tears forming. She did explain how she'd awakened, knowing someone was in the room with her, and had been unable to get to her weapon to protect herself, then felt the cloth over her face. But it was impossible to remember much else.

Dr. Locklear leaned back a few moments later.

"Well, sweetie. I have good news for you and a little bad news—but only a little. The good news is, your virginity is intact."

Kat closed her eyes, relieved, tears forming. "Thank you. And the bad?"

"The bad is that you'll probably be quite uncomfortable for a few days because of the way you were tossed about and tied, but that's the extent of it. I'll send over a copy of the report in the morning, as soon as I get the results back from the lab. And everything else is in good shape. Your shoulders and your hips hurt because of the way you were tied down. A few hot baths will probably take care of those aches and pains. You can take ibuprofen every four to six hours. That's all."

"That's not even bad news," Kat said softly, "I was expecting something terrible. Thank you, Dr. Locklear."

"Dove," Dr Locklear leaned forward and hugged her. "Call me later this afternoon. I want to hear your voice, and know how you're doing. Furthermore, call me any time you feel as if you need to talk to someone."

"Yes, ma'am." Katie reached down and picked up her boots. She pulled the left one on, but when she began to struggle with the right one, she reached down into it, realizing the .380 was still inside. She pulled it out and set it on her bedside table. "I tried to get it last night when the man came into my room, but I wasn't able to get to it before..." she trailed off, and Dove reached for it.

"I'll take it to Gabe for you. By the way, Shelley may need to talk, so open up to her if you can." After standing, she leaned down to give Kat a kiss on the cheek. "Call me," she said softly, before leaving the room. At Kat's nod, she smiled and left.

∽

When Dove left Kat's room, Gabe was waiting for her at the end of the hall.

"If you don't mind, one more thing—I just wanted to show you Kinsey's arm. He was sliced with a knife early this morning."

"Show me," she said, an expression of worry on her face.

He opened the front door. "Kinsey? Your arm?"

Kinsey came inside, taking the piece of Josie's shirt off his arm. "I know you told me to wash it up, but I haven't had a chance."

"Tsk-tsk," Dove said. "Into the kitchen with you. I want a better look."

Kinsey let her drag him into the kitchen and clean up the wound as he studied her, frowning.

"Take off your shirt. When was your last tetanus shot?"

His face lost its color.

"I take it that's a 'Never'?"

"I think I was ten." His face grew even whiter when she put her bag up on the dining room table and pulled out a syringe and a vial. Drawing it up, she reached for him and nudged him down into a chair.

"You know," she said, grinning, "real men take shots."

"Don't laugh at me."

"Who said I was laughing?" she scowled at him. "I'm trying to save my reputation, that's all. Can't have a tall, strong, good-looking man developing tetanus because I didn't do my job."

Kinsey's face was now turning a deep shade of red. "I see."

"Here, let me show you something." She pulled a small container from her bag and shoved it into his hand.

"What's this?"

"It's a new kind of glue for skin. Keeps people from having to have stitches. It's the coolest thing."

"Glue for skin?"

"Yep. But you'll need another tetanus shot within ten years. Sooner if you keep fighting criminals armed with knives." Dove popped the syringe into a red container and back into her bag, taking the container from his hands. "Watch." She applied it to the wound and waited for it to dry, anchoring it with steri-strips.

Kinsey sat there as it dried, and then looked at her. "When are you giving me the shot?"

Dove grinned at him. "I did, already. You missed it while you were examining the glue. I warn you, though, you'll probably have a sore arm for a day or two."

She pulled out a band-aid and covered the injection site, but when Kinsey saw it, he grinned up at her.

"Snoopy? You're all right."

"Gee. I'll bet you say that to all the girls." She returned his grin. "Gabe, keep an eye on this and call me if it gets infected. I'm leaving a prescription for an antibiotic."

"Will do."

"Well, I hate to go, but I've got an office full of patients to see tomorrow." She closed up her bag and smiled. "Oops. Make that today. Gabe, I need to speak to you for a minute. I have some instructions for you. And I need your signature on some papers."

Within a half-hour, Will and Cynthia were waiting at the hanger, and Gabe drove her over.

"How much do I owe you?" he asked as he approached the plane where Will and Cynthia were waiting.

"Your first-born child. No, I'll make it easier than that. I want to be invited to the wedding. And I'm telling you, I wouldn't let Kat out of your sight if I were you.'

"I don't intend to."

"For more reasons than this one. And don't forget to call me later today when the girls are wide awake. I'll want to talk to them. And don't be surprised if they're both emotional for the next few days."

"Got it."

"And call me if you sense they need someone to talk to. I'll stop what I'm doing. And if I feel like they need a counselor that's closer, I'll recommend someone."

"I'd appreciate that." He paused. "Anything else I should watch for?"

"I'll call you if I think of it. And when the lab results are back, I'll send you a copy, along with the sheriff's office. Take care, Gabe."

He tried once more. "I didn't intend for you to come for nothing, you know."

"I'll send you a bill unless the wedding occurs first. So, get on the stick and propose already." She grinned as Will helped her into the plane, and waved goodbye.

Kinsey was waiting for him as he approached the front door and pointed to the sky. "You have a couple of hours," he said. "There's a little time to rest. By the time Will gets back, it'll be first light."

First light...

Gabe kept an eye on Kinsey, who was kneeling by the tracks. The obvious drag of the left leg and the shortness of the steps as they went on were definite signs of distress.

"Slowing down more and more," Kinsey muttered. "Aaron, you and Will go east. Come out at the entrance to the pond. It's dry right now. Tim, Gabe, follow me."

Gabe nodded, and Will followed Aaron in the direction Kinsey had indicated.

Kinsey motioned for silence. They slowed their steps more. Kinsey was sure they would find him soon, either waiting in a trap for them or dead.

In the dim light, they heard screams, a man's screams, coming from dead ahead. Kinsey looked back. "Careful. It may be a trap."

The screams continued as the three of them ran, worried for Will and Aaron, who should be up ahead by now.

Suddenly, Kinsey stopped, throwing out his arms to prevent the others from going further.

They all saw it at the same time.

Heraldson had run out into an area of barren land on the adjoining property and fallen.

The screams, however, weren't the only sound they heard. The ominous sound of rattlers filled the air as they writhed around Heraldson's fallen body. He was attempting to beat them away with a stick, but appeared to have been bitten numerous times, and was still screaming as they watched helplessly.

His battle had clearly been lost.

Gabe shouted to him. "Don't move, Heraldson. We're throwing you a rope. Grab it—it's your only hope!" He threw the rope, covering the distance and landing within reach of the helpless man. "Grab it!!"

But Heraldson only sat there, staring at the rope now lying within his grasp. Instead of picking it up, however, he let it lie there. In the silence, he raised his gaze to where Gabe stood. He was no longer scream-ing. His face, void of all expression, clearly mouthed the words, "You win."

A few seconds later, Heraldson raised his weapon to his own temple, and pulled the trigger.

Gabe and his men stood there as the sound echoed through the woods. None of them spoke as they stared at the gruesome sight. No one, even one as evil as Don Heraldson, deserved to die like this.

Gabe turned away from the scene, closing his eyes briefly.

Tim put a hand on his shoulder. "Go back to the house, Gabe. You can't do anything for him now. Call the sheriff for a rescue squad."

Gabe didn't say a word as he moved toward the house. He heard Will's voice as he spoke quietly to the men standing there.

"This is exactly where his mother died," he said, "and with the exception of the gunshot—" he ceased abruptly, and Tim continued, finishing for him.

"This is exactly *how*."

Gabe called Sheriff Burns, who promised to be there with a team of men quickly. "By the way, we picked up Josie this morning, waving a baseball bat and mumbling incoherently. But no one seems to be talking about what happened last night at the house. And Gabe," he added, "Get some sleep. You've been up all night long."

"So has everyone else."

"I don't care. Go hide out until you've rested. And one more thing. Don't try to come to the hospital to see Joseph Lowell."

Gabe frowned. "Why?"

"Just don't. I'll explain later."

Finding Cynthia in the great room, he finished his call and dropped his phone in his pocket.

"That was the sheriff. They found Josie and took her into custody. Joseph is still in the unit. Apparently, he's not doing well. And *apparently,* no one is talking. Not Josie, not her mother, not Joseph, and not Raine, so no one knows what happened. I'd considered going up to the hospital, but he doesn't think it's a good idea. In fact, he suggested something else. Cynthia, how does next week look for you?"

She looked at him, surprised. "I don't have any appointments scheduled for interviews, if that's what you mean. Why?"

"I was thinking of taking Katlynne to Yellowstone, and I'd like you, Will, Shelley, and Tim along. Even Ted and Lorina might enjoy it. I think Kat would be more comfortable if we all went."

"Gardner, at the north end of the park, has a few new hotels. Want me to see if I can get a couple of suites?"

"Please. Even if it's just for a few days, I think it would be good for Katlynne and Shelley to get away for a bit and see the park."

"Gabe, you're a sweetheart," Cynthia said, picking up her laptop to look for hotels. Within thirty minutes, she looked up from it. "We're all set. The confirmation should be printing."

"Good job. Thanks." Gabe went to peek in on Kat. She hadn't moved, but Shelley had gone back to her own room. Every muscle in his body complained of weariness, and he stepped inside the room and closed the door. Climbing into bed behind Kat, he drew her next to him and wrapped his arms around her.

Within seconds, he was asleep.

Twenty-Four

L aw enforcement...

Kat lay there, listening to him snore softly above her
head. She decided to try to get up, but was pulled more
tightly into his arms. Finally, she relaxed and closed her
eyes. When she opened them again, it was nine o'clock.
Gabe had rolled over on his back, his hand entangled in
her hair. Carefully, she managed to release her hair
from his fist, and moved carefully off the bed.

She didn't immediately see her boots. Limping to
the door, she managed to open it. The living room was
full of people, and she saw several deputies pacing.
Finally, she managed to catch Cynthia's eye.

Cynthia got up and leisurely wandered down the

hall, as if going toward her own room, but she veered off toward Gabe's door on the way. Looking back, she made sure no one was looking, and helped Kat across the hall into her room.

"Thank you, Cynthia," Kat turned to her as soon as the door was closed. "I didn't have anything to wear."

"Gotcha covered, sweetie," Cynthia grinned. "I'll be right back." She wandered down the hall and spoke to Mariah, loudly enough so the others could hear. "Kat's in my room, Mariah, after the mess during the night. I'm getting her some clothes, but could you pour her some coffee and throw something on for her to eat?"

"Sure thing, Miss Cynthia." Mariah began heating up a burner and throwing some eggs into a pan.

A moment later, Cynthia was headed back down the hall with an armful of clothes and Kat's boots. Mariah handed her a cup of coffee as she passed by, which she took down to her room.

"Here you go, kiddo. Drink up before you go out there and face the mob."

"Oh, Cynthia, I owe you, *big*."

"You can pay me with another sketch of Will," Cynthia said, laughing. "Here, Mariah sent you some coffee. Smells like hazelnut. I'm going back to get some for me."

"Oh my. Tell Mariah I owe her, too."

By the time Cynthia returned and sat down on the wicker bench to enjoy her coffee, Kat was dragging her clothes over her head and pulling on her jeans. Sliding her feet into her boots, she turned to Cynthia. "Gabe is asleep. Do they need to talk to him?"

"If they do, they'll have to come back later. Sheriff Burns has already told them he has to rest first." She turned suddenly to Kat, her expression serious. "Kat, someone needs to tell you what happened this morning. And I think I'd better, before you see Gabe again." She leaned over and patted the wicker bench gently. "Sit."

Wide-eyed, Kat gasped when she heard the news about Heraldson, and how he had killed himself in the exact spot Gabe's mother had died. Kat put her hand to her mouth, and tears filled her eyes.

Cynthia put her arms around Kat, hugging her. "I know. It must have been ghastly. But he's handling it well. Anyway, drink your coffee and relax before showing your face. But remember, Mariah's fixing your breakfast, so don't take too long."

Kat nodded. She sat there, staring through the patio door. From here, she could see the little cove outside, and realized how lovely it was. After a few moments, however, she became restless and rose to go down the hall.

"Hey, Kat," Jason smiled down at her as she passed them, "Where's your other half? I never see one of you without the other."

"He's still asleep," she answered. "Sheriff Burns said not to wake him."

He looked at his watch. "Give him a little more time. We'll talk to him last. I know he's had a few rough nights lately." He turned to the officer behind him. "Hey, Ian. How's the head?"

"Tolerable. I'll be glad to take her statement."

But Jason only shook his head. "I'll get them both at the same time, Ian. Thanks, anyway. You should probably go sit down for a minute."

"I'm fine." Ian extended a hand. "Hello. I'm Ian. We've spoken on the phone."

Kat took his hand. "It's nice to meet you."

Ian gave her a smile, and moved to the sofa to sit down.

Kat leaned forward. "What's wrong with his head?"

"He got into it with a prisoner during the night. But I'm sure he wouldn't appreciate me telling you that."

Kat nodded. "I won't tell."

The sound of raised voices caused both of them to turn. Sheriff Burns was staring at Ian.

"What are you implying, Ian?"

There was a frown on Ian's face. "I wasn't implying anything. If we get this show on the road, we can get it over with and get that poor soul's body out of the snake pit."

"That poor soul, as you call him, helped kidnap two—three, if you include Josie Lowell, innocent girls, kidnapped, molested, and killed a juror, and killed a convenience store owner and assaulted a clerk and left her for dead, and came back to try it again last night, shooting one of Gabe's ranch hands in the process. Shall I go on?"

When the men returned after retrieving Heraldson's body, it was the sheriff who came into the kitchen to see Kat. "I hate to ask you this, Kat, but would you go and wake Gabe up? We won't keep him long."

"I'll be glad to." She moved to Gabe's door and planted a soft knock.

"It's open." His voice from inside sounded groggy. Opening the door, she peeked in.

"Gabe? Sheriff Burns wants to speak with you. I thought for a minute he and Ian were going to have a fistfight in the great room."

He reached out for her, and she moved closer. "What do you mean?"

She frowned. "I'm not sure exactly what happened."

"All right." His gaze rested on her face. "Hm. Sometimes, Ian can be a pain in the ass."

"Ahem," Kat interjected, grinning. "You wouldn't let me say that."

"You're right. Give me a few moments in the shower, and I'll be ready. Don't go out there until I'm with you."

"That's what Cynthia said, too. All right. I'll wait."

He pulled himself up and stood. Grabbing her suddenly, he kissed her ferociously and released her. "Stay put."

Kat lowered herself into the chaise, closed her eyes, and leaned back to wait. When she opened them again, Gabe's face was inches from hers.

"Sorry, sweetheart. You'll have to wait until this afternoon to grab a nap. Up you go." Taking her hands in his, he pulled her to her feet. He opened the door and gave her a little nudge in front of him through it, and then tucked her under his arm.

"There you are," Jason waved. "I need statements from both of you. In the dining room?"

"Sure," Gabe settled Kat into the chair where he usually sat, and sat across from her.

Kat gave her statement first, but it was short. All she remembered was dreaming someone was in the room, and the hand over her face. Gabe's was next.

"Where's Ian?" he asked curiously.

"The sheriff sent him out with the rest of the men."

Tom Burns approached Gabe as the great room emptied. "The rest of the squad have already retrieved Heraldson's body. They're on the way to the morgue with him now. Kat should be safe now, but I have a feeling that isn't the case. I don't know exactly why I feel this way, but my sixth sense tells me you still need to keep a close eye on Kat and Shelley. Even with Miller and Heraldson dead, she may still be in danger."

Gabe looked back at Kat. "I have the same feeling," he said, scowling. "Has Josie's laptop revealed anything we didn't know?"

Burns nodded. "It was incriminating, if that's what you mean. There were multiple e-mails back and forth to Heraldson, and her phone showed multiple texts. She gave him Kat's location, and told him where her bedroom was located at the house. But as far as Joseph

Lowell is concerned, a piece of advice? Stay away from the hospital. Send flowers or a get-well card from the family. But don't make a personal visit—to the hospital *or* to the house."

"You said earlier you'd explain why."

"Because Josie's talking now, and she's trying to implicate you in her father's assault. No one is listening at present."

"Your advice is always worth listening to," Gabe nodded seriously. "Thank you. But Ian arrived at the Lowell house before Tim and I did. He was really helpful."

"I know, and I wasn't but a few minutes after that. I'm just saying, be careful."

Gabe nodded. "I'm planning on taking Katlynne and the family to Yellowstone for a few days. Is there any reason I shouldn't?"

"No. The more people you and Kat have around you, the better it will be. When are you planning on leaving?"

"Tomorrow, at the latest, if the girls can be ready by then."

"Okay. Have a good trip, and keep your cell phone with you."

"Will do."

Gabe watched Burns disappear down the hill

toward the bunkhouse a few moments later. He closed the front door and turned back toward the kitchen where Kat was sitting, deep in thought. She was staring down at an empty tablet and grasping a pencil in her right hand, but was making no move to use it.

"Come here, sweetheart," he said, reaching for her. "I need to talk to you."

She rose to her feet, moving toward him. Taking his hand, she followed him into the great room.

"I need *you*," he said, "to spend the afternoon packing your bags."

Her eyes widened and took on a look of sadness. "You're," she whispered, "sending me away?"

"What? No. Come here." He put his hands on her waist and pulled her closer. "I have a surprise for you." He watched as she continued to look up, nodding. "I'm taking you to Yellowstone tomorrow. Will, Cynthia, Shelley, and Tim are going with us. Also, Lorina and Ted if they'll come. Shelley can help you pack. I think we all need a change of scenery for a day or two."

Twenty-Five

Yellowstone...

Ted and Lorina decided not to go when Gabe approached them that afternoon.

Ted answered Gabe thoughtfully. "Gabe, I can't tell you how much we appreciate the offer, but I think we'll take a few days and rest up from all the excitement. Lorina's eager to get back to the cabin, too. Perhaps next time."

Gabe nodded. "I understand. But I feel like I need to get Katlynne away for a few days, and she wants to go. Let me know if you change your mind."

Lorina and Ted went back to the cabin that afternoon, and Shelley helped Kat pack for Yellowstone. Kat fell asleep shortly after supper that evening, and Gabe was thankful he'd insisted the girls talk with Dove earlier. Instead of putting her in her room, Gabe took her down the hall and put her in his bed, bundling her up under the covers.

He stood there watching her, listening to her even breathing before he went outside to take watch until midnight.

It was six in the morning when he came back down the hall. Glancing into the great room, he saw Tim leaning back on the sofa, his long legs stretched out in front of him.

"Did you sleep?"

"As well as it's possible to sleep, I guess. I swear, Gabe, your sister is killing me. If I don't marry her soon, I'll die a slow and agonizing death." He sat upright, staring at Gabe. "So, do I have your permission to marry her?"

Gabe stared at him for a moment, and then chuckled. "About time you asked." He disappeared into the kitchen, but before he could even say good morning, Mariah handed him two mugs of coffee, grinning. He took them back and handed one to Tim, who leaned forward.

"You didn't answer me."

Gabe looked over at him. "Didn't I? Hm." He took a sip, frowning, and then looked over once more. "Well..."

"I'm waiting. *Impatiently*."

"I can tell." Gabe was grinning. "And the answer, my friend, is yes."

Tim's face split with a wide grin. "Thank you, Gabe. I'm trying to figure out a good spot in Yellowstone to pop the question."

"Do you have a ring yet?"

"Actually," Tim's grin was wider still, "I do. I've had it for almost a year."

"A year?"

"I know, I know. It was so delicate and feminine and elegant, just like Shelley, and I had hoped to ask her before she went away to school last year."

"I doubt I'd have given my permission last year. Neither of you would have been ready then."

"I figured that. It's why I waited. So," he looked at Gabe, "what's *your* explanation?"

"For?"

"For looking so haggard and exhausted?"

"Same as yours. Only she's smaller with dark hair, and has a different name."

"Ah. I figured that." Tim held out his coffee mug as if in a toast, and Gabe did the same. Both of them took a sip. For a long time, they sat in silence, before Gabe continued. "As soon as the Baxters are up, I'll pay them a visit. They're as close to parents as Katlynne has now."

"Here you go." Mariah appeared with the coffee pot, pouring each of them another cup. "For good measure. Both of you look like you need the extra-strong stuff this morning."

"Thanks, Mariah." He waited until she was gone before leveling a gaze at Tim, "You didn't seem to have any trouble asking," he observed.

"Are you kidding me? I've been working up my nerve for a solid year. I haven't been able to sleep for weeks, even before all this mess happened. I know we discussed this in the barn the other day, but you didn't expressly give your permission, and I didn't exactly ask for it."

Gabe rose to his feet. "I haven't slept since my camera found Katlynne coming in at her graduation." He rose and advanced toward the front door. "If she wakes up, tell her I'll be back in a few minutes."

Tim looked at the clock. "You do know it's six-thirty? You sure they'll be up?"

"Nope. But I figure they'll forgive me. Eventually."

~

They weren't. Lorina answered the door in her nightgown and robe, and peeked out the window to see Gabe's truck before opening the door. "Gabe, what's wrong? Is Kat all right?"

"Katlynne's fine," he answered. "She's still asleep, but I needed to speak with you both."

"All right."

Gabe could hear her voice as she went back to the bedroom. "Sweets, Gabe is here, and wants to talk with us."

Ted stumbled in as Lorina quickly poured the water through the coffee pot. A moment later, she handed each of them a cup.

"Thank you. And I'm sorry for waking you. But see, the thing is..." he said uneasily, and paused.

"Yes? Go ahead, Gabe." Ted leaned forward.

"Well, you two are the nearest thing to family that Katlynne has now, so I figured it would be appropriate to ask you...." He trailed off again.

"Gabe Ingrahm," Lorina grinned. "Are you asking our permission to propose to Kat?"

Gabe stared at her. "Yes," he said, finally.

"You've got it," Ted answered, rising. "Good luck.

Let us know what she says, but later. Right now, I'm going back to bed."

Gabe looked from Ted toward Lorina.

"Ignore him," she grinned. "Gabe, we couldn't be happier. Now, all you have to do is ask Kat."

He was still staring from one to the other. "Whoa. That was easy," he said, grinning. "Well, now that I've disturbed your early morning, I'll go disturb Katlynne's." He began heading toward the doorway, "We'll try to leave around noon or so. If you need anything at all, feel free to call my cell phone. We should be back in a few days." He went through the door and then poked his head back in. "Thank you," he said. "Both of you."

The table was an animated cacophony of sound this morning. Kinsey and Terry were full of questions about the running of the ranch, Will and Cynthia were chatting with each other about the trip, Cali and Mariah were making plans for things to do on their days off while everyone was gone, and Tim and Shelley were whispering to each other. Gabe was adding his two cents to Kinsey's questions as well.

This was heaven. As she looked around the table,

Kat realized everyone here was extremely dear to her. How would she ever, ever be able to leave them? The days since she'd arrived here had flown by, yet there was still so much to be done on Cynthia's book. That, hopefully, would keep her here for another month. At least, she hoped so.

She wished... oh, how she wished she could stay forever.

Yellowstone was a wonderland. They spent the first few days photographing elk and bison, and she even found a moose, grazing with its head underwater, occasionally coming up to study the visitors on the bank. Elk, old and young, with velvet dripping from their antlers, grazed on the hotel lawn in the late afternoons. By the end of the second day, Kat had snapped a one-terabyte SD card full of photos, and Gabe was thrilled to see her so excited.

As they stopped that afternoon at the desk, however, the clerk glanced at Gabe. "I believe I have a message for you here somewhere," he said, checking the computer. Then, he frowned. "No, not for you specifically, but someone asking whether you were here, and looking for a young lady named," he glanced down. "Katlynne Abramson."

Gabe stared at him. "There are only two people who would be looking for her. I'll get in touch with them. Thanks."

A call to the Baxters, however, proved negative.

"No. We hope she's enjoying herself," Lorina said, "but we haven't called."

Gabe hung up, glancing at Kat with concern.

"What is it?" she asked.

"I'm not sure, sweetheart."

As Gabe and Kat were leaving the hotel the next morning, the desk clerk stopped them.

"Good morning, Mr. Ingrahm. Did the gentleman find you yesterday afternoon?"

"I'm sorry?" Gabe stared back, obviously puzzled.

"Actually, he was looking for a young lady staying with you. He said he was her cousin." He looked down at Kat, who was as puzzled as Gabe.

"I'm an only child," Kat said, her voice flat. "And so were both of my parents."

"If anyone asks about any of us," Gabe responded

quietly, "We aren't here. I know it's probably too late at this point. Did you tell him what room we were in?"

"No sir, we're not allowed to do that. And I didn't tell him you were here either, any of you. We don't do that unless you leave a message that says you're expecting someone. He didn't seem convinced, however. And he is staying at the hotel." He continued to observe Gabe's face. "Should I involve security?"

"I don't know," Gabe replied. "But if he asks again, I'd like to know about it. And you may not be able to tell me his name—"

"In light of the circumstances, I believe it would be all right." He slid the hotel roster around so that Gabe could see it. The line read, 'Jim Jones'. "I can also give you a description. Tall, muscular, dark brown hair. I don't remember the eye color."

Gabe shook his head. "It's an alias, but thank you. And thank you for the description."

He was scowling when he got into the car, putting Kat in first.

"Gabe? Who do you think it might be?"

He turned to her. "I don't know, sweetheart. But I want you to stay within my sight, every minute, today. Understand?"

"I will."

Kat listened to the chatter as they ate a late lunch at Yellowstone Lake, realizing it was the first time a meal had not centered on what was happening at the ranch. She was surprised to find that she missed it. As much as she was enjoying herself, she loved the family life at Gabe's home.

"Katlynne?" Gabe brought her back to the present. "You all right, sweetheart?"

"Yes," she looked down sheepishly. "I was just thinking about the ranch, and wondering how everyone was doing."

"Do you miss them?" He wrapped an arm around her and pulled her close as their drinks and sandwiches arrived.

"I do miss them. A lot."

Gabe paid and stayed with Kat as she perused the gift shop, looking to see what was there. Fifteen minutes later, he realized she had her arms full of packages.

"What have you found now?"

"Stuff," she responded. Going through the items, she showed him what she'd found for each person at home.

"And? What did you find for Katlynne?"

"I'll find something, but it hasn't spoken to me just yet."

"Fair warning. I'm not taking you home until you pick out something for yourself."

Kat giggled. "I'll find it. I did see a hooded sweatshirt with a moose on the front, and one with a bear that I liked a lot, back at the hotel gift shop. That might be it."

He followed her up to the counter to pay for her purchases, and took the bags, carrying them for her. "We'll put these in the SUV, and then you can take some pictures of the lake."

She laughed, a musical sound.

Gabe grinned down at her and reached for her hand. Waving to the others, he led her outside.

"Now," he said, closing the trunk, "Photo time. And be thinking about where you'd like to spend tomorrow, because," he paused, "tomorrow, I intend to have you all to myself. It'll just be you and me, sweetheart. We may run into the others, but we won't be staying with them."

"I look forward to that," she said softly, taking his hand.

≈

They ended up at the Lodge later that afternoon, enjoying pecan pie at the cafeteria. Afterward, they spent a leisurely afternoon at the museum and gift shop. Kat was thrilled at watching the geyser rise into the air time after time before going back to the cafeteria for supper.

"How are you, sweetheart?"

She looked up into his face. "I'm fine, Gabe. At least, I think so. This is wonderful, in spite of what happened this morning at the hotel."

"You haven't seen anything unusual today?"

She shook her head. "No, I haven't. Have you?"

His gesture matched hers. "No. But I'm still keeping my eyes open every minute—and my hands on you." He grinned suddenly. "That's not necessarily a bad thing, however. I quite enjoy it."

She raised her brows. "Gabe Ingrahm," she scolded playfully.

"Yes?"

"Behave yourself," she tossed her head at him, and he laughed.

"Or you'll what?"

"Or I'll..." she trailed off. "I'll think of something." She was thoughtful for a moment. "Hm. There isn't anyone I can tattle on you to, is there? Not even Cynthia."

"No. It stinks being in charge sometimes, but I suppose that one is a perk. There's no one to report me to." He wiggled his eyebrows, making her giggle.

"Not fair. Then there's me. I have no clout, and I always seem to be in trouble."

He chuckled. "It's your own fault, you know. If you'd just be a good girl and behave yourself..."

"Pfft."

Gabe threw back his head and laughed. "Shall we go find the others? And have you shot Old Faithful until your heart's content, or do you need another 1 terabyte SD card?"

"I think I have all I need. I'm eager to download these to my laptop, and start tomorrow with a fresh SD card. I've heard so much about the Grand Canyon of Yellowstone, and I can't *wait* to shoot it." She rose from her chair, taking Gabe's hand.

Surprises...

As they got out of the car, however, an elk was perusing the parking lot; stopping to look at the camera Kat focused on him. She caught the shot, but only for a second, before he turned away and clipped across the lot, head held high.

"Next stop is to get these on my laptop," she said, grinning.

"I'll come in and watch you—I'd love to see them too," Gabe said in her ear. "But I'm taking you up the steps to the room the back way, sweetheart. Then I'll go down to the lobby and talk to the clerk and see if there have been any more questions." He walked her into the back of the hotel and scooped her up in his arms as she carefully held her camera bag in her lap. The others took that route, too.

Gabe disappeared a few moments later, but was back within fifteen minutes. Kat looked up, full of questions.

"He returned to the desk and asked again today," he said. "The hotel clerk told him we had checked out. He said the man checked out shortly after that."

"Hm," Tim nodded, frowning.

Will was scowling. "You think he really left?"

Gabe looked down at Kat, who was frowning and biting her lip. "I don't know. I'll keep an eye out every minute, anyway."

They spent the evening looking at slide shows of the photos Kat had taken since the beginning of the trip, and decided to go to bed early. Gabe looked in on

Kat just before retiring to his room, relieved to see that she was already asleep. A smile had crept across her face, and she looked totally relaxed.

He went back into his suite, fighting the urge to take her in his arms and kiss her senseless.

Twenty-six

Kat opened her eyes to see Cynthia pulling back the curtains. A gorgeous sunrise was visible outside the window, giving them a beautiful view of the mountains across the river.

Kat was torn between shooting the sunrise and snuggling under the comforter in the warm bed, but eventually, the bed won out. Shelley giggled as Kat pulled up the covers and curled up into a little ball. They lay there, chatting until Will's voice was heard on the other side of the door.

"Wake up, girls. A man could waste away to normal here. Gabe says to get a move on."

"My hero," Cynthia had just come out of the shower, wrapped in a giant bath towel. "Hate to tell you this, my dear, but you'll have to *waste* until we all

324 · TESSA CARR

get showers. Besides, it's early yet. Go back to bed for a while."

Will sighed. "No respect," he said. "Besides, I thought you'd like to see the sunrise."

"I'll see it some other time. Patience."

Shelley laughed and looked over at Kat. "You look comfortable. Stay warm while I hit the shower."

"Sounds lovely," Kat murmured, snuggling down further and closing her eyes. She opened them for the third time as Shelley came out of the bathroom. By then, both Tim and Gabe had rapped on the door, asking whether or not they should leave and go by themselves.

Kat sat up on the side of the bed and pulled her boots on. Stomping over to the door in her nightgown, she pulled it open.

"You leave without me, Gabe Ingrahm, and I will never speak to you again."

"Ah. I see. But Katlynne..." he paused.

"What!"

Gabe's grin at her made her even more irritated. "Um, your nightgown and your Indy boots are a great combination. A new fashion statement?"

Kat looked down, remembering that she was dressed in only her thin cotton nightgown, and gasped. She quickly shut the door between the suites and shook her head. Gabe called through the door to her as she marched away into the bathroom.

"Get ready, young lady."

In response, she slammed the bathroom door shut.

"And where to, sweetheart?"

She looked up. "I'd like to see the Grand Canyon of Yellowstone."

"We can do that."

"And if there's time this afternoon, could I please see the Cascade Falls? Shelley said they were beautiful, and this may be my only chance."

"Why do you say that?" Gabe was leaning down, his face close to hers.

"Well," she said softly, "the summer will be over soon, and I suppose…" She looked down, her teeth troubling her lower lip. "I mean, I can't intrude on your family forever…" She frowned again, "Um, could we run next door to the gift shop?"

"Next door it is," he grinned. Gabe wasn't sure exactly what was going through her head, but he gently helped her up and paid, guiding her toward the gift shop. She didn't know, he realized, that he had no intention of allowing her to go back to Washington.

"Now, I expect you to pick out something for yourself."

He began following her around the store, grinning as she picked things up and put them down again. She finally located the hooded sweatshirt with 'Yellowstone' printed across the front and picked it up. It was a deep, rich rust color, with a moose on the front. However, she set it back down. Then, she moved over slightly to pick up the one with the bear on it. Once again, it rejoined the pile in front of her.

"What are you doing?" Gabe asked, curious.

"Oh, I'm just not sure," she said, biting her lip. "I love it, but..." Shaking her head, she moved over to the next aisle. Finally, she found a tri-colored necklace that caught her eye, with tiny leaves woven in and out of each other in a choker style. "I like this too."

He watched, grinning down at her, as she smiled. "I'm ready." But as she went toward the cashier, she picked up a cap with a *Yellowstone* label the same color as the sweatshirt she had put back. Smiling, she paid for the items just as she spotted a rack of postcards and calendars. "I want to look at these," she said.

He nodded, but said into her ear. "Take all the time you want, but do *not* move."

Accustomed to hearing him say those exact words,

she wandered over to the rack. A moment later, he was beside her with a big bag in his hand.

"You've been shopping too?"

"Yes. Ready sweetheart? Or did you find something else you wanted?"

"I'm ready. But I might come back and look at these again later, if it's all right."

"Absolutely."

He led her out to the car, watching as she took the necklace out of its package. "This is so pretty," she grinned, trying to fasten it.

Gabe took it from her and brought it around her neck, turning down the mirror so she could see it.

"I love it," she said softly, fingering the tiny leaves.

"And," Gabe said, handing her a bag, "this is for you."

She looked up, surprised, as she took it. "What is it?" she asked, as she pulled it open. The sweatshirt she had admired with the bear on it looked back at her. "Oh, Gabe, you shouldn't have."

"Just say thank you, Katlynne," he said with a chuckle.

"Thank you."

"Good girl." A few seconds later, he handed her another big bag.

"Another?" She gave a delightful laugh when she

328 · TESSA CARR

opened it and pulled out another sweatshirt, this time with a moose on the front.

"Oh, but—"

"Ahem. What are you supposed to do?"

"Thank you."

"You're welcome."

"Oh," she said as she handed him a smaller bag, "and this is for you."

He took it and smiled at her, pulling out the hat that matched her shirt.

"Ah. And thank *you*, sweetheart."

She looked down at her sweatshirt. "We match."

"Good. Then we should be able to spot each other easily. I wanted you to have the sweatshirt because it's a little cool outside today. And now, off to the Grand Canyon of Yellowstone."

He said nothing more until they had reached the upper canyon and parked. The car was quite far away from the steps that led upward, and the parking lot was full. Buses peppered the parking lot. Turning to her, he leaned forward. "There are a ton of people here today, sweetheart. I want you to stay extremely close to me. Don't let go of my hand, for any reason."

"I'll stay close," she promised.

Gabe answered her by leaning down and tilting up her chin, possessing himself of her mouth. She reached down and found the latch to her seat belt, releasing it so she could lean closer to him. By the time his lips left hers, she was breathless, and her heart was pounding fiercely in her chest.

"*Oh, Gabe,*" she whispered, leaning her head on his shoulder for support.

"Breathe, Katlynne," he was smiling; she could tell by the sound of his voice.

"It's hard when you kiss me like that," she whispered, "to do anything that even remotely resembles breathing."

It was several minutes before he let her up from his grasp. "Ready to go shoot the Grand Canyon?"

In answer, she held up her camera, and he laughed. Kat put the camera strap around her neck, and Gabe took the bag, carrying it for her. As he took her hand, he led her out of the car and across the length of the parking lot. Gabe took the lead, but matched her pace. He knew she would try to keep up, no matter how fast he walked. By the time they reached the steps up to the canyon, he stopped for a moment, allowing others to walk past and giving Kat a break.

Kat decided Gabe was right. The number of people here today was enormous. When she tugged on his hand, he leaned down toward her. "What is it?"

"Look," she said, pointing to an opening through the trees. "That would be such a lovely shot."

He nodded. "If you like. But I can't let you get too close to the edge. And I'll hold on to you." He led her over and stood behind her, cushioning her from the crowd passing by.

Gabe watched as she raised the camera to focus. Just then, the crowd got extremely close, and someone shoved him forward. He grabbed Kat, moving her quickly to his side to keep her away from the cliff. Turning, he looked over at the crowd. No one was looking at him. It was as if no one even realized they had pushed them toward the edge.

"What—what happened?" she gasped.

"I'm not sure. The crowd got a little close, I guess. No one seemed aware of what happened. That's what I mean about crowds of people." He took her hand tightly again and moved back a few more feet, steering her away from the crowd. He moved upward, close to where the overhang was, and waited until the number of people had thinned out before taking her down the steps to it. The railing was high, but Gabe wouldn't release her or let her lean on it. He moved her in front of him, holding her by the waist.

"Shoot away, sweetheart." He leaned down in her ear. "There are your upper falls. Beautiful, aren't they?" He waited until she had taken several shots and pointed down and to the left. "There—I don't know if you can see it—is a mama osprey and her nest of babies."

"I see her!" Her excited voice rang out. She focused carefully and caught the mama leaning down toward her offspring, feeding them.

"Only a few more shots, sweetheart. There's a huge crowd headed this way. We'll need to get up the steps until they've cleared, and then, if you want, we can come back down again and take more." He guided her away and up the steps, clearing the overhang just as a group of Japanese tourists excitedly descended the steps with cameras in hand. They were very polite, but Kat noticed the jostling that happened as they tried to get photographs of the falls.

Gabe wrapped his arms around her from behind as they watched one group of tourists after another descend to the platform. Finally, he sat down on a large rock, pulling her into his lap. "People-watching is almost as much fun as seeing the sights," he chuckled into her ear.

Kat nodded. Finally, as the crowd thinned, he led her back toward the steps. "You might want to get some shots this way of the canyon and the river at the bottom. I've always liked those trees growing out of the side of the cliffs."

"They're almost as fascinating as the ones at the hoodoos growing out of the rocks," she grinned, snapping away. When she finished, she stood, leaning back against him, just admiring the view. "Thank you for bringing me here, Gabe. This is so beautiful."

Tim and Shelley walked, arm in arm, across the parking lot, avoiding the large crowds of people getting on and off the buses.

"That looked like Gabe's SUV," Tim said, glancing back toward the end of the lot. "They must be here somewhere."

"I wouldn't doubt it." Shelley smiled. They had reached the steps upward just as a group of people went past and disappeared down toward one of the buses. "This was where Kat wanted to come today."

When they reached the top, there were so many people there that Tim looked around. "Here. Let's go this way. Maybe we can find someplace quiet."

They smiled at each other and walked toward some of the far-away benches in the distance. "Ah. I see a chance to be alone. Come with me." Tim wrapped his arm around her waist and pulled her close.

They were free of the crowds when Shelley turned and looked up at him, lifting her face to his. Tim, smiling, lowered his lips to hers, drawing her closer. "My girl," he said softly. "I have something to tell you... and something to ask you."

"Yes?" Her heart was beating faster, she realized, as she gazed upward into his eyes.

Tim lowered himself onto one of the huge rocks and pulled her into his lap. As she leaned against him, she realized that his heart was beating thunderously, even more so than her own.

Tim took her hand into his, entwining his fingers with hers. "Shelley," he began softly, gazing down, I don't know exactly when I began loving you. The first time it hit me in the face was last summer when you got off the plane after your spring semester, and I watched you come bouncing up to the house. Your hair was blowing in the wind, and your eyes had gotten so intensely blue, I..." he paused, looking down at her small hand in his. "I just fell," he finished. "It was all I could do to speak to you. But I went out the next week and began looking for a ring. I didn't find it until the end of the summer, and then I couldn't bring myself to give it to you."

"And then, I went away again," she looked down at their hands thoughtfully.

"And I swore to myself that when you came home this year, I'd never allow you out of my sight again.' His voice was quiet, but his lips held a grin. "You, my sweet girl, haven't allowed me to get a wink of decent sleep for over a year now."

Shelley grinned up at him.

"Which is why," he said, looking down into her eyes, "I am asking—no, I'm ordering you to marry me."

Shelley giggled. "*Ordering* me?"

"Well," he grinned, leaning down to kiss the tip of her nose, "Okay, I'm begging you then. Marry me?"

She scowled, "I think I liked it better when you *ordered* me."

Tim pulled her closer with one arm, while he raised the other to give her bottom a sharp pop.

"Brat." He laughed, reaching into his pocket for the tiny grey velvet box. "Ow," she frowned, rubbing her bottom. But as her eyes lit on the box, she gasped, looking up.

Tim opened the box, smiling at her gasp. A one-carat oval diamond solitaire with tiny side stones peeked back at her.

"Oh, Tim." Tears sprang to her eyes. "It's gorgeous."

"Not as gorgeous as you," he said, taking it from the box and gently placing it on the third finger of her left hand. "So, young lady, does this mean you'll marry me?" He lifted her chin, brushing away her tears. "Sweetheart, are you okay?"

Slowly, her arms reached up around his neck. "Yes," she whispered. "*Oh, Tim, yes!*" Eagerly, she threw her arms around his neck.

Kat was thankful for the firm grasp of Gabe's hand on hers.

"Stay close, sweetheart," he said. But another group was headed toward them, very tightly clustered together. Gabe moved her over to the side to avoid them, but it was difficult.

Suddenly, her hand was jerked away from his, and she was yanked backward, away from his secure grasp. She found herself in the middle of a group of people who were chattering away to each other in German, completely unaware that she was in their midst.

"Katlynne!"

"Gabe!" she called out, trying to edge her way out of the crowd. Keeping an eye out for the hat she'd bought for Gabe, she was disappointed when she couldn't see it.

"Katlynne? Katlynne! Where are you?"

Gabe's voice! It grew louder and sounded frantic.

"*Gabe*?" Her answering cry was as loud as she could make it. But was it loud enough?

She could hear him calling her, but his voice sounded more distant now. Suddenly, a man appeared in front of her in grey sweats. He stood, unmoving. His presence alone was threatening, and she tried to back away. Again, she screamed as loudly as she could as he took a menacing step toward her.

Kat threw up the camera in front of her and flashed a picture in his face. Trying to take off around the edge of the mass of people whose language she did not understand was unsuccessful. Next, she dived back into them, trying to avoid him.

A large man from the crowd stopped in front of her at her scream. He had sympathetic eyes and had small children with him. He spoke, but she had no idea what he said.

In a split second, Kat shoved her camera into his hands and cried, "Security!"

The group was at the overhang now, and there was no way she could keep from descending the steps along with the crowd. She faltered, stumbling before she realized they were underneath her.

Kat screamed once more, unable to stop her descent. The mass was excited, and before she realized it, she was pushed up against the railing on the overhang.

This time she heard Gabe's voice calling her. He seemed closer now.

Her voice broke with the next cry she uttered.

Suddenly, hands were on her shoulders, and she felt herself being turned around.

He had found her! She took a deep breath and sighed with relief. "Gabe—I'm so glad..."

"Looking for someone?" a deep, familiar voice said above her head. Kat looked up and gasped as she recognized him. A hand clapped over her mouth as she felt herself being held against him and lifted off the ground.

She kicked and clawed as he lifted her higher off the ground and over the railing. His hand had moved away from her mouth and she took a deep breath.

"*Gaaabe!!*"

~

Gabe was running, elbowing his way through the crowd as fast as he could, when he heard it. A long, terrified scream came from the direction of the overhang, and his heart felt as if it had stopped.

Katlynne!

He had no concept of time. How long it had taken him to reach her, he didn't know. All he knew was that the crowd was gasping and pointing downward. When he reached them, they parted. He was climbing over the rail toward the edge when he heard a shout.

"Wait!"

Gabe had no intention of waiting, but as he looked up, a park ranger grabbed his arm, holding a rope. Gabe paused long enough to grab it from his hand and tie it around his waist before throwing the other end into the ranger's hand.

"The rescue squad is on its way," the ranger responded as he tied the rope through the rail and around his own waist. Calling for rescue on his two-way radio, he began giving directions.

Tim and Shelley both stiffened.

"Tim?" Shelley looked backward, toward the canyon. "Did you hear—"

"Yes."

"It sounded like—"

"Yes." He took her hand and began dragging her toward the direction of the canyon. People were stopping, staring toward the overhang that overlooked the canyon, far ahead. Shelley's heart sank as she heard people shouting for Security, and saw one man running, frantically climbing over the railing.

It was Gabe.

And he was alone.

Gabe watched the small figure as he grew ever closer. "Oh, *dear God*!" was all he could say aloud. She was lying, completely still, far, far down below him, her small body askew, her face deathly white. Gabe was alarmed at the amount of rope left in his grasp, knowing he wouldn't have enough to reach her.

But as he was jerked to a halt, he heard a shout from above.

"Wait! We're extending the rope!" came the call from above, and Gabe gave his portion a little slack, waiting. He watched Kat to see if she was breathing, but was still too far away from her.

"All right!"

As soon as the shout came from above, he scrambled the rest of the way down, reaching her. He knew not to move her, but tried to ease her right arm out from behind her, straightening her out a little. He lowered his head to her chest, listening. She was still breathing, and her pulse was regular.

"Katlynne," his voice broke into a whisper as he leaned down next to her. "Sweetheart, I'm right here. I won't leave you." He fought to remain calm as he gently stroked her cheek, brushing her hair back from her face.

Hearing shouts from above, he looked up to see a crew of three men descending the cliff with a stretcher. At that moment, he heard a whimper from below him and looked down. Kat had opened her eyes.

"Gabe?" It was barely a whisper.

"I'm here, sweetheart... I'm here."

She managed a smile. "I knew you'd find me," she said, as she closed her eyes. Gabe checked once again, listening for her heartbeat. It was still there. Reassured, he kissed her forehead.

"I won't leave you. I won't *ever* leave you."

Gabe helped the men get the stretcher down to her and load her onto it, fastening her down to secure her. Slowly, *slowly*, they guided it upward, back toward the top of the cliff.

As he glanced downward, he managed to suppress a gasp. If she had fallen another ten feet, she'd have gone over the side of the slight overhang and landed a hundred and fifty feet below. He managed to stay calm as they pulled her up. The crowd had backed away from the concrete overhang above, watching the rescue operation in progress. They were completely silent now. Gabe continued speaking softly all the way up the cliffs during the rescue, hoping she could hear him. The sound of a helicopter in the distance barely registered.

It seemed an eternity before they reached the top. The crowd heaved an audible sigh of relief when the rescuers got her over the top and up to flat ground. There was an ambulance waiting in the parking lot to take her to the waiting helicopter.

Security briefly asked him questions as they took her toward the ambulance, and he ran toward it.

"Name's Jim." The EMT from outside the ambulance called to him. "She refuses to leave without you. We're not supposed to let you ride, but since she says you're an EMT as well..." he shrugged and got into the back, motioning to a spot next to Kat for Gabe to sit.

Gabe didn't hesitate. He climbed in and sat next to her, reaching for her left hand, since the IV had been started on her right. They had pulled the sweatshirt off over her head because she had refused to let them cut it, and handed it to Gabe. And they had her top open and were putting electrodes across her chest to monitor her. Kat was trying to cooperate with the EMT who was checking her pupils.

He shook his head. "Pupils unequal but reactive."

The helicopter reached the heliport at Billings before Gabe could pull out his cell phone. It was blinking. Looking at his calls, he realized there were multiple calls from Tim. He pressed the call-back button.

"Gabe! I've been trying to get hold of you. Where are you? Where's Kat? How is she? What happ—"

"Tim, slow down. We're in Billings at the medical center here. They're coming to get Katlynne for a CT. They brought us up by air. Call Will and Cynthia and tell them what happened. He has a key to my SUV. Look, I have to go. I'll call you back when I know more." He hung up the call, feeling frustrated and helpless.

He waited impatiently outside the CT room while they scanned her. It didn't take long, and he looked up to see the ER physician coming toward him with films in his hands.

"Hello, sir. Dr. Matthews." He held up the film, showing it to Gabe.

"This area," he said, "shows a lot of swelling. And this," he pointed to the area on the right side is a hemorrhage. She must have hit hard. And with all the bruises on her, she obviously bounced and tumbled when she fell. But this area is close to the brain stem, and I'm concerned about her breathing. I'm going to put her in ICU to monitor her. It's a private room so you can stay. She awakened once in CT and was really upset when she didn't see you. I'm not going to put her on a vent, but I want her monitored closely. Can you stay?"

"I won't leave her. She's very precious to me."

Dr. Matthews looked at the chart. "It says here you're her guardian. I assume your relationship is more than that?"

Gabe nodded. "Much more."

"I see."

Dr. Matthews scribbled something on the chart and then nodded to Gabe. "I've written an order that says you can stay with her 24/7. Now, here's what we need to do regarding her care. I've ordered a full body scan to make sure there are no major injuries. We did x-rays, but there is more to trauma than just broken bones. The bad news is that she's going to be really uncomfortable for a while, and we can't give her much for pain because we can't risk masking symptoms."

They brought Kat back as he was speaking. She opened her eyes and whimpered at the jolt of the stretcher.

"Gabe?" she whispered.

"I'm here, sweetheart." His gentle voice calmed her.

Kat looked toward his voice. "I can't... see you very well. You're fuzzy." Her breathing was fast now.

The doctor leaned over. "Katlynne, I'm Dr Matthews. The reason you can't focus very well is because there is some swelling in your brain that's putting pressure on your optic nerves. It should get better soon, but we're going to do another scan after a bit—possibly several more, to keep track of the swelling. And I'm going to bring in a neurosurgeon and an ophthalmologist to see you."

"Can Gabe stay with me? Please?"

"Absolutely. I've already written an order that says so."

She reached for Gabe and latched on to his hand.

"It's all right, sweetheart. I'll be with you every minute I can," he said softly.

That seemed to give her comfort, and Dr. Matthews noticed it. Smiling, he patted her arm. "They're going to come and get you, Katlynne. You'll go to ICU, but you'll have a private room, and they can put in a cot so Gabe can stay."

This time, Kat remembered not to move her head. "Yes, sir," she whispered, "Thank you."

Kat's sleep was broken by a familiar male voice.

"Katlynne?"

Her eyes fluttered open, but she was unsuccessful in focusing. "Yes?"

"It's Sheriff Burns. Do you feel like talking to me for a few moments?"

"Yes, sir. Aren't you supposed to be at home?"

"I came up to see you," Burns had a gentle voice, "I just need a brief summary of what happened this afternoon. If you can."

Step by step, and in a halting voice, she described the horrors of the afternoon. Her voice was soft, her hand pressed to her head. There was an intense silence over the room when she finished.

Then, Sheriff Burns leaned forward.

"Can you identify the man who dropped you over the side?"

"Yes."

There was more silence. Burns glanced at Gabe before turning back to her.

"Who was it, Katlynne?"

She opened her eyes, trying to focus on his face.

"It was Ian Winslow."

"You said there was a picture," Dr. Matthews said quietly, "Is it still on the camera?" Gabe spoke quietly. "Katlynne? Does anyone have an idea where your camera is?"

"As a matter of fact," Burns said, "I spoke with security at the Park Department before I came. This was turned in this afternoon." He reached down for the leather bag he'd brought with him and brought out a camera. "Several witnesses confirmed that the man who dropped her wore grey sweats and sunglasses." He pushed the buttons on the back of the camera to pull up the last shot and held it so they could see it.

"It's Winslow, all right," Gabe declared, his mouth grim.

Twenty-seven

B*ad news...*

Things rapidly took a downhill turn as the evening wore on. The neurosurgeon brought in the films, showing them to Gabe.

"She needs surgery, and she needs it now. Who is willing to sign for it?"

"She's under my care," Gabe realized he was fighting to keep his voice calm. "But the caregivers that have been responsible for her since her father died are also staying on my property. I'd feel better if you spoke with them."

He left Kat in the hands of Dr. Willis and the OR crew, and kissed her gently as they took her away. She had watched him until she lost sight of him. He'd stood there, lost, for a while, his hand gripping the small velvet box in his pocket.

He'd been carrying it for a week now, waiting for just the right time to take it out and give it to her. He'd been clutching Kat's small hand in his left hand, and the box in his right, when she'd been so fiercely jerked away from his grasp.

The next few hours were spent in fear. Cynthia went down to the cafeteria with Will and Dove Locklear, who had arrived, and they brought up meals for everyone. Gabe was unable to make himself eat.

"Gabe, you haven't had anything since breakfast." Cynthia's voice cut through his thoughts suddenly.

He frowned. "I'll eat when she's out safe. Not until then. You all go ahead."

Cynthia knew better than to push. She passed out the food to the rest of them, as a nurse came into the room.

"Ingrahm family? With Katlynne?"

"That's us." Gabe jumped to his feet.

"I'm Nancy. Katlynne is fine. She's sedated but not completely asleep. They need to be able to ask her questions. But she keeps asking about you. She wants to know if you've had something to eat."

Gabe stared at her.

"Sir? Are you all right?"

"I'm fine. Please tell her I'm fine," he swallowed hard. "How long will the procedure take?"

"I hate to give you a time limit, but it shouldn't be too long. Can I get you all some coffee? Cookies?"

"Yes, please," Dove nodded toward her. "I think everyone could use some."

"I'll be back in about ten minutes with another report—I'll bring them with me."

She was true to her word. "They've had to shave a spot on the back of her head, but it's small," she said, bringing in a large carafe in her right hand. In the left was a big basket of individually wrapped cookies, and under her arm were some styrofoam cups.

"Was she okay with that?" Cynthia wanted to know.

Nancy smiled. "She said, 'It'll grow back'. Anyway, I wanted to let you know she's doing very well. Gabe, she said to tell you you'd 'better have eaten something when she sees you, or you're in big trouble'." She winked and disappeared, saying, "Be back in fifteen."

Gabe began to relax slightly, and accepted a cup of coffee.

Will chuckled softly. "That's our Kat."

Gabe smiled; it was the first time he had done so in hours. "Yes, it is," he said.

On the next trip in, Nancy notified them the procedure was nearing an end. Kat's vision would take a bit to clear up, but it should start getting better instead of worse. She already had some relief from the pain. With that, she disappeared.

Gabe felt as if a tremendous load had been lifted from his shoulders. He didn't realize he had sighed with relief until he looked up to see the others staring at him.

"Food?" Cynthia asked again.

"No, but I would take more coffee." He took the cup as she poured it for him.

It was fifteen minutes before Nancy put her head back in. "Finishing up," she said, grinning. "After she's been in recovery a few moments, you can come in. Since she's in ICU, we won't keep her up here very long. I'll come and get you when you can see her. I suggest one at a time until she gets back downstairs."

The last remaining moments were the longest. Gabe's fists were clenched when she at last put her head in. He shot to his feet and followed her as she led the way. As he approached, he saw that Kat had her head turned the other way. There was a large bandage wrapped around her head, and dark reddish drainage had soiled it an inch or so behind her right ear. But her dark hair peeked out through part of it. Nancy had been right; they had not had to shave it all off.

"Sweetheart?" he whispered gently, leaning over the stretcher.

"Gabe." She smiled at him as he reached out and touched her cheek gently. "Did you eat something?"

"You probably already know the answer to that, young lady," he said softly, meeting her eyes.

"Tsk-tsk," she tried to grin. "Shame on you. I left express orders."

"I know," he kissed her hand gently. "And now I'm giving you some. *Rest*."

She frowned. "I don't want to rest. My head hurts less now than it has all day."

"Then take advantage of it and get some sleep."

"Spoilsport." She scowled at him.

"I know. Want me to send someone else in who won't give you orders?"

She thought a moment. "I'd rather have you. But I probably ought to see Shell."

"I'll send her in, sweetheart. I love you."

"I love you too," she whispered.

He leaned down and kissed her mouth ever so

gently, and left her bedside. Dr. Willis cornered him outside recovery.

"It went well, Gabe. Basically, all we did was relieve the pressure. She'll need to take it easy. I'd like to keep her for a few days, but if she's better tomorrow, we might be able to get her moved into a step-down unit. I just want to make certain she's on her way to a complete recovery before we let her go home. And she may not remember any of the procedure."

Gabe shook his hand vigorously. "Thank you, Dr. Willis. I can't tell you..." he stopped, his voice full of emotion.

Dr. Willis put a hand on his shoulder and turned on his heel. "No need," he grinned. "I'll be down to check on her shortly."

The rest of the family left to find a hotel as Kat was settled into ICU. There was a roll-away bed in the corner, but it was too far from Kat to be able to touch her, and she kept reaching for him. When the nurses asked her if they could get her something, she promptly asked them to bring Gabe something to eat. In spite of his protests, the nurse looked from one to the other. "I know this scenario well," she said, grinning. "If you don't eat something, she'll stay awake and worry about you all night. So, what would you like to have?"

He ate the chicken salad sandwich that arrived from the cafeteria a few moments later just to satisfy Kat, but found it unappetizing. When he finished, he caught her eye. She was grinning.

"Feel better now?"

"Yes."

"Good. Then, sleep," he ordered.

Kat didn't need any encouragement. She closed her eyes, smiling.

Gabe stood there, watching her. He wondered how long it would be before the sedative wore completely off. When he asked, they assured him that it might be in her system for another few hours.

The next time Kat's nurse came in, however, she saw Gabe standing by the bed. Grabbing a chair, she pulled it up next to the bed. "You look pooped," she said. "We could move the roll-away closer, but I still don't think you'd sleep. We wouldn't care if you climbed into bed with her."

Gabe shook his head. "I don't want to take a chance on bumping her head."

"Understood. But you wouldn't hurt her. She's not as fragile as she looks."

He nodded, but was unconvinced.

Hours later, however, when Dr. Willis came in and Kat was able to pass his neurological exam, he left an order that she could have something mild for pain. To his delight, she said she didn't think she needed it.

"My head doesn't hurt now, just my shoulders and ribs and neck and arm and..." she said, pausing abruptly. "And I'm cold."

"We'll get you another blanket. But I'm bringing you something for pain anyway. Gabe, get some sleep. Crawl into bed with her if you want to. You won't hurt her."

Gabe stared after him. But he stood there until Dr. Matthews came back in.

"You guys don't ever sleep?" Gabe waved at him.

"Doctors? Sleep? Funny," he said, looking over Kat's chart. "Katlynne? Need anything for pain? We can give you something now."

She looked thoughtful. "Just something warm against my neck and shoulders would be wonderful."

Dr. Matthews looked up as a man in a brown uniform came into the room.

"Hello Katlynne. Deputy Hanes. I just wanted you to know that Ian Winslow has been taken into custody. He's on his way back to Big Horn County Jail with Sheriff Burns."

Katlynne stared at him, surprised. "How did they catch him?"

He smiled at her. "He was detained by a group of German tourists who saw him drop you over the cliff. Yellowstone security has had him in custody all afternoon. There was an interpreter there, but it still took all afternoon to get their statements. The main thing is, they *got* him. It was, apparently, a circus between the language differences. But the Germans hung in there, determined to wait. Nice folks. It was important to them to be able to help."

Kat reached out with her free hand to the deputy, and he took it.

"Please," he said to Gabe, "take good care of her?"

Gabe nodded back. "I'll do my best."

A moment later, everyone had left the room. A nurse came in and turned the lights down so that Kat could rest. She smiled at Gabe. "We'll be in and out, but we'll try not to disturb anyone. It's shift change. I'm going home, but Cathy should be in shortly. She'll be the night nurse." She pulled the curtains to shut out as much of the light from the hallway as she could, but left the door open to the room.

Gabe stood there, looking down at the sleeping Kat, conscious of what the Dr. and the nurse had said. Even though she was asleep, she had his hand clutched tightly, and each time he moved to sit down in the chair, she whimpered. As the moments passed, one of the nurses came in to check on her. She witnessed what happened when Gabe tried to pull away to allow the nurse access to her.

"I'm Cathy, night shift," she said softly to Gabe, "and you're *tired*." She lowered the railing on the side of the bed where he stood and smoothed out the top of the sheet that covered Kat, patting it. "Here. Climb in. Your warmth will probably help her back and shoulders." She walked around the other side and helped Kat gently onto her left side. After removing his shoes, Gabe edged his left arm under her pillow so that her head rested on it, and Cathy covered both of them with warm blankets.

"Now. Call if she, or you, need anything." She smiled and left the room before Gabe could answer. He scooted up as closely to Kat as he could, gently putting his other arm around her waist. When she leaned back against him and sighed, he knew she was comfortable.

Within seconds he, too, was asleep.

Twenty-eight

~~~~~~~~~

I *an...*

Sheriff Burns locked Ian into one of the empty cells before moving into his adjoining office. He purposely left the door between them open a bit. He waited a few moments, hoping Ian would speak.

But the first voice he heard didn't belong to Ian.

"Well?" It was Josie's voice.

Ian's followed a moment later.

"I failed."

"You *failed?*"

The sarcasm in Josie's voice grated on the nerves of even the sheriff, outside the room.

"I dropped her over the cliffs. But she lived. She identified me."

A string of curses erupted from Josie, directed at him. "I asked you to do one lousy thing! One! And you screwed it up." She was screaming now.

"This might surprise you," Ian said through clenched teeth, "but I didn't do it for you."

She stared at him. "Of course you did."

"No."

"Then who did you do it for?"

Burns moved slightly closer to the door to hear a little better.

"None of your business."

A curse from Josie was next. "You bastard. You're lying."

"Josie, I'm not in the mood. Stop it."

She whirled away from him. Her cursing, however, didn't stop.

On the other side of the door, the sheriff shook his head. It wasn't the first time he'd pitied Joseph and Mrs. Lowell.

But she kept on. It was moments later when Ian exploded in his cell. "Stop it, Josie. I did what you wanted. *Now stop*!"

"But you said you didn't do it for me. Who, Ian? Who did you do it for?"

Burns waited. A few seconds later, Ian spoke again. "Sheriff?"

Burns waited a moment before moving toward the door and putting his head in. "You need something?"

Ian swiveled to face him. "I'm ready to talk, under one condition."

"Oh? What's that?"

"Get me away from Josie Lowell. That's all."

When Gabe opened his eyes, the room was light. Cathy was inside the room, replacing Kat's IV bag with a full one. She grinned at him.

"Katlynne barely opened her eyes all night long, except when we came in to check her pupils. I don't know that she even remembers that. But she said she wasn't hurting. When we asked her how she was doing, she said," Cathy grinned, "she felt delightful. *You*, now, I think you were sleeping with one eye open the whole night."

He smiled. "I usually do that anyway. But I think I probably need to get up."

"Well, don't get up unless you want to. You have another two hours before breakfast. They're going to give her some liquids this morning, until Dr. Willis comes in. Then he might let her have something more substantial. Want us to bring you a tray?"

"Yes, please," Kat said without even opening her eyes. "He needs to eat."

Gabe only glanced at her and shook his head.

Cathy grinned. "I think she has spoken." Chuckling, she left the room.

Gabe glanced down at Kat's bandage, noticing that the stain had seemed to progress only slightly more during the night. He lowered his head back down and closed his eyes.

The next time he opened them, Dr. Willis was in the room, standing on the opposite side of the bed and studying Kat's bandage. Gabe sat up, slowly easing his arm from under Kat's pillow. "Sorry," he said.

Dr. Willis raised a brow. "For what? You being there was most likely exactly what she needed. Warmth *and* security, both."

Gabe was smiling when Dr. Willis left. The bandage around Kat's head was new, and Dr. Willis had drawn a jewel on the front with a purple pen. Reaching for her table, he pulled up the mirror and angled it so she could see it. "There you are, Princess Kat," he said with a grin as she let out a giggle. "We'll talk about you going home tomorrow." He waved at Gabe as he disappeared.

"Tomorrow," she suddenly frowned, "I was hoping for today. Where are we, anyway?"

"Billings, Montana."

"Everyone here in the hospital is very nice."

"You're an easy person to be nice to, sweetheart." He leaned over and kissed the tip of her nose. "Sometimes," he added, grinning.

She scowled at him. "What does that mean?"

"It means," he looked down, "behave yourself." He felt the tiny box in his right pocket, and closed his hand around it. Before he could speak, however, a female voice was heard from the doorway.

"Good morning, Kat. I just need to check your eyes, and grab some vitals on you."

Sheriff Burns stood at the end of Kat's bed an hour later. "I have some news for you both. Kat, do you feel up to hearing it?"

"I'm ready," she said, nodding eagerly. "And I hope you're ready for my questions."

Burns grinned. "I'd be disappointed if you didn't

have any. Ian, by the way, has confessed. Here. I'll read it to you." Pulling up a chair, he began to read. As he reached the part about Ian's motive, however, he paused. "He said, and I quote, 'I did it for my family.'"

"My family?" Gabe stared at Burns, echoing the statement Ian had made. "Who does that include? I thought Ian was an only child."

Burns leaned back in the chair. "Not entirely. Ian's mother's first husband was," his expression was grim, "you guessed it; a Heraldson. She left him and married James Winslow. They had one son, Ian. But she and her first husband had two sons, a few years older than Ian."

Gabe continued to stare. "Half-brothers," he said.

"Ian admired them, and he always tried to emulate them. They were rough and tough, and always in trouble. The oldest son's name was Alan. He was a big kid, and strong. When he was a freshman in high school, Alan began getting into trouble. That led to being in trouble with the law. One thing led to another, and eventually he killed a girl in college. And the judge's name who presided over the case? Katlynne, you can probably guess it."

"My father," Kat added softly, in dismay.

"Yes. I'm sorry. Don Heraldson was younger then, but he was consumed with the thoughts of vengeance, and he filled Ian with them, too. When Ian began working in Sheridan, no one knew of his family history. And when he was transferred, we didn't know about the Heraldsons either. Then, enter Josie."

Gabe frowned. "Go on."

"She was delighted when Ian was transferred home, and she began hanging around the sheriff's office. They began seeing a little of each other, and he told her about his family in Seattle. Ian was already livid that Alan had been imprisoned. But when he found out Alan was killed while serving out his sentence, his hatred only increased. Then Ian found out Don had been imprisoned too, and vowed to get even with everyone involved in the trial."

"Which included Katlynne," Gabe added grimly, "since she testified against Don at the trial."

"Yes," Burns nodded. "He carried that hatred around for years. When Josie told him a girl named Katlynne Abramson was here, and staying with you, they both began to plan. A few emails later, and Don Heraldson was on his way here. That's how he found Katlynne. By that time, Ian had already been listening to Josie far too much. When I told you she'd been trying to implicate you in Joseph's beating, I wasn't kidding. I knew better than to believe her. But Ian, unfortunately, didn't." He paused a moment. "But you'll be interested to know it wasn't Ian who sent word to Heraldson. It was Josie. We found her laptop full of emails."

"Dear God," Kat whispered.

"Yes," Burns said solemnly. "But there's more to it than that. Ian and Gabe had been at odds since high school, and he sought revenge for that. His original plan was to get into the family. If he married Shelley, he'd be family, and there would be a better chance of getting the piece of land his father wanted."

"But why?" Gabe interrupted. "I always knew they wanted it. What I didn't know, was why."

Burns nodded. "At one time, your father and Mr. Winslow were good friends. It seems there's a pocket of your land which adjoins their property."

"All of the western border of our land adjoins theirs." Gabe leveled a gaze at him.

"True," said Burns, "but what he's interested in is the northwestern twenty-five-thousand acres. Winslow discovered a small bit of gold underground that leads into your land. He wants it. Desperately. When your father refused to sell it, Winslow was determined to acquire it another way. Ian said all he heard growing up was that your father was keeping them from becoming rich, keeping them from accomplishing their dreams. He grew up resenting your whole family."

Gabe shook his head. "I never knew that. I only knew they wanted the land, and Dad said never to sell it to them."

"That was why," Burns said thoughtfully, "But then, Ian stopped by to visit and saw you, Katlynne. When Josie told him you planned to marry Katlynne, it irked him."

Kat stared at him. "She said that to me, too. But I had only just gotten there, and the reason I was there was to do sketches for the book Cynthia's working on. That's all."

Burns nodded. "But Ian didn't know that. He took it as fact. When he came by and saw you, he figured if he could get rid of you, it would be one more way of getting at Gabe.

"And that was the day Josie dragged me down to the barn. I told her I couldn't go because of the asthma, and can't be around hay."

Gabe glanced at Sheriff Burns. "And Josie proceeded to sneak into Katlynne's room and take all of her inhalers with her. When she brought them back, they were empty; every one of them."

Burns stared in disbelief. "You're not serious."

"I am. Extremely."

Burns rolled his eyes. "Good Lord. Add Josie's lies

on top of it all, and Ian knew he'd kill several birds with only one stone."

"Yes."

"Also, there's Josie. Mr. Lowell heard about it too, years ago. Mrs. Lowell was determined there should be a marriage between you and Josie, and they'd eventually be rich. So Josie was egged on by her mother."

Gabe could only stare. "I see. Was Joseph Lowell involved in it?"

"No. Not Joseph. But he didn't believe the story about the gold, either."

"That's crazy," Kat said in disbelief, "but somehow I believe it."

"Greed does strange things to people." Burns smiled. "If it helps any, Katlynne, Ian confessed to several things. Gabe, you'll also be interested to know he also confessed to slipping Miller a firearm. That's how Miller got it."

Gabe narrowed his eyes. "So that explains it. When Miller and Heraldson both showed up with a weapon after Tim and I searched them, I couldn't believe either of us had been so negligent."

"Not so. Ian waited until we were distracted, and Jason was reading Heraldson his rights. Then he took the opportunity to slide the gun into Miller's reach. When they put Heraldson in the second car, Ian waited until Jason was on his way back to the house, and gave him a weapon and the keys to the handcuffs. And that's how he got away."

Kat gave off a hiss of irritation. "That's amazing," she said quietly. "Ian seemed like such a nice guy. I was in shock when he dropped me over the side of the overhang."

Burns grinned. "Never trust a nice guy; especially one who wants to be in power. But that's not all. Katlynne, I want you to hear this. He also said, and I quote," he pulled out a notebook and began to read.

"Josie had filled me with her lies. I never should have listened. It was my fault, and mine only. I saw the truth in Katlynne's face the moment I held her over the railing and dropped her to what was to be certain death." Burns paused before continuing.

"Those innocent eyes said it all."

Kat was about to get her wish. When Dr. Willis looked in on her the next morning, he laughed. The first words on her lips were, "When can I go home?"

"Somehow, I knew you'd ask that. Well, let's take a look at you and see, shall we?" Dr. Willis winked at her and nodded toward Gabe. He had found her in one of the chairs, and pulled the other one up to face her. "Ah. My drawing is a little worse for wear, I see. Not unusual, however." He brought his scissors underneath it, loosening the top layer, and then began to unwind it, bit by bit. At last, he leaned back.

"Little Miss Kat, I'd like to do one more CT of your brain. If it looks good, I will allow this gentleman to take you home. I'd really prefer for you to stay in town until tomorrow, and come see me in my office in the morning. But let's get the CT first, all right?"

She nodded eagerly.

"How's the headache?"

"Gone."

"Completely?"

"Yes."

"Vision?"

Kat frowned. "Much better. But not perfect. I can see when Gabe's scowling at me now."

Dr. Willis turned to Gabe. "I believe she's about ready for you to take her home," he said, "depending on the CT, of course."

By four o'clock, they had arrived at the hotel. Dr. Willis had released Kat with a small bandage behind her ear and a proclamation that she was good to go. But as soon as the elevator door closed, Gabe picked her up in his arms and didn't let her down again until they were in the suite.

"Sleep tight, sweetheart. I'll awaken you before supper."

"I'm not sleepy."

"Oh?"

She sat up, scowling. "I feel like a bird out of a cage. How could I sleep now?"

"Are you serious?"

"As a heart attack."

"All right, then. I have something to discuss with you." Sitting on her bed, he lifted her into his lap.

"Uh-oh. Is something wrong?"

"Not a thing. It's just that I've been attempting to get you all to myself for weeks now, and without exception, I've been interrupted every single time. So now..." He clamped his mouth shut as the phone on the bedside table rang.

It was Sheriff Burns. "Joseph Lowell is awake and talking now. It seems Josie let the three men into the house the night they kidnapped the girls. They were the ones who beat Mr. Lowell, and the first one they kidnapped was Josie."

"Dear God."

"And now that he's talking, he's incriminated his own daughter. He knew she'd been speaking to the parolees and giving them information. Just wanted to let you know."

Gabe hung up, explaining the conversation to Kat.

She nodded. "Um, you were about to ask me something."

"I was, wasn't I, before I was so rudely interrupted."

The phone rang again. Gabe's expression showed exasperation. Promptly, he took the cord out and disconnected it. "Now. Let's try this again."

A knock at the door brought his mouth into a flat line. Setting Kat back on the bed, he rose and opened the door.

"Room service."

"I didn't order room service," Gabe announced, closing it again.

A second later, there was another knock. Kat giggled, watching him as he opened it once more.

"It's from a Dr. Dove Locklear."

This time, Gabe opened the door wide, and waved him in. "Be my guest."

The tray positioned on the small coffee table, the gentleman left. Gabe closed and locked the door behind him and turned to Kat.

"Make it fast," she laughed, "before someone else comes. It's a conspiracy."

"I believe you."

Gabe moved to her. This time, he knelt on one knee, pulling the little box from his pocket. "I'll make it short and sweet."

"Please do."

"Be quiet."

She only giggled.

He held out the box, listening to her quick intake of breath. "Marry me, Katlynne."

"Oh, Gabe," her left arm crept outward and around his neck. "Really?"

"Really. I want you in my arms, and in my bed," he said, "and in my life... forever."

"She nuzzled into his neck. "Can I make it short and sweet, too?"

He grinned. "Please."

Kat leaned forward, whispering in his ear.

"Absolutely," she said.

Epilogue

∽

"**D**early beloved, we are gathered together..."

Kat stood next to Gabe in the little garden cove near the back of the house, facing him. He held her hands tightly in his as they faced each other, and kissed one hand at a time as she smiled up into his face. Maddie and Jude stood on one side, Shelley and Tim on the other, as they witnessed the wedding.

It had been only weeks since Gabe had knelt in front of her at the hotel suite and proposed. Her long white dress hid the braces, but it didn't really matter. She knew Gabe accepted them as part of her, and loved her in spite of them.

This man was the kind of man she wanted, the kind she'd dreamed of. He reminded her of her abilities when all she could think of were her disabilities. And yet, he wasn't afraid to lecture her when she deserved it. He was the man who loved her unconditionally, and thought she was beautiful, even if she didn't.

So many things had happened here on the ranch. The shadows that had once hung over her head were no longer there. Ian was awaiting trial and had agreed to testify against Josie. The Lowells had legally disowned her.

Justice, at last, had been served.

The future was bright, as Kat attempted to listen to the minister's words. Her mind, however, kept wandering.

Lorina and Ted had decided to stay in Wyoming, but were planning a trip to close up the house permanently and sell it. Before long, they'd be bringing back Kat's little VW with them. Ted was thrilled with the greenhouse, and often said so.

Shelley's wedding to Tim was coming up in two weeks; Cynthia's to Will, right after that. Cynthia had insisted on waiting until both girls had their own weddings. Kat thought she had never Cynthia and Will quite so happy. Maddie was expecting, and Jude was thrilled, hovering over his little bride. And Dr. Willis and Dove were now seeing each other, and were making plans on how to fund a hospital for the reservation.

"Katlynne. Oh, Katlynne," Gabe leaned down, whispering. "Where are you?"

She sent a rueful grin his way and stuck out her tongue. When he raised a brow, she struggled to keep from giggling. But when she forgot his middle name during the ceremony, she was mortified, and Gabe couldn't stop his chuckle as he reminded her of it.

"Tsk, tsk, children," Cynthia muttered under her breath.

Lorina and Ted had heard, and Kat could hear them chuckling at Cynthia's comments.

The minister paused, forgetting his place in the ceremony, and was forced to go back several lines and start over. When Shelley let out a giggle, so did Kat. Gabe once again leaned down.

"Behave yourself, young lady. Do I have to take you outside at your own wedding?"

The minister, however, had had enough. Raising his voice, he glared at them. Tersely, he spoke. "I now pronounce you man and wife. You may kiss the bride."

It was all the encouragement Gabe needed. Kat was lifted off her feet as he took her mouth with his, demanding submission from her.

"You, Mrs. Ingrahm, are a brat. Did I ever tell you that?" he whispered playfully in her ear.

"Oh yes, Mr. Ingrahm. I believe you have." She grinned upward mischievously.

"But only once or twice."

The End

Meet the Author

Hello!

I'm Tessa Carr, and I grew up reading everything I could get my hands on, (including the phone book). I also began writing early, and entertaining my friends with stories about themselves

Libraries were my best friends, back then. They still are.

If you've found some of my books no longer available, it's due to the fact that they are being rewritten and recovered. They should be back in bookstores before long!

I hope you enjoy book two of the Wyoming Arms Series! Book One has also been rewritten and recovered, and will be available along with this one!

Much love,

Tessa

Milton Keynes UK
Ingram Content Group UK Ltd.
UKHW022036301123
433552UK00015B/489